Caroline Jones Lewis

The Dream Robbers

THE DREAM ROBBERS

THE DREAM ROBBERS

Caroline Jones Lewis

Caroline Jones Lewis

The Dream Robbers

Copyright © 2011 by Caroline Jones Lewis

Caroline Jones Lewis the author asserts the moral right to be identified as the author of this work. All rights reserved.

This novel is entirely a work of fiction.

The names, characters and incidents portrayed in it are the work of the author's imagination. Any resemblance to actual persons, living or dead, events or localities is entirely coincidental.

All rights reserved under international and Pan-American Copyright Conventions.

By payment of the required fees, you have been granted the non-exclusive, non-transferable right to access and read the text of this book. No part of this text may be reproduced, transmitted, downloaded, decompiled, reverse engineered, or stored in or introduced into any information storage and retrieval system, in any form or by any means, whether electronic or mechanical, now known or hereinafter invented, without the express written permission of the author.

www.thedreamrobbers.com

caroline@thedreamrobbers.com

Caroline Jones Lewis

The Dream Robbers

CONTENTS

Chapter One: The Beginning

Chapter Two: The Gathering Gloom

Chapter Three: Challenges Ahead

Chapter Four: Growing Unease

Chapter Five: Fallout

Chapter Six: The Road to Redemption

Chapter Seven: Unfamiliar

Chapter Eight: Fated

Caroline Jones Lewis

The Dream Robbers

Had I the heavens' embroidered cloths
Enwrought with golden and silver light,
The blue and the dim and the dark sloths
Of night and light and half light.
I would spread the cloths under your feet:
But I, being poor, have only my dreams;
I have spread my dreams under your feet;
Tread softly because you tread upon my dreams.

W B Yeats

The time had come once more. The time for winds of change to blow away an old order to welcome in the new. There had been so many times since the world had begun. It seemed that men never learned enough to prevent it happening. And it was always greed at the root of the problem. Greed. Lust - for power, for territory, for money and possessions, when the hearts of men gripped by the desire to possess more and more blinded their eyes and their conscience to the injustice of their actions. Lust - the worst sin of all since it leads to all others, to covetousness, to injustice, to cruelty - and to murder. History is littered with the names of such men. Now the time for change was here once more. There would be winners, there would be losers. And there would be casualties, of course. Innocent casualties. It had always been so. But it had to be if a world order were to be restored. If the world were to be cleansed. The winds were gathering pace already, breezes swirling together over the Atlantic and licking the lands of North America as far as the Canadian border. No-one yet had clearly defined it - but change was the clarion call of the day.

Caroline Jones Lewis

The Dream Robbers

Chapter 1 - The Beginning

September 2007

In the Bailey household, the morning began as any other morning. As they drew back the curtains there was no hint of the winds that were blowing, of the storms that were brewing and the changes that would threaten to overwhelm them in the months ahead beginning quietly on this very day. The landscape looked as comfortable and familiar as any other morning.

From her office in the High Street Emma Bailey doodled flowers on her blotter as she chattered excitedly to her mother on the 'phone. Her eldest and musically talented daughter Isobel was the subject of their conversation. "She's so excited, Mum. It's the chance she's been working for."
Great blousy blossoms and acuminate leaves on slender sweeping stems flowed across the whiteness of the otherwise pristine blotter as she spoke, flowing from the tip of her pen like the ribbons of joy that flowed tangibly from the very heart of her. She was happy. So happy. She had always had an artistic bent. There was a time when she had contemplated art college to forge her career. But there had been Pete. Always Pete. And she had never regretted the choice she had made. But the art had stayed with her as a reflection of her moods and emotions, of her successes, her failures and her fears. She doodled with regularity.

The letter about the bursary at the academy had arrived in the early morning post, fluttering onto the doormat in a distinctive white envelope bearing the academy crest. It had lain there in silent invitation and in contrast to the dour manila of the gas bill and yet another flyer for solar paneling.

Caroline Jones Lewis

The Dream Robbers

Its message had been greeted with whoops and cheers by a family migrating around a breakfast table that was cluttered by a meal in full flow. Pete and Emma were preparing for their departure to work and their children for another day of learning and gossip with friends at school. At 16 and the eldest of their offspring, Isobel had her sights set firmly on a musical career, practicing on her flute for long and invasive hours despite the protestations of her 13 year old sister Hannah and 11 year old brother Joe.

"Well done, Izz," whispered her father, planting a kiss on his daughter's forehead as she edged past between him and the table carrying a jug of orange juice retrieved from the 'fridge.

"Cool, Izz," gasped her brother through a mouthful of cornflakes. "Does that mean she'll have to live at the school?" he quizzed his mother.

"Yes, but she'll be home for weekends and holidays, won't you, Izz?"

"Oh, great. Can I have her room then?" chirped Joe. "It's bigger than mine," and he spluttered a giggle through a mouth crammed full.

"Oh. God," exclaimed Hannah. "You're so mercenary."

"Hannah don't swear," censured her mother.

"I didn't," she protested.

"You know what I mean."

Joe continued good-humouredly.

"No I'm not, but she won't need a big room if she's only here at weekends, will she?"

"Joe, please don't speak with your mouth full."

Their mother's voice again.

"Well, your room isn't exactly small, Joe. Is it?" Emma continued.

"No - but it isn't as big as Izzie's."

Isobel laughed and flipped her brother's hair with her free hand as she passed him on her way to her chair, placing the jug of orange juice on the table in front of her.

Caroline Jones Lewis

The Dream Robbers

"You know very well you'll miss me, you wretch," she grinned, confident in the closeness that she shared with her family. She glowed with happiness. A pretty girl at any time, at this precise moment with blue eyes sparkling beneath generous lashes and cheeks flushed pink with excitement she looked positively stunning as she tipped the box of Kellogg's over a cereal bowl and nipped the odd cornflake or two from the shower that cascaded into the dish.
"Have to go. Have a good day, you guys," called Pete from the hallway.
"Celebrate tonight, Izz," he added softly, sticking his head around the kitchen doorway to smile at his talented eldest girl.
"Thanks Dad. See you later."
"Might be a bit late, Em," he added. "Chamber of Commerce meeting at 4."
"OK. See you later then," and Emma moved across the kitchen to kiss her husband as he left.

When Emma had arrived at the estate agency where she worked, bursting with the news and impatient to transmit it to both Isobel's proud grandmother and her Aunt Sophie, she had lost no time in picking up the telephone, firstly to call her mother.
"Oh, Em. That's wonderful news. Well done, Isobel. She's worked so hard. She really does deserve it. Dad will be thrilled."
An archetypal mother and grandmother, Kate Gray had invested her life in her family, their success and happiness the only reward she craved. Emma was the elder of her two daughters and along with her husband Pete and the three grandchildren they had gifted her, was the centre of Kate's universe. They were a family irrevocably moulded together, the embodiment of middle England, a mixture of conservative tradition and family values but with commercial aspiration towards progressive and new. Kate's younger daughter Sophie was a different case,

Caroline Jones Lewis

The Dream Robbers

frequently the cause of hurtful disappointment. Not in her achievements. She had done well in her career and Kate was justifiably proud of her for that. But Sophie's attitude towards the family was often one of hurtful derision that was a source of pain.

"Will you manage, Em," Kate went on. "Financially, I mean. Now that she has this bursary?"

"Well, it's going to cost us, of course. The bursary's only for 40%. But then we've known it would be either this or university. It's just come a bit earlier than uni would have done, that's all. At least we have a while to go yet before we're faced with university for Hannah. And Joe isn't really academic, is he? I think Pete's hoping he will go into the business with him rather than pursue the academic path. He'd be better suited to doing day release at the local tech. With me earning good commission we should be alright. I'll work a night shift if I have to!" she exclaimed with a grin in her voice. "This is the kids' future we're talking about, Mum."

"Well, if we can help in any way you know we will. You will let us know, dear, won't you?"

Minutes into the conversation Emma was interrupted by the opening of the agency door.

"Mum, I'll have to go," she whispered urgently. "A client's just come in. Speak to you again later," and she cut the conversation short. She recognised the anxious-looking young woman who had entered and who left the door swinging violently behind her as she approached Emma at speed. Emma replaced the receiver and turned to welcome her with a disarming smile.

"Good morning. It's Mrs Carpenter, isn't it? What can I do for you?"

The diffident Mrs Carpenter settled herself stiffly on the edge of the chair before Emma's desk - as though she were afraid of being comfortable in case she might be tempted to

Caroline Jones Lewis

The Dream Robbers

stay and knew she shouldn't. In her hands she wrung the straps of a copious striped fabric shoulder bag that now rested untidily in her lap. The brightness of its colours drew Emma's eye and registered in her mind for no apparent reason. She was an untidy woman, Mrs Carpenter, Emma noticed. Ungainly. Everything about her was cluttered. The unruly wavy blondness of fly-away hair framed features free of make-up in the anxious face and long blue beaded ear-rings drifted downwards towards a white blouse of Indian cotton that in turn met a voluminous soft cotton skirt of varying shades of blue. The cotton had that slightly crumpled look that the fabric made impossible to avoid. Everything about her was a total contrast to Emma's sleek and groomed hairstyle, the neatness of her business clothes and a figure kept trim by frequent visits to the gym, a convergence of the rustic rural of mother earth with the slick urbanity of commerce.

"Is Gavin in?" asked Mrs Carpenter breathlessly. "I really need to speak to him."

"I'm afraid he isn't at the moment. Is there anything I can do for you? It's Walnut Grove that you're buying, isn't it?" Walnut Grove, thought Emma. She just doesn't look like Walnut Grove. People are so surprising. She had never met Mr Carpenter and wondered whether he was a Walnut Grove person, a pin-striped business type, an upwardly mobile. She couldn't visualise it beside the mother earth of Mrs C. Mrs Carpenter nodded and caught her breath.

"It's our mortgage offer," she blurted. "It's with Northern Rock and after the news this morning ... well, we're really worried that it won't be honoured."

She delved into the depths of the gaudy bag and withdrew a letter which she unfolded shakily, leaning across the desk towards Emma to show her its contents and in an obvious state of alarm.

"The news," echoed Emma.

"Yes. Didn't you see it this morning?"

"Actually no, I didn't," admitted Emma. "We had some

Caroline Jones Lewis

The Dream Robbers

special news of our own in the post this morning and I didn't get around to listening to the radio," and she smiled encouragingly into the network of worry lines criss-crossed on the forehead in front of her.
"It was on the TV," Mrs Carpenter continued, ignoring Emma's 'special news' and intent on pursuing her own agenda.
"Northern Rock's in difficulties."
"Really? Oh, I see." Emma hesitated, surprised, somewhat in disbelief, her own countenance shifting from one of abject joy to that of vague confusion.
"We don't have the TV on in the mornings," she mused - as much to herself as to Mrs Carpenter - "so I missed it. Are you sure?"
She tidied her blotter unnecessarily as she spoke, struggling to shift her mind into gear as rapidly as possible.
Why didn't I put the car radio on like I usually do? she silently chided herself. So wrapped up in Izzie's letter. I should have listened to the news, then I'd know what she was on about. A British bank in trouble. It can't be right. The woman's exaggerating. They're always doing it, these nervous clients. She hardly looked the sort of person likely to have total grasp of the business world. *What was it* that her husband did now? Emma had no idea and her thoughts rambled on until the drone of Mrs Carpenter's voice broke through them. She caught the last vital sentence.
"People are queuing already to withdraw their money."
Emma caught her breath, covering her ignorance and disquiet with a defensive twiddling of the ends of her sleek blond hair.
"Umm, look," she began, "Gavin will be in shortly, I'm sure. Shall I ask him to ring you? He'll know what's going on. I'm sure he'll put your mind at ease. You know how the media over cook these things," and she smiled a conspiratorial smile in an attempt to put the woman at ease. It failed. The face before her remained resolute in the light of Emma's obvious ignorance of the current state of play.

Caroline Jones Lewis

The Dream Robbers

Emma took Mrs Carpenter's telephone number and watched her disappear through the heavy glass door back into the street, shoulders hunched tensely and the careworn expression still etched across her features. A sudden breeze caught the hem of her skirt as she hovered on the pavement waiting to cross the road, brushing the pale skin of her bare legs. She wobbled, clutching the stripy bag close to her chest and shifted in the flat black pumps on her feet to steady herself as the breeze turned into a wind that caught her slightly off balance. The wind lifted the strands of her hair as she turned her head left, then right to check for approaching traffic. Emma pondered her thoughtfully, then clicked deftly on the internet explorer on the computer on her desk and googled 'Northern Rock'. She was concerned at what she read. The bank, it seemed, had gone cap in hand to the Bank of England for a temporary loan to cover a short-term shortfall of funds.

When the news had leaked out, anxious investors, fearful of losing their hard-earned savings, had assembled outside branches country-wide intent on withdrawing their money, milling around on the pavement while waiting for the queue ahead to stagger forward at a snail's pace. It was indeed developing into a run on the beleaguered bank that could only propel it into even greater jeopardy. Emma's mind worked quickly. Gavin had been using Northern Rock regularly in recent weeks. There were several other sales that could be affected. It was distressing to people when their plans fell through and it was she and her colleagues who would be at the forefront of their concerns, trying to retrieve their dream home, trying to calm the choppy waters. Mrs Carpenter was only the beginning. There would be other anxious clients on the 'phone and invading the office. And for herself, if the Carpenter's purchase fell through then their sale would also be threatened not to mention others, which would mean her commission for next month would be hit. She needed to earn as much as she could at the moment,

Caroline Jones Lewis

The Dream Robbers

with her Dad due to retire and the gift of a celebration party for him and Mum to pay for. And Christmas was not that many months away. She had already started making 'the list' which grew ever longer and more expensive with each passing year as the children grew and their own circle of friends and family expanded. And of course there were the bonuses for the men. Pete was drawing as little as possible from his business right now. "The Tythings" development was almost near to completion but as yet none of the properties had been sold. Marketing had only started a week ago with the first open day for viewings scheduled for the coming weekend.

"Damn," she muttered. "Damn. Where the hell's Gavin when I need him?"

She rang his mobile number but there was no response. She tried his home number and got his answer machine.

"Gavin, it's Emma. Please can you call me. It's urgent," she breathed into the machine.

Impatient to reach him she tried his mobile number again but still there was no response. Then as if he had read her mind, as though her thought waves had reached out to him through the ether and drawn him in, Gavin burst through the front door like a rocket on which the blue touch paper was already lighted, his mobile 'phone beep-beeping urgently in his pocket. She replaced the receiver and the beeping ceased.

"Gavin," she began. "Where the hell have you been? Mrs Carpenter's been in looking for you. She's worried about their mortgage offer."

Her voice trailed behind Gavin as he sped past, followed by the swiveling gaze of his concerned colleague. He threw open the door into his office behind her and dropped his laptop case onto the desk with a resounding thud.

"Well she might be," retorted his muffled voice from behind the partition wall. "It's with Northern Rock and well, haven't you heard the news this morning. That's where I've been - on the telephone at home to my contacts."

"What exactly does all this mean?" Emma quizzed,

Caroline Jones Lewis

The Dream Robbers

addressing her query into the vacant space that stretched between them.

Gavin came back out into the main office, striding past Emma to stare bleakly out of the window into the High Street, thrusting his hands into the pockets of his trousers and hunching his shoulders. He gave out a deep sigh.
"It means that Northern Rock are in the deep doodoo, that's what. I've been trying to get a realistic picture but they're all giving out the official line. Bank is stable, just a temporary shortfall that will right itself, etc etc," he went on, turning around abruptly to pace his lean form to and fro across the dark blue carpet, his footsteps leaving a trail of indents in the freshly vacuumed pile.
"But as they're short enough of funds to ask the Bank of England for help you can bet your life there won't be any money at Northern Rock for new mortgages. I'll have to get the Carpenters file out and see who else I can go to. They're pretty tight on their budget, though. Might not be that easy. That's why we went for Northern Rock in the first place. And," he added pointedly "they're not the only ones. We've got half a dozen sales in the pipeline that could be affected."
He stood before Emma's desk fidgeting with the stapler while she muttered her disbelief. A moment of tension hung in the air.
Emma sighed.
"Well, I know you'll do your best, Gavin," she concluded.
"Bugger," he exclaimed. "Bugger, bugger, bugger," and disappeared back into his office leaving a perplexed Emma gazing absentmindedly ahead. She heaved another deep sigh.

******

The day passed extraordinarily with reports of anxious investors continuing to queue outside the branches of the

Caroline Jones Lewis

The Dream Robbers

stricken bank in a scramble to withdraw their money.
"A run on a bank - can you believe it," exclaimed Pete that evening as he and Emma watched the unfolding drama on the late night news. He had come home even later than expected after an impromptu site meeting, a development of six prestige houses in the Kent countryside being built by his company and aimed at the commuter earning big money in the capital less than an hour's train ride away. At approaching 40 years of age with a company he had set up ten years earlier, he considered his life secure. He and Emma had met while she was still at school and he at university, brought together by an obliging spin of fate when his family had moved into the same neighbourhood. Neither had given anyone else more than a cursory glance since their first meeting. It had always been a passionate relationship and when passion had overwhelmed their sense of responsibility and Emma became pregnant at the end of the sixth form - to the dismay of her teachers who had envisioned a talented career - there had been no question of anything but marriage. It had been a struggle in the beginning, while Pete had completed his training and as the other babies had come along. But for two people endowed with common sense and tenacity the mountains had never appeared too high nor too rocky to climb. And Emma's parents, Kate and Andy, had always been at hand to help in any way they could. When the good times had come, together they had designed the house they now lived in, built by Pete's company five years previously on a plot of land they had searched for diligently for over a year. It sat on the outskirts of a pretty village, sheltered from the winter winds by woods to the north of them, the south-facing windows looking out over rolling countryside beyond the patio and the garden and overlooking in the distance a farm on the opposite slope of a shallow valley ahead. Now gratefully they were without mortgage and Emma's part time job at the estate agents after Joe had started school had fitted neatly with Pete's own involvement in house-building. They

Caroline Jones Lewis
The Dream Robbers

enjoyed a comfortable standard of living that had been carefully planned and worked towards over the years of their marriage. Even so, with growing children and the inevitable increase in the cost of living teenagers imposed, the news on Northern Rock came as a shock to two people whose livelihoods were linked so closely to the mortgage market.

"Can you believe it,' repeated Pete. "In this day and age. What the hell have they been doing, for God's sake?"

"I'll ring Soph in the morning," yawned Emma, padding barefoot towards the kitchen and followed by her husband on the evening security routine. "She'll know what's going on. It's probably not what it seems."

"I hope you're right, love," Pete observed.

"In the meantime, I think I'm ready for bed," Emma added.

"Didn't you ring Sophie today?" asked Pete. "Thought you'd have been on the 'phone straight away with Izzie's news."

"I did try but she apparently had meetings all day and you know that she and James don't get home until fairly late. These high flyers in the City - they work such long hours."

"Mmm. They're welcome to it if you ask me. Can't be much of a life, can it?" Pete muttered. "I know they earn fantastic money but the quality of life! It just doesn't exist. Well, not as we know it anyway."

"Oh, I don't know. It has its benefits when you think of the luxury holidays they have - and the champagne suppers out at trendy restaurants, when we make do with last minute package deals and shepherd's pie made from the left-overs of Sunday's joint."

Pete locked the back door and turned to face her.

"Ah, well, that's the difference having three children makes for you, isn't it? I daresay we could have those things if it didn't cost five times of everything instead of two. If we didn't have university fees and weddings to plan for. But I tell you what, Mrs Bailey. *I* wouldn't swap, that's for sure. What about you?" and he wrapped his arms around his wife

Caroline Jones Lewis

The Dream Robbers

and kissed her cheek.
"You know I wouldn't," she grinned.
"Good. So let's go to bed then." He placed a lingering kiss on her upturned mouth.
"Is the front door locked?"
"Think so. Is the cat out?" she quipped.
"We don't have a cat."
"I know," she responded. "But don't tell the mice."
As the lights went out on another day, the implications of the day's events had not yet sunk in.

******

Over the ensuing days the subject of Isobel's bursary and impending departure to the music academy was the main topic of conversation within the family. When at last Emma managed to catch her younger sister Sophie on the telephone, the subject of Northern Rock was secondary to that of Isobel's career progress and perfunctorily dismissed by Sophie as 'bad management and unwise investment'. In fact she was surprisingly reluctant to address the subject at all.
"Remarkable really," Emma commented to her husband. "I thought she'd really enjoy the opportunity to annihilate the reputation of a rival bank. She hardly said a word about it."
Sophie Gray worked at a high level in the London based investment arm of a long-established bank. She lived in a luxury mortgage-free apartment in the Docklands with her boyfriend James. He a dealer on the stock market, they were two career people with no interest in leading what they saw as Pete and Emma's tedious and parochial life, a life restricted by extended family expectant of their attention and with the burden and expense of children. The two sisters were as disparate in personality as they were in looks.
Emma featured her father whose height was limited to 5 foot 8 in, a temperate man of average build whose blue eyes, fair hair and colouring and fastidiousness of habit sat well with

Caroline Jones Lewis

The Dream Robbers

the mildness of his manner. Sophie, it had been deemed, was a throw-back to her maternal grandmother now deceased, a tall feisty lady whose striking looks of chestnut locks and rich brown eyes matched an almost reckless character that had defied convention.

She had brought Kate up in a ramshackle cottage bequeathed her by her long deceased parents, earning her living by selling flowers and produce nurtured in the expansive garden and home-made wines fermented in a brick-built shed. Kate had been her only child, a child outside of marriage at a time when illegitimacy had been a cause for social exclusion, the issue of paternity unresolved to a family kept deliberately in the dark as to the identity of the absent parent. It was a safely guarded secret with which Kate's mother had confounded the local gossips and taken with her to the grave giving rise to speculation amongst family and friends that he surely must have been a man already married, probably a local man with whom she had had furtive assignations though they knew not who or where or when. The only person it had never really bothered was Kate herself who demonstrated an uncomplicated acceptance of a father's absence and a lack of curiosity that had surprised even her mother. Given the diversity of the pool of genes on which they drew, Emma and Sophie were inevitably destined to pursue very differing agenda in life.

As children the girls had slotted quite naturally into their respective roles. Emma the elder and responsible sister calmly rescued her rash younger sibling from countless escapades as a matter of duty of care and Sophie, the rash younger sibling, sustained a kamikaze path through life content in the knowledge that her elder sister was a dependable safety net. The pattern had remained constant from infancy through adolescence until finally Sophie had jettisoned the ever-present guardianship of her sister and family in favour of pastures new.

Caroline Jones Lewis

The Dream Robbers

Their mother, Kate, an equally temperate parent as their father, had long since given up any hope or expectation of more grandchildren from the youngest of her daughters and husband Andy had learned to disguise his disappointment at the selfish lifestyle that so hurt his wife by the infrequent visits and excuses trotted out to explain absences on birthdays, Mother's Day and other events that might have prompted a visit from a more caring daughter. Sophie's long working hours and high salary provided her with a luxury city apartment, designer clothes and a fancy open-topped sports car but most importantly of all with a six figure annual bonus. Together with James' equally immense salary as a trader and his equally enviable bonus structure their joint annual income was beyond her parents' wildest dreams or comprehension. It was the annual bonuses that had bought and paid for the flat and maintained a healthy deposit account with an offshore bank. Together they enjoyed a life free of worry or responsibility and Sophie eased her conscience by making generous donations to her two nieces and nephew, of whom she was undeniably fond - albeit at a distance. For the girls she gave generous cash donations on their birthdays and for Christmas expensive designer clothes and jewellery that made her sister tut-tut at the extravagance but that meant both of the girls adored her. And for Joe, James could always get his hands on the latest piece of technology whatever the cost.

"You shouldn't indulge them like this," Emma would protest. "Life isn't about money. It's you they want to see. I wish we could see more of you, Soph. And I know Mum wishes you'd come more often. Can't you pop down a bit more? After all, it isn't far, is it?"

They had chatted on one of Sophie's rare flying visits without James in tow.

"To *Royal Tunbridge Wells*, you mean," scoffed Sophie. "No, I suppose not".

She bit into a rock cake that she had sneaked from the griddle in the kitchen on which the fruits of Emma's Sunday

The Dream Robbers
Caroline Jones Lewis

afternoon baking was cooling. Though she would be reluctant to admit it, visits such as these prompted the luxury of nostalgia. The smell of fresh baking reminded her of Sundays at home as children, of their mother's weekly baking session while the Sunday joint roasted in the oven and she and Emma sat at the kitchen table shelling peas or slicing runner beans. Good days, they had been. But not, she insisted, what she wanted for her own life and not what she wished to encounter too often.

"You'll get indigestion - eating those while they're still warm," Emma chided.

"Rubbish," her sister retorted. "Old wives' tale, Em."

"Can't you, Soph? Can't you pop down a bit more often?" Emma persisted. "Mum and Dad aren't getting any younger, are they? Mum hasn't been too well lately. Pete and I were a bit worried about her last week. She had a sort of giddy turn."

Sophie swung around to look out through the kitchen window at her youngest niece playing with her pet rabbit in the garden. It was easier to divert the subject and the routine censure by avoiding Emma's gaze and with her back to the source of the question.

"Did she go to the doctor?" she mumbled through the remnants of the rock cake.

"No - you know what she's like. I'm alright, I'm alright. I don't need a doctor. But I can tell you she looked as white as a sheet. If Dad had been home he'd have made her go but he was at the allotment."

"Tending his cabbages as usual," Sophie tittered.

Emma let the subject drop. She disapproved of her sister's disdain for her parents' lifestyle but had learned that her disapproval made no impression and elicited no promise of reform. Why Sophie was so derisive she had no idea.

Born to their parents a little later in life perhaps than many of their contemporaries, their parents were, true enough, closer to elderly than the parents of their friends. In their parents' day most people married younger than their generation had

Caroline Jones Lewis
The Dream Robbers

done but life had not brought them together until Andy was almost 30 and Kate not many years behind. At first his family had been disapproving of the match, of his marriage to the illegitimate offspring of what they saw as a wild and unconventional woman.
"She's just different," Andy had told them of Kate's mother. "But she's decent enough," and with time and patience the couple had won them round. And what difference did their age make as parents? They had had a perfectly happy childhood, she and Sophie and their parents had never really censured Sophie in any way, to Emma's knowledge, despite her propensity to create endless crises. Emma was sure there been no discord between them. Their mother surely would have confided in her had that been the case. Any estrangement would have distressed Kate. But there had never been any mention of such a thing.
"Well, she seemed OK this morning," Sophie countered. "You'll keep me informed, Em, won't you? Let me know if there's anything wrong? I'd better be off now. By the time I've driven back to town James will be back from his afternoon's golf with his buddies."
Yes, go on. Walk away again now that I've mentioned the taboo subject, thought Emma but which she refrained from voicing. A pointless exercise, she silently acknowledged.
"Won't you wait and see Pete and Joe?" she asked instead. "They'll be back from football any minute now".
Sophie lied in response.
"I'd love to, Em, but if I don't go now I'll get caught up in the traffic. All the weekenders making their way back into town ready for the working week - you know what it's like."
"No, I don't actually," thought Emma, "but I know *you* well enough."

In reality Sophie's return to London was delayed by a visit that she had fully intended but concealed from her sister. It was her habit on such occasions, when she was visiting without James, to call on Robert before setting off for home,

Caroline Jones Lewis
The Dream Robbers

a habit she considered a cherished secret from all but the two of them. She hugged the secrecy of her visits to her bosom like a treasured possession, a favourite childhood toy or a dream privately nurtured. A childhood friend and former lover, Robert ran the livery stables he had now taken over from his retired father. As Sophie approached she could see him in the yard, grooming a splendid chestnut stallion and she acknowledged to herself that familiar flip of the heart the sight of him still caused.

He was a handsome man, dark haired and healthily suntanned from his work out of doors, of slim but muscular physique, so different to James' fair skin and blonde hair and a lean figure kept healthy in the gym. Robert cut a dashing figure in snug jodhpurs and an open-necked rugby shirt. A modern day Mr D'Arcy, thought Sophie - still waiting to meet his Elisabeth Bennett. It should have been me, her mind protested before she could stop it. It should have been me. She allowed the car to crunch lazily to a halt on the gravel drive and stepped out to greet him. Robert turned at the sound of her car and smiled, a sensual familiar smile.

"Hi, Piglet," a childhood nickname that had endured between them, a relic of days spent playing Pooh-sticks at Pooh bridge in the Ashdown Forest and Pooh tales related by Sophie's mother by the fireside in the sitting room in the days when Robert came for Sunday tea.

"Hi, Pooh," and she planted a kiss on his cheek. Robert resisted the temptation to wrap his arms around her, running the thumb of his one hand instead across the sharp bristles of the brush he held in the other.

"So what brings you down to the sticks from the big City?" he ventured. Not me, I'll be bound, he thought wryly.

"Oh, family visit - you know. And I couldn't go without a visit to 'the estate'," teased Sophie.

"James not with you, then?"

Caroline Jones Lewis
The Dream Robbers

It was a rhetorical question.

"Golfing with his buddies," she confided, and stroked the mane of the beautiful chestnut stallion Robert was grooming. "I bet you're a joy to ride, my beauty," she crooned to the animal.

"Is he a new addition?" she asked.

She had ridden as a child, welcomed to 'the estate' by Robert's family until disapproval had set in.

"Mmm. New client. They're grooming him for the show jumping circuit."

"Yes, I'd love to ride you," she repeated. "He reminds me of Brandy Boy. Remember? Those heady summer days riding out on the weald. You on Brandy Boy and me on Nickel?"

"How could I forget?" he grinned. "He's a different temperament to Brandy Boy, though. More tranquil. Brandy Boy could be difficult some days, couldn't he?" and he paused at the memory, of two horses tethered to a tree while they lolled together against its trunk and gazed out across the valley.

"If only," he thought. If only the cold winds of separation had not sent her gusting towards the City and a different life. The memory caused his eyes to cloud, his smile to dim just a little, the memory of family discord and disapproval.

"She's a gold-digger. An avaricious little strumpet," Robert's father had thundered. "She's not cut out for this life, it's just the money that appeals and you'll rue the day if you go ahead with this proposal and she accepts you. She'd have you bankrupt in no time," he had proclaimed.

Robert had been angered by his father's blunt appraisal of Sophie's character, wanting to protest but secretly afraid that indeed his father could be right. For all his good looks and obvious assets he lacked self-confidence in the shadow of his father's effortless presence. But still he loved her and still he hoped that one day his parents would accept her as his wife.

Caroline Jones Lewis
The Dream Robbers

"So you don't think it's possible she could simply *love* me. For myself. For the person I am?" he managed.
His father had turned away, hurt in his eyes at the obvious insult he was paying a son he so loved.
"She may well love you - now. At least she thinks she does," he countered. "But it wouldn't last. She'll want more than this life can give her and then what? Son, you're worth better. So much better."
Brian Welling had hoped that with his last few words he had in some way cauterised the wound that his rebuttal had inflicted on his son but remained adamant in his opinion of Sophie. Now they lived two vastly different lives, Robert and Sophie, but still a tie remained - for both of them. A tie that James viewed with suspicion.

On the drive back to London, Sophie pondered just why it was that she had such an aversion to a lifestyle she had grown up in. A happy childhood, cared for by loving parents. Good people. Why did she feel so alien to that life now, so uncomfortable that within an hour of arriving all she wanted to do was leave? Too long in the City perhaps? Too set in a life of smart restaurants and sophisticated people. Smart people who operated on a different level, she thought. Like herself. Like James. Her parents just couldn't relate to the way they lived. Neither could Emma and Pete any more than she would relate to their lives. Any more than she would want to. Pete disapproved of her, she was sure.
"He's so damned provincial," she had told James with contempt. "Thinks himself a big player with his little development company building a dozen or two homes a year. What can he possibly understand of your world and mine. Billions of pounds flow in and out of our bank every day, much of it at my bidding?"
"Well, at least Emma is happy with her life and with Pete," said James.

Caroline Jones Lewis
The Dream Robbers

"Yes, and I'm glad about that. Glad for Em. But I'm not her and I don't want for my life what she has. I wouldn't be happy with her life. I know it's what she and Mum would wish for me, a life like Emma's and another clutch of grandchildren."

James winced. He had made it very plain that children were not on his agenda. Nor indeed marriage, so far as Sophie was aware.

"We're fine on our own, aren't we? We don't need children to be happy?"

"Yes, darling," he had replied. "We're fine the way we are."

Sophie had been with James for six years now, six contented years through which they had shared a mutual enjoyment of all life's best rewards. James' parents had retired to France, to a renovated chateau in Brittany which afforded the couple some wonderful holidays in glorious countryside. The flight into St Malo was quick and easy and the Freyers kept a motor launch at Dinard for sailing the bays and canals in the area. What more could anyone wish for? She lived a life so distant from the one her parents had envisaged for her as to be a different world. No wonder *their* world was one that she was reluctant to return to. Perhaps it was her guilt about that that made her feel such discomfort. She didn't know. She didn't feel in the least guilty when she was living her life in town. But when she came to visit there was always that feeling that her parents were judging her, that her sister was judging her, resenting her rejection of the future they had expected of her. And then - there was Robert.

She could not envisage a world without Robert being a part of it, Robert and his world of horses and country and small town values. She should view him and his life in the same way that she did her parents - but that was not the case. There was a part of her that still hankered for Robert and Robert's world and when she came to Kent without James,

Caroline Jones Lewis
The Dream Robbers

try as she may to resist she could never leave without visiting Robert. There was always that little fillip when first she saw him, a need for the affection they had always shared. She tried to leave it behind her, but it dogged her and she failed each time she promised herself she would leave without seeing him, like an addict struggling against addiction but failing. What was it that still held her? Why was it she had never left behind a family that had snubbed her? Once she had entertained the notion that Robert was about to propose to her. But it had never happened. It was the parents, she was sure, the parents who did not think her good enough for their public school son. His mother was gone now but the father ….. The father she remained wary of.

Maybe that was what brought her back, the need to show them what she had made of her life without them, the need to drive into their world in her luxury car dressed in her designer clothing and obviously expensive jewellery. It was different, she knew. Robert's family was old money, tradition and establishment. But she didn't care. It made her feel good to come back flaunting her success, her new money. She felt differently about driving into their estate than the reluctance at visiting her own family. Whatever it was about returning that irked her she was glad that she had once more done her duty by her parents for a while, had briefly sated her need to see Robert and was now heading back to the world she knew, the world in which she felt comfortable and was respected without question. With the roof down on the cabriolet, she adjusted her Gucci sunglasses, relaxed back in the seat and let her hair billow in the breeze as she sailed along the A21 towards home. Little did she know then the changes that lay in store.

Caroline Jones Lewis

The Dream Robbers

Chapter 2 - The Gathering Gloom

Over the ensuing weeks the sorry tale of the demise of Northern Rock transpired to be only the tip of a hitherto undisclosed iceberg loose and deadly on the Atlantic horizon. Stories of massive losses by bank upon bank emerged and were reported graphically by all areas of the media. Blatant greed and foreseeably disastrous investments in what had been dubbed the American sub-prime market, unbelievably irresponsible lending to vulnerable sections of society, began to unravel and impact on the availability of mortgage funds for genuine prospective buyers. The housing market was propelled into free-fall. Across the Atlantic banks were already writing down their losses, and the US Federal Bank had cut its discount rate to banks to downside risk to growth. The American dream had turned into a nightmare. The Bank of England offered an injection of funds of £10 billion and Germany's Deutsche Bank recorded losses on its loan book of up to a billion euros.

Back in Emma's own back yard, chain after chain of house deals wobbled and swayed until eventual collapse as banks withdrew mortgage offers or raised repayment terms to a level that potential buyers could no longer afford. Like a house of cards, the market was collapsing all around them. Mrs Carpenter was forced to accept the inevitable - in great distress. How could she tell Gavin what this meant to her life? How could she confide that while she still liked the relaxed homespun comfort of the house she and her family currently lived in and while the tree-lined avenue in which it stood still appeared calm and friendly, their failure to move to Walnut Grove meant living daily in sight of the neighbour with whom her husband had been having a torrid affair; that every day, stepping outside of her own front door was another stab in the heart for her and that every time she saw the pretty and stylish divorcee from no 53 pass by, her

Caroline Jones Lewis

The Dream Robbers

self-esteem sank a little lower. How could she tell him that in her dreams she pictured herself in the house in Walnut Grove as a new person, metamorphosed from her current self to a made-over version that would be more to her husband's liking, a change of hairstyle, a neater more fashionable style of dressing, a new image to fit the new home and future. For Mrs Carpenter the move to Walnut Grove had not just been a house move. It had been essential to sustaining her marriage. For without it she doubted her husband's ability to keep his promise that the affair was over and - more importantly - that without it she doubted her own ability to put the past behind her and rebuild her own self-worth and her marriage.
"Those bankers," she fretted. "They've played with peoples' lives."

******

"No wonder Sophie didn't want to talk about Northern Rock," Pete observed later. He was raking up leaves in the back garden. Splashes of the gold and yellow and orange of autumn littered the brilliant autumn green of the lawn. Emma followed behind him, scooping up the multi-coloured heaps with a pair of large green plastic hands.
"They've all been at it," he continued. "Profligate spending on bad investments, the lot of them. And guess who's going to end up paying the price? The likes of us, no doubt."
"Where on earth did all these leaves come from?" Emma was protesting in an attempt to divert his attention. "We don't have that many trees in the garden."
Pete stood upright, flexing his back.
"It's all these high winds we're getting," he said. "I don't remember an autumn as windy as this one. We hardly seem to have a calm day nowadays. Look at your washing. It's almost horizontal."
They regarded together the row of school clothes fluttering on the washing line, Joe's white shirts and the blue and white

Caroline Jones Lewis
The Dream Robbers

stripes of the girls' school blouses.
"It seems to have been windy all year," Emma mused.
"Remember that bar-b-q at Neil and Gemma's? When the tablecloth disappeared over the hedge the minute it was put on the table. It had to be retrieved from next door - then anchored in place with rocks from the rockery?"
Pete held open the black plastic bag into which the offending leaves were being deposited.
"Climate change again, I suppose," he ventured. "That's what the boffins and the politicians would tell us. It's all our fault, of course. The likes of you and me. For driving gas-guzzling cars and burning too much fossil fuel. Never mind that they can't agree on policy and ratify Kyoto."
"You sound really grumpy this morning," Emma chided. "What's wrong with you today? You're not usually so negative."
Pete huffed.
"I'm just fed up with carrying the brunt of everyone else's disasters. Pollution isn't just down to us driving a 4x4. It's historic. It's been growing since the industrial revolution and it's still going on in countries like China. It's down to the policy makers. The planners. All that smog being pumped into the atmosphere from the dark satanic mills; by the entrepreneurs we need in the world but who've overlooked the effect on the planet in their pursuit of wealth," he dramatised.
"Oh, no. According to the powers that be it's the likes of us. Joe Public. We are the cause of global warming. And we have to mend our ways. So we should give up the 4x4 and drive a mini because if we don't our children will suffer. Talk about emotional blackmail. Now it's the same with this banking crisis. The bankers have caused it and the government stood by and allowed it but who do you think's going to carry the can?"
"Do you think Sophie's bank have made these massive losses?" Emma continued. "She hasn't said anything about

The Dream Robbers

it - Sophie. She's responsible for some of the investments. Perhaps even she ….."

"Oh, no doubt," Pete interrupted bitterly. "She's probably up to her neck in it and if she is you can bet your life she'll justify herself somehow. Just as long as her own selfish lifestyle isn't affected. Responsible for - Sophie, responsible for? God help us."

"She isn't that bad," Emma defended, a duty to defend because the accused was family, whether guilty or not.

"Is she not?" Pete queried. "Well, we'll see how you feel when we're in difficulties ourselves, Em, because the way things are going at the moment it won't take that long. Do you know how many houses we've sold at The Tythings? One, that's all. One. And that's provided their mortgage offer holds. We should have reserves on the lot by now. Sold off plan. I can't even think about starting on the site at Burwash. There's no point even if we had the capital reserves, unless the market gets back on its feet. It just makes me seethe to think what these banks have done. But it's Joe Public's fault again. People wouldn't have been able to borrow so much if the banks had been regulated properly."

They bundled the tools back into the shed and headed for the back door.

"Lunch?" suggested Emma.

"Yes. I'm starving. It's a wonder the kids haven't been hollering."

"Oh, I'm sure they're alright. They've probably raided the crisp box - or the biscuit tin," and Emma laughed as they strolled across the garden arm in arm.

"Won't have been the fruit bowl, that's for sure," retorted Pete with a wry grin.

The conversation continued indoors as Emma tossed a salad and Pete laid the table, uncorking a bottle of pinot grigio and reaching for the wine glasses from the cupboard on the wall. Emma watched him as he distributed the place mats, that

Caroline Jones Lewis

The Dream Robbers

little tell-tale sign of threatening anger in a normally controlled man clearly visible. His mother had told her when they were engaged.

"You'll know if he's agitated, if he's getting in a temper," she had told her. "You'll notice. It's his leg. His left leg - it shakes, just a little tremor. His father does exactly the same."

True enough, there it was now - that little tremor fluttering the leg of his trouser. She did her best to divert his attention, ever watchful of his blood pressure.

"Is the planning permission for Burwash through yet?"

"No, but it should be next week when the Planning Committee meet. I don't anticipate any problem. It's a shame we bought the site when we did - but no-one has a crystal ball, do they? We'll just have to sit on it for a while - until house sales get going again, however long that takes. We might even have to rethink the type of housing we build there, depending on how the market develops. With any luck the government will kick-start the economy for the first-time buyer. Suspension of stamp duty and a cut in interest rates, that's what we need. That would do it. But we really need to sell some of the stock at The Tythings - we need to recover some of the build and development costs. Otherwise I'll be laying the men off and that's going to give them a problem. And anyway how on earth would I decide which one should go?"

"Oh, dear. That would be awful," fretted Emma. "Especially Martin. His wife's just had another baby."

"Well, they're nearly all married with mortgages and families to support. Martin isn't the only one. I dare not draw anything for *our* needs, Em. We'll have to get by on yours for essentials and dip into the piggy bank for extras. And that won't be easy. Look how your commission's gone down in the last few months."

"I know. It's halved since May. Sales are really falling away now that the pipeline sales have completed. I'm

Caroline Jones Lewis

The Dream Robbers

really beginning to worry how we're going to pay for Izzie's place at the academy in the New Year. Things should be better by then, though, shouldn't they?"

Pete shrugged his shoulders.

"Not sure. Not if the doom and gloom merchants are right. Nationwide are predicting stagnation in the market - tough times ahead in 2008. As the biggest lender they have the broadest statistics available. They reckon zero growth in house values. Rightmove are in agreement. It isn't looking rosy."

"Yes, but if you're buying and selling, values don't really matter, do they? It's swings and roundabouts. There should still be some deals that go through. Let's not get too despondent."

"No, you're right, Em. But it's the first time buyers, isn't it? They're the key. They're going to be reluctant to come onto the property ladder right now, aren't they? They'll want to wait and see if property values fall further and they can get a better deal so that will inhibit the sales above them. I don't have to tell you how the market works. And the banks are insisting on bigger deposits now. Remember how difficult we found it - that first step?"

"Yes, I know. I was just trying to stay optimistic. We've weathered storms in the past. We'll weather this one."

Emma insisted on positive thinking.

"Yeah, sorry, love. I'm being a pain, aren't I? But it was all so much easier in the past. We didn't have so much at stake then. Do you think I'm getting old, Em? Letting things get me down?"

"Don't be daft, of course you're not. It's just …. Well, you're right. We're responsible for other people's lives now instead of just our own. It's a big responsibility."

"The guys are getting a bit edgy. They're obviously worried about the future. They don't say much but there's the odd remark, the odd furtive look. They're guessing that it won't be long before I have to put the ones on the payroll on short time and they're right. I can manage not to do it

Caroline Jones Lewis

The Dream Robbers

before Christmas. That would be just too awful. But I think we'd better keep our own Christmas to a fairly modest affair, Em. You won't go spending out too much, will you?"

"I'll do my best. But I've all but promised Hannah a new computer. The old one's groaning and she really needs it for her homework. I was thinking of a laptop."

Pete sighed. And what we do for Hannah, he thought, we must do for the other two.

"Is a laptop a good idea?" he asked. "Too easy to use in the bedroom - out of sight and all that. She'd probably spend most of her time on Facebook."

"Hmm - you could be right," answered Emma. "I'll have to think about that one. But let's concentrate on Dad for the moment. Have you ordered the champagne for his retirement party?"

Pete gave another sigh and mentally calculated his credit card balance.

Emma walked to the door and called out into the hallway. "Come on, guys. Lunch is ready."

"I saw Robert Welling in town yesterday," Pete mentioned casually. "We had a mutual grumble. He was saying - things are getting tough for his business, too."

******

Above the neatly manicured counties of the British countryside and the icy waters of the Atlantic, through the streets of cities on both sides of the ocean, the winds continued gathering momentum, dusting away the cobwebs of one after another ill-founded regime. Around the world banks grudgingly admitted their involvement in the badly-advised American market.

******

In her office in the City, Sophie Gray ran her finger

The Dream Robbers
Caroline Jones Lewis

nervously down the list in her investment portfolio for, unlike her sister, she had known full well the reasons for the financial disaster that had caused Northern Rock to flounder. The extent of her own bank's exposure across the Atlantic filled her with trepidation. There would be an inquisition, of course, by a Board that had until now been blissfully ignorant and uncaring of the actions of their subordinates, content simply to take the resulting spoils. She would be amongst the first in the line of fire. A knock on her door interrupted her train of thought.
"Come in," she called.
Leo Trask stepped into her office with an air approaching reverence and padded across the carpet to place a sheaf of paperwork on her desk.
"This morning's mail, Miss Gray," he breathed, "and last night's stats."

Leo was a trainee investment banker. In his mid-twenties, he had a boyish quality about him that was not dispelled by the baby face and the light brown curly hair that framed it. Of slight build and stature, the spring in his step was fired by an eternal optimism and an immaturity of personality. Sophie Gray was his idol, the role model he strove to emulate, her success legendary in the staff room and her lifestyle one that he coveted. He followed her every career move like a puppy dog that shadowed its master. He lived only streets away from her penthouse apartment in a small property that he had bought only months before with his partner Tess. A secretary in the Directors' suite, Tess had fancied Leo from the moment they had met, their eyes coyly appraising each other in the lift between the first and second floor. She was all that he was not - mature beyond her years, a pretty and petite realist who saw the world in virtual black and white. Leo was the romance and excitement in her life, the pastel hues of the gentle and the vibrant shades of boldness. She was the stability in his, the feet that remained firmly on the ground in the face of fantasy. The

Caroline Jones Lewis
The Dream Robbers

relationship had escalated at speed. Now they were expecting an unplanned first baby and were assessing their collateral and income. Tess would take maternity leave from the bank for as long as they could afford it and Leo was intent on climbing the career ladder sooner rather than later. The future looked rosy and the idea of the baby was exciting.

"Thanks, Leo," Sophie answered absentmindedly, oblivious to the quietly reverential retreat that ranked on a par with the backward exit from the company of royalty. She reached for her mail, hoping for some good news though in reality expecting none and leafing quickly through confirmed the negative expectation. Something in the exercise jogged her memory about the square cream handwritten envelope that had arrived this morning at home and which she had stuffed into her handbag in her haste to leave for the office. She reached down to retrieve it from her bag in the bottom drawer of her desk. Slicing open the envelope with the letter opener on her desk, she found herself fingering an invitation to her father's retirement party.
"Oh, damn," she breathed. "I'd forgotten that."
It was not an occasion that she contemplated with joy, nervous of the inevitable probing and innuendo attending the event would bring. Pete in particular, she guessed, would be aiming for the jugular.
"We have you bankers to thank for this lot." She could hear him say it now, his voice terse with reproach. Within the confines of the bank's cavernous London headquarters the gathering clouds over the business dealings of Sophie and her colleagues' were casting lengthening shadows over her entire universe. Losses in the billions of pounds sterling for her bank had focused attention on their activities and their over-zealous investment in a market that now appeared to have always been untenable. At the time of investment it had somehow presented an opportunity of making millions to eyes greedy for an ever-fattening purse and minds dismissive of the obvious flaws in the strategy. The

Caroline Jones Lewis
The Dream Robbers

collapse in the US housing market in which this money had been so woefully and ill-advisably poured had left the bank reeling. She and her colleagues now glanced fearfully over their shoulders on a daily basis.

"You can almost hear the knives being sharpened in the board room," she grumbled to James.

"What's the damage?" he asked her.

"Billions," was the succinct reply.

"There's no outward sign of discord yet, but you can feel the tension in the air. It's hanging over us all like the sword of Damocles."

Each of her colleagues was busily and hastily engaging in nifty foot-work to divert the blame from themselves to elsewhere, potentially on each other. 'Could not have been foreseen' and 'a situation not of our making' were phrases that would echo empty in the light of commercial fact and common sense. It was only a matter of time before the reality of the bank's plight became common knowledge to staff and media alike and it was quite enough being stalked in the corridors of commerce without having to face it from her family too.

Turning down the invitation, however, would illicit condemnation on a hitherto unprecedented level unless supported by a water-tight alibi, an unavoidable and unalterable business commitment somewhere, indeed anywhere, in the farthest reaches of the country or preferably even outside the UK. There was nothing in the offing and nothing she could invent since investment was now in a state of stagnation. To the party she would have to go unless an urgent summons of importance provided a timely excuse. James sighed at the news as they imbibed in a trendy wine bar later in the evening.

"Oh, God. Do we have to?"

"Yes, we do have to."

"A village hall, for God's sake. Much as I respect your parents, Soph, I really don't relish the idea of spending the biggest part of a day with a load of country yokels and their

Caroline Jones Lewis
The Dream Robbers

offspring."

"Don't exaggerate," Sophie laughed. "They're hardly that."

James grinned at his own embellishment. But he, too, had reasons for not wanting to be out of town right now. There were rumblings in his world too. They had begun as whisperings, mutterings, then developed into clearly spoken concerns and now were growing into accusation. He didn't see what all the fuss was about, he had argued to himself. Insider trading had always taken place - ever since he'd been a trader. So many people he knew did it, though no-one else at his firm, as far as he knew. So the knives were being sharpened in another boardroom and other axes were poised to fall. Others had indulged, he excused himself, and no-one had batted an eyelid - until now. It was what made the world go round - money and its dealings. So why suddenly all the fuss? He knew the answer well enough so he, too, needed to keep his ear to the ground, his eye on the ball, so to speak. Like Sophie, he was watching his back for the knives and the hatchets and an absence from the battlefield, however brief, could mean he might miss something vital. He regretted his involvement now. It was not as if they had needed the money. But the rewards were enormous and when the right information had come his way - well, the temptation had been too much to resist. He had mentioned nothing to Sophie. She was worried enough for her own well-being, he knew.

Reluctantly he conceded that a visit to 'the family' was inevitable, particularly as Christmas would be spent with his own parents in Brittany prompting an expression of displeasure from Pete and Emma. But somehow he would find a reason for this visit to be the briefest of affairs.

"Right, Cinderella," he conceded. "You *shall* go to the ball."

******

Caroline Jones Lewis

The Dream Robbers

Emma had misgivings of her own with respect to the celebration, for a confidence by her mother had identified another source of concern.

"Your Dad's pension forecast is almost half what we had expected it to be," Kate had fretted.

"He spoke to his financial advisor. Apparently it's because of all the falls on the stock market, because of this credit crunch thing. All these banks in trouble. That's bad enough, Em, but we've just had a letter to say that the price of our gas is going up again. That's the second time in the last few months. And the electricity. And the cost of petrol! Well. How we're going to manage I just don't know. We've got the rest of the money from selling the house in the bank but if we keep dipping into that it isn't going to last very long. And then what?"

She sniffed into a tissue, the remnants of a cold adding to her discomfort.

"We've both been so looking forward to his retirement, to having time to do all the other things we've always wanted to do. Worked all our lives for. We've paid into his pension for years and years. We thought we'd done all the right things to provide for old age but now I really don't know how we're going to manage. There won't be any spare money for the holidays we were intending. That cruise we were planning for next year will have to go on hold. Your Dad's talking about getting a part time job somewhere. The local supermarket, or something. But then if there are lots of young people needing work they won't want oldies like your Dad, will they?"

"Oh, Mum. This really is too bad. This US housing thing seems to be affecting everybody. But you know how things go. The market will probably come up again in a few months - when things have stabilised a bit."

"I hope so. Em. I really hope so."

Emma said no more. She and Pete also had anxieties. The housing market had remained sluggish to the extent that most of "The Tythings" remained unsold. For the first time

Caroline Jones Lewis
The Dream Robbers

for many years they faced a major cash flow problem over
the coming months. The salary bill for the current month
would take them to the edge of overdraft even without Pete
drawing a penny for their own household expenses. As if
that were not enough to worry about, Emma's commission
had shrunk further to leave a salary that would barely cover
the normal monthly outgoings of a family of five let alone
extras like a retirement party and Christmas. The savings
account, which hitherto had been sacrosanct and for the
children's' future needs, would be the next port of call.
With Isobel's departure to the Academy looming, they really
needed things to pick up - and soon. But the pundits were
promising nothing positive, the more pessimistic amongst
them predicting long and hard days ahead. The timing
could not be worse.

******

Oblivious to the financial facts of life, Isobel sauntered
through the local shopping centre with best friend Abi,
rifling through the clothes racks in their favourite boutiques
in search of that 'special' little outfit for the festive season's
parties.
"How about this one, Izz," Abi suggested holding out a
skimpy, fitted little black number with thin shoulder straps
and spattered with sparkle.
"Hmm. Quite nice. But I need to wear it to my granddad's
party as well and he and grandma don't like me in black.
They're always saying it. 'You young people, you wear too
much black. Black is for funerals'," she mimicked and she
pulled a face, then giggled.
"Good excuse to have two then!" grinned Abi.
"Don't think the allowance will stretch to two, Abs. I want
to keep some money back for when I get to the Academy."
"Oh, Izz. I'm really going to miss you. You will come
home at weekends, won't you?" she pleaded.
"Well, not every weekend. We'll be doing concerts some

Caroline Jones Lewis
The Dream Robbers

weekends which I'm really looking forward to. But I will be home sometimes. I'll still see you, Abs. Anyway, you could come up to town. We could go to the Kings Road, and stuff."

"Oh, cool. If Mum and Dad will let me, though. They might not be too keen on the idea of us wandering around town unsupervised - you know what parents are like."

"Well, mine will be coming up sometimes, you could come with them. I'm sure they'd let us off the lead for some of the time."

"Great. Sorted. Heh - how about this blue one. Fab colour. That would really suit you with your blonde hair."

The day of the retirement party dawned beneath skies laden with November fog. After the drive down from town at midday through a swirling mist trapped in the glow of still-lit street lamps or caught in the headlights between berried hedgerows as the streets of town gave way to country lanes, Sophie and James parked the cabriolet beside the duck pond in view of the village hall. Another couple was just arriving, making their way towards its door, the woman clutching a wrap thrown around her shoulders and piled up under her chin. Her husband coughed against the inclement weather expelling the heat of his breath in great clouds that dispersed into the haze around him.

"Well - here goes," sighed James, turning to grin at Sophie in the passenger seat beside him. Sophie pursed her lips in a tight smile and turned to face him.

"At least we have the excuse of the weather to leave early," he observed.

Sophie nodded.

"OK. Here goes," she echoed, stretching to grasp the extravagantly wrapped gift on the seat behind her.

They opened the car doors in tandem, James uncoiling his tall, slim suited frame to stand to his full six foot three. He shivered as the cold air hit him after the warmth of the car. Sophie swung her long, silk-clad legs out onto the tarmac,

Caroline Jones Lewis
The Dream Robbers

raising elegantly onto stiletto heels and smoothing down the skirt of a Prada dress.

"Quick, Soph. It's freezing out here."

She grabbed her handbag from the foot well, the present from her seat and slammed the door closed. With a click of the key fob to lock the car, they hurried hand in hand to the scene of celebration.

Kate and Andy Gray welcomed their guests at the door. Sophie was surprised at how smart and youthful her normally homespun mother looked. She had obviously had her hair done for the occasion by someone other than her usual hairdresser, her soft grey hair shaped into a stylish bob. Her dress was a departure from the usual small print pleated skirt and top in manmade fibres, substituted by a sleek shift of purple silk and complimented by pearls and pearl earrings. Her father had exchanged his usual trousers and cable cardie for a suit and tie, albeit a tie that James would not be seen dead in but no matter, she thought. At least he had made the effort. Sophie bent to kiss her mother on the cheek.

"Hello, you two. You look marvellous, both of you. Mum, you're a dark horse. Have you been raiding the piggy bank?"

Kate blanched a little, reminded of the protest she had made to Emma on their shopping spree, at the cost of the dress she was now wearing in the light of the financial state she and Andy were about to find themselves in.

"Oh, Emma took me shopping," she explained. "You know what she's like. She insisted this was *the* dress, the only one that would do."

"Quite right, too," Sophie encouraged. "You look wonderful. And Dad. Quite the dapper gentleman," and she kissed her father lightly, thrusting the present into his hands.

"Just a little something for all those relaxing days ahead of you".

Caroline Jones Lewis

The Dream Robbers

"Thanks," he managed, already feeling somewhat overwhelmed by the entire occasion.
"Mrs Gray, Mr Gray," James ventured, holding out his hand to shake with two people he still could not manage to refer to by either their christian names or anything more familiar. Andy shuffled the bulky gift awkwardly in an attempt to return the greeting.
Hello, James. Nice to see you. Thank you for coming. Good journey? Fog, oh yes, awful. Such nasty weather but glad you made it. Yes, Emma's over there. She'll find you a drink but help yourselves anyway. Until all the politeness of the niceties were interrupted by new arrivals behind them. Oh, Sandra. Come in, come in out of the cold. Dreadful weather, isn't it? George, nice to see you. We were worried you might not make it, whether you'd be out of hospital in time.

Looking around the eclectic mix of the company above whom he stood, almost without exception, a head and shoulders taller, the nearest to match him in height being Sophie herself and brother-in-law Pete, James found the company were much as he had expected. Andy's erstwhile colleagues from the printing firm rubbed shoulders with former neighbours from the old house and new ones from the estate where he and Kate now lived in their neat and compact little bungalow. Various friends they had accumulated over the years chatted amiably with his former boss and wife and Pete's brother Tony and his family. And of course, Emma and Pete themselves and the children. Had he been in London at this end of the working week, James mused, he would have met Sophie at the wine bar to launch their weekend with a glass or two of fine wine, possibly a dish of pasta or a favoured fish dish and conversation amongst friends to challenge the intellect, tinged with wry humour and the latest City tittle-tattle. What could he find to say to this lot, he wondered? Inwardly he sighed. At least, he thought, he was spared the presence of the handsome and

Caroline Jones Lewis
The Dream Robbers

successful Robert Welling, the man, he was ever-conscious, who still harboured affection for Sophie and threatened his own ability to hold her. Sophie was the love of his life but he was not, he recognised realistically, the love of hers. She had never confirmed it, but her manner when they came into the company of Robert Welling, and his suspicion that whenever she was in Kent alone she called on Robert at his home, had always fuelled his imagination. He played his hand coolly, kept his suspicions close to his chest, never allowing himself to play the jealous lover. Sophie was not a woman who would respond well to possessiveness. It was not easy, but he reckoned it was his best hand. At least Robert Welling was not amongst today's merry throng, hardly within the Gray's social circle.

Putting his thoughts aside, he followed Sophie who was edging her way through the still gathering assembly towards the impromptu bar, passing a table on which a growing collection of presents covered in an array of gaudy wrapping was displayed.
"What did you do with the present?" he whispered.
"I gave it to Dad."
"What was it, by the way?"
"A water feature for the garden and a voucher for the garden centre. He'll enjoy setting that up in their little garden."
"Oh. Right. Fine. Thought I should know in case they say something. Now - I need a drink. And since I can only have one then I hope it's a stiff one."

Sophie sidled up to her sister with James close behind her.
"Hi, Em. Hear you're handing out the drinks, then."
Emma swung round to face her sister.
"Well, Pete is. Hi. Glad you're here safe. Mum was a bit worried about you travelling in this fog."
"It isn't as bad as you might think. We only really picked up any dense fog about Sevenoaks. It was reasonably clear until then, wasn't it James?"

Caroline Jones Lewis
The Dream Robbers

James nodded, shooting her a warning glance.

"Have to watch it as it drops dark, though," he added, neatly planting the excuse for an early departure from the outset.

"These country lanes are a bit hairy in the dark let alone with poor visibility. And fog always gets worse at night, doesn't it?"

Arriving at Sophie's elbow with a tray of drinks in time to catch the comment, Pete raised his eyebrows at an uncomprehending Emma. Don't let us keep you, James, he thought.

"Last time we were down a deer shot out right in front of us, didn't it, Soph?" James continued, determined to press home his point.

"Oh, yes, you're right. It did. James had to brake quite hard to avoid it. It was scary. It just appeared from between the hedges along the main road. Lucky it wasn't foggy like today or we might not have seen it in time."

"Yes, I must admit I wouldn't like to have a journey to do in this weather. At least we've only got to drive back to our village," Emma conceded. "Still - you made it. That's the main thing."

"Izzie looks marvellous," Sophie observed, casting her eyes around the room to where her niece stood laughing and gesticulating to a group of attentive guests. Izzie, the virtual replica of her mother, popular, calm, an all-together individual who knew just what she wanted from life and was entirely focused on getting it, she thought.

"Who chose the dress?"

"She chose it herself," Emma answered proudly. "She went shopping with Abigail and came back with that little gem. Clever, isn't she?"

"I'll say. That blue really suits her. Hmm. I'm impressed. She's going to turn a head or two when she gets to the Academy."

"Mmm, if she gets to the Academy," Emma muttered. Sophie turned her head sharply towards her sister. "Why? Why shouldn't she?" She was perplexed, aware of how

Caroline Jones Lewis
The Dream Robbers

enthusiastic had been her sister's encouragement of Isobel's ambition on Isobel's behalf.

"Finances are looking a bit shaky," Emma confided. "I surely don't have to tell you what's happening to the housing market - to the economy."

Until now Sophie's only thoughts on the matter of the credit crunch had been in readiness to defend her own position. The effect on others had not really occurred to her, not even in respect of her own family. She changed the subject abruptly, turning her head away from her sister's gaze to scan the assembly.

"Where's Joe and Hannah?"

"Oh, among the crowd somewhere, both of them. Hannah looks lovely, too though I took her shopping for her outfit myself"

Emma's eyes darkened somewhat at the recollection of the tantrum prompted by her choice.

"No, Hannah. I am not paying that price for a dress that is patently unsuitable for the occasion and for a girl of your age. We'll get the other one. It looks lovely on you - and it's a more reasonable price."

"But this is the one I want," Hannah protested vehemently and just short of a foot-stamping exhibition. "I'll ask Aunt Sophie. Aunt Sophie will buy it for me."

"You will **not** ask your Aunt Sophie, Hannah and that's final."

"Oh, Mum," Hannah had growled.

"And Joe," she continued to Sophie. "Well, anything more than an open-necked shirt and black trousers is suspect as far as Joe is concerned."

Sophie glanced around the room until she spotted them, Joe a miniature of his father in looks and personality, destined already in all probability to follow in his father's footsteps and join the family firm. The Bailey dynasty, thought Sophie with a lightly mocking smile. And then there was dark-haired Hannah who featured neither of her parents but strongly reminded Sophie of a photograph on her mother's

Caroline Jones Lewis
The Dream Robbers

mantelpiece, a photo of the maternal grandmother she had never known but was constantly reminded that she herself resembled.

Yes, it's you Hannah, she thought. It's you who carries on that line, the gene with a legacy of rebellion and unconventionality that is already making itself apparent. Good for you, girl. You be your own person.

Dusk sank rapidly into early evening darkness as greeting arrivals gave way to affable communion, then to speeches and presentation and the popping of corks from champagne bottles for a toast to long and healthy years ahead. Only a little after the last drop of bubbly was wrung from its bottle did James seek out Sophie who was holding audience with her two nieces. He whispered in her ear that maybe now they could "make an escape."

"Sssh," Sophie admonished. "Someone might hear you."

"Oh, come on, darling. For God's sake, we've done the necessary. Can't we make a move now? I've looked outside and the fog is like pea soup - we need to get going before it gets any worse."

"OK. I don't need any convincing - but just don't make it too obvious. We don't want to hurt their feelings in front of their friends, do we?"

With the weather a plausible excuse for departure and with Kate and Andy nodding their understanding, Sophie and James took their leave. They slipped out of the hall into the descending gloom, leaving the host of friends and family coiling serpent-like in the conga, weaving between tables and chairs and the less energetic members of the party who remained seated, Hannah hanging laughing on the shirt-tail of her Uncle Tony who led them around the hall.

"Thank God that's over," James breathed as he sank into the driving seat and closed the car door.

"Oh it wasn't that bad," sighed Sophie as she sank into the passenger seat with equal relief. "At least we've kept them happy."

Caroline Jones Lewis
The Dream Robbers

"You're beginning to sound like your sister," James was teasing now, relaxing now that the event was over.

"You needn't go that far," Sophie guffawed.

Within minutes they were edging warily onto the A21 at the fog-ridden junction and heading for home.

"By the way," said Sophie, "I gave Emma a cheque for £300. towards cost of the party and I only had the cheque book on the joint account with me. Just so that you know when the statement comes in."

"What on earth did you do that for?"

"I think they're finding things a bit tough at the moment, the housing market being the way it is. I thought we should make the gesture - half shares and all that. And we can afford it, darling, can't we?"

James said nothing for a moment, suddenly stung by a recognition that events in the City were truly beginning to impact on the lives of others. He, too, was reluctant to address the issue further.

"Yes, of course we can," he said. "No problem," and the subject was dismissed.

Loading dirty dishes into the dishwasher in the kitchen at the village hall, Pete expressed his annoyance to Emma.

"With all the money those two have, don't tell me they couldn't have stayed in a hotel for the night and graced your parents with their company a little longer. They really do annoy me, your sister and James."

"Yes, I know, love, but there's no point in agonising over it," protested Emma. "They're not likely to change, are they? Anyway, Mum and Dad have us and we make up for everything that Sophie isn't. *You* make up for it, for everything that James isn't," and as he bent to slot a pile of plates in the bottom rack, she planted a kiss on the crown of his head, just where his hair was beginning to thin, she noticed; where the pink of his scalp was now visible through the strands of brown hair. Time was marching on for them too, she thought wistfully. Time was flying by. They had

Caroline Jones Lewis

The Dream Robbers

always talked about retiring at 50, when the children were independent and they would be free to do all the things that so far had been denied them, tied to the costs of a growing family, a school timetable and all the demands of the children's' other activities. She thought of her parents, of the hopes they had had before economics had altered their agenda. Pete had become really grumpy these days. She had never known him like it before. But stress had become his ever-present companion and it showed. Who knows what's ahead for any of us, she thought. Who knows.
"By the way," she went on, "Sophie gave me a cheque towards the cost of the party."
"Hallelujah. At least that's something even if they can't be bothered to put in any other effort. It's more than they usually do, I suppose. Perhaps there is a conscience buried somewhere beneath the designer bling."
Emma said nothing more. Her husband's growing irritation with her sister was becoming an obsession she was finding hard to bear but her loyalty to him prevented candour. It dismayed her to contemplate the row that was clearly brewing and the possibility of a greater rift within the family. She could not know, it was better for her not to know, the direction that life - and death - would eventually take.

Caroline Jones Lewis

The Dream Robbers

Chapter 3 - Challenges Ahead

December 2007

With the retirement party over and planning for their Christmas in full swing, Emma's attention was constantly on their diminishing bank balance. With no improvement in her pay packet Pete agreed with her that a withdrawal from the savings account was the only option. After drawing up a comprehensive list and budget, which Emma handed to him with a wry grin and some misgivings, he went online and made the transfer.

"Nothing more," he insisted. "You've got presents there for Uncle Tom Cobley and all," he added, prodding the list with his forefinger.

"Well, after this year we're bound to have to cut back, with the fees to pay for Izz at the Academy. So I thought we'd have a last fling, so to speak. Alright?"

Pete grinned wryly. "Is that right?" he questioned. He knew his wife had all the best intentions but he also knew that she would spend whatever was needed to make their Christmas full of cheer and that next year would be no different. And he would let her because she had always been able to twist him around her little finger.

"Alright then, as long as it is."

He pulled out up a scrap of paper caught in the paper clip holding together Emma's papers.

"There's a 'phone number on here, Em. Is it important?"

"Oh, it's the local dairy," she explained. "I thought we might start having our milk delivered. It would be quite nice, I thought. To have the milk arrive fresh on the doorstep every morning."

"Oh, ok. What prompted that idea?"

"Well, it was the supermarkets really. Several of them have just been fined millions for price fixing. It was on the news.

Caroline Jones Lewis
The Dream Robbers

They tried to make out it was to help the farmers by raising the price of milk but the FSA didn't believe them. I didn't either. Just more profit for themselves."

"More greed in the corridors of power," Pete muttered.

"The supermarkets have so much control over people's spending I thought the only way to help the farmers is to cut them out altogether," she continued. "So I thought, milk from the local dairy and vegetables fresh from the farm shop. It's a bit more expensive, I'm afraid, but then sometimes you just have to take a stand, don't you? If more people did it the supermarkets would get the message."

"Right. Quite the little campaigner then, heh?"

He smiled, a proud smile for the wife he respected. She's so much more socially aware than I am, he thought.

"And does that mean bread from the local baker as well?" he continued.

"Actually I'm thinking of getting a bread maker and making my own."

"Mmm, that sounds good. I wouldn't mind having a go at that."

Emma smiled.

"It will be really nice, don't you think? Nostalgic. That clink of milk bottles landing on the doorstep early in the morning while you've still got your nose under the bedclothes. Just like when we were kids. The smell of bread baking in the kitchen. Mum used to bake bread sometimes. Did yours?"

"Can't remember her doing. Nice idea though. Let's give it a go."

It had already been agreed that the first term's fees for the Academy would also come out of the savings account. From there on it was the intention that efforts must be made to manage without more piggy bank contributions. Kate and Andy, it was insisted, would come to them this year for Christmas and not the other way around as had been the

Caroline Jones Lewis
The Dream Robbers

practice in previous years. Now they were in the bungalow and not the family house of previous years, where Emma and Sophie had spent their childhood and Pete had called a-courting, there was no room to host a large congregation. And with their current financial concerns and the lack of a monthly income apart from Andy's state pension, the extra burden would be unfair. Since Sophie and James would be in France, it was down to Emma, Pete and the children to make the family Christmas merry. It would not be difficult, particularly with Isobel bubbling over with excitement at her impending progress towards her future career.

******

At the Guildhall in London, the Guild of Freemen and their guests assembled for their annual banquet in a glow of glitter and sparkle. The evening frocks of the ladies swished and swirled through the entrance to assemble at the security barrier beside their evening suited men - a smart and glittering affair. The warm brickwork of the building glowed mellow in the light that flooded the courtyard from inside, its arched façade smiling a welcome. James and Sophie, elegant in their finery, alighted from their taxi onto the cobblestones and joined the merry throng.
"Where are we meeting Charles?" asked Sophie.
"He said he'd find us inside. In the Old Library. The champers is served there before we go in to dinner."
"Oh, good. I don't really want to wander into dinner on our own. It will be far nicer to break the ice beforehand. It's alright for you. You know them already," she mused.
"**Him**. I know **him** ,"James stressed. "I've never met his wife"
They passed through the security check in a queue, deposited their outdoor clothes downstairs in the respective cloakrooms, then met back at the top of the stairs to wander contentedly along the ambulatory towards the assembled throng in the Old Library. A buzz of conversation and

Caroline Jones Lewis
The Dream Robbers

laughter greeted them as they entered through the heavy wooden door. Sophie studied her surroundings. It was her first visit inside the Guildhall and she took in the ambience enthusiastically, the enormous oil paintings, the chandelier, and the décor. James scanned the crowd ahead for their host, Sophie at his elbow still entranced by everything around her. She smiled contentedly. She loved the pomp, the ceremony, the tradition that typified the establishment, such a contrast to the fast-moving contemporary world of banking that was her usual environment. Accepting a glass of champagne from a tray offered by a waist coated waiter, they squeezed
through the laughing, chattering crowd towards the far side of the room.

"Impressed?" James asked her with a grin.

"Impressed," she confirmed. "Very impressive. And not a blue rinse in sight."

James laughed, a genuine head-thrown-back laugh.

"So - these are the good people who may wear their swords unsheathed within the boundaries of the City and drive their sheep over Tower Bridge," Sophie continued.

"Apparently so," James replied. "Well, some of them anyway. I suppose some are just mere mortals like you and me."

Across the room, half concealed behind a pillar, Charles Forsythe watched the couple enter and make their progress towards himself and his wife.

"Damn," he thought. "He's made it. Damn."

Since extending the invitation to this son of a former associate, there had been rumours, whisperings in the corridors and washrooms of the City institutions in which Charles was involved. Whisperings of malpractice, of investigation by the Financial Services Authority. The name James Freyer had cropped up more than once but only as an aside, not as a main protagonist. If he is a bad egg, thought Charles, as a newly elected member of the Court of

Caroline Jones Lewis
The Dream Robbers

Common Council it is not a name right now I should be associated with.

He had wondered whether he should ring Giles Freyer. Let him know about the rumours, that if was possible his boy might be in trouble. Perhaps he owed him that much. But then he decided against it.

"Best to keep mum," he had concluded. "At least until there was something more definite than just a City rumour. Everyone knew how prolific the City rumour machine could be, and not always correct at that.

Oh, well, best get on with it, he thought. I'll wait until just before dinner and then 'find' them, so to speak. And after tonight, I can ease back from an alliance best kept at arm's length - at least for the time being. He sipped his champagne thoughtfully.

Grace will suss him out. She's a far better judge of character than I am. Cracking girlfriend, though, he acknowledged. Stephanie, isn't it? Or Susan? Something like that.

"Do you know anyone, darling?" Sophie asked.

"Yes - one or two. Old boys from school mainly. There's another dealer over there. I've seen him at the Exchange but we're only on nodding terms."

"Ah," she sighed, raising her eyebrows. "The old school tie. The public school network."

"Well, the City runs on the old school tie network, darling. It's a boys' club. The right school, the right background. You know how it goes."

"You're OK then."

"No, not really." James sounded disappointed. "I only went to lowly Musgrove, you know. There is a pecking order, of course. Most of these guys went to one or other of the more important schools. Then there's the next stage of the apprenticeship. I missed that one out altogether."

"Which is?"

"The Honorary Artillery Company. That's the route to

Caroline Jones Lewis
The Dream Robbers

take. The right school, service with HAC, and an interest in public service. Then you're in."

"Why didn't you?"

"Not really my scene, is it? Can you see me taking military orders? Committing my spare time to public service?"

She shook her head and laughed.

"No. Definitely not," and he grinned, a wry grin, half in pride and half reluctant. Maybe, he thought. Maybe if I had. Maybe if I had been less of a maverick, I would not be faced with the problems facing me now, these problems of which Sophie is so far unaware. But indulging in 'if only' was a useless pursuit. He cut dead the train of thought and concentrated on finding his host. A voice behind him caused him to turn.

"Ah, James, old man. You made it. Wonderful. Found you just in time. I think we're just about to go in to dinner. May I introduce my wife Grace. Grace, James Freyer."

Grace Forsyth extended her right hand in greeting, her left clasping a champagne glass still half full. An immaculately groomed lady, late 50s at a guess, thought Sophie, elegantly dressed in the conservative little black dress and accessorised with a quiet suite of diamond jewellery. Her whole manner spoke of dignified money. Old money, James noted.

"Pleased to meet you," he responded. "And this is Sophie Gray, my partner. Sophie - Charles and Grace Forsythe."

Grace Forsythe eyed Sophie critically from behind a smiling mask. No competition, she decided. Attractive though she was, the designer clothing, the exuberant jewellery, this self-assured woman was not the type that Charles usually went for. She would probably frighten him half to death. Grace Forsyth relaxed into her natural friendly manner.

The banqueting hall was a revelation to Sophie, its vaulted interior adorned cathedral-like with the banners of the many livery companies of the City. Immense statues of Churchill and Wellington sat between the doorways along the length of

Caroline Jones Lewis

The Dream Robbers

the hall. In the library, they had scanned the table plan to find their places at table, and Charles, familiar with the layout, led them directly to their seats at a sprig central to the top table. From the minstrel gallery above, strains of orchestral music floated out over the assemblage between two huge twin statues of Gog and Magog that stood guard over the proceedings at either side of the gallery. Charles trotted out a commentary of the proceedings and the surroundings.

Sitting beside her husband and facing their guests, Grace Forsythe noted the enthusiasm in her husband's voice as he spoke. She listened silently to his performance and was proud to hear it, for despite the one and only fly in their marital ointment, she adored him and all that he stood for. He had a genuine love of the City and devoted endless hours to its protection and well-being. As a Common Councillor, he now sat on a host of Committees that his father had served on before him - a family tradition. As a Member of a Ward Club, he promoted the interests of the Ward and encouraged a wide membership with the motto 'Open to All.' A fine man, she considered him. A good man. The investiture with the freedom had called for vetting, which had caused him no problem, coming from an old established family and estate as he did, already familiar to the City institutions. His acceptance had been guaranteed and he was regarded with respect by all. It was just the other women that were the problem. No full blown affairs, so far as she was aware. They never came to that. Just silly little dalliances that she feared one day might catch him out and bring scandal and disgrace on an otherwise pristine reputation and honourable character. Adultery of the heart, she believed, especially when it were only of a temporary nature, was not really adultery at all. Knowing him as she did, she doubted that any had progressed even as far as the bedroom door, but others would be unlikely to believe it. No smoke without fire, that's what others would say whatever she believed to

Caroline Jones Lewis

The Dream Robbers

be true. Men, she pondered. Such fools when confronted by a pretty face and a youthful figure. So susceptible to artful flattery. He was still an attractive man in her eyes, a former military man with a military bearing. And his connections and influence would appeal to a certain type of female. He would never leave her - she was secure in that. To do so would be against everything he believed in. Duty, responsibility. One simply did not do such a thing in the circles in which they moved. But it was more than that, for no less genuine for his window shopping was the love they shared between them, a comfortable love that neither would abandon. Whether he realised she was aware of his little philanderings she doubted but really had no idea. He would not have wanted to hurt her in that way and probably believed that discretion kept his secrets safe. Things might have been different, she would muse, had they had children. A son and heir to carry on the family estate or a daughter for him to spoil and cherish. But it was never to be, for no reason that anyone had ever been able to explain. Perhaps he saw her as she saw herself, she wondered for a millionth time. Incomplete. An incomplete woman.

A burst of laughter from her guests brought her back to the moment and she smiled, a Mona Lisa smile that Sophie caught and found quite poignant, detecting a sadness about this woman despite a life of privilege and the trappings of old money with a husband who appeared to adore her.

The evening was one of warm hospitality, good food, good wine, amusing speeches. Sitting to Sophie's left, James to the right of her, was a porter from Billingsgate, with a wealth of interesting tales to tell that she would relate to James later. Then the novelty of 'the ceremony of the loving cup' had the couple transfixed. Raised to their feet, their hosts passing the cup along the diners at each table, standing back to back with their neighbour before them, both hands on the cup while they sipped from its contents.

Caroline Jones Lewis

The Dream Robbers

"The history is," Charles explained to James and Sophie, "that in days of yore when stopping at a hostelry for sustenance and taking a drink in insecure company, your back would be protected from any would-be assassin behind you. When you pass the cup to the next member of your company, both your hands are engaged and in view, as are theirs, thereby showing no ill intent by either party. In other words, you can't stab them in the back while they are drinking, nor they you."

James and Sophie engaged in the ritual enthusiastically. "We should have this at lunches in the City," whispered James as he passed the cup to Sophie. "All the potential knives for the back that are being brandished at the moment ... Invaluable!"

"How true," Sophie smiled a response, their eyes twinkling in shared amusement over the rim of the vessel they held between them. She took the cup, wiped the rim with the napkin provided and turned to her neighbour. The porter from Billingsgate took the cup from her with an open smile. James turned his back to her back in assumed protection and the symbolism of the gesture did not evade him. He would do this for her always, he thought. Always. Protect her. Cherish her. For he loved her life more than his own. His own careless life that he had not protected as well as he should, had not led as well as he could. Try as he might, he could not dispel the darkness that hung over him, a day of reckoning that was threateningly near. The evening, in the company of good men and true, hit home the fact that money for the sake of money could not buy respectability and while he knew that there were rogues amongst the assembled congregation, the majority were decent honest people engaged in decent honest trade and profession. For the first time in a career and life led totally to suit his own wants and agenda, a tinge of conscience and regret pricked his heart.

They walked arm in arm down towards the embankment after the banquet. Cars at 10.45 pm, the invitation had told

Caroline Jones Lewis
The Dream Robbers

them but they walked instead, briskly in the chill night air through the streets of the City, looking to pick up a taxi to home.

"They're all the same, aren't they? Their type of people. All set in the same mould," Sophie mused.

"Mmm. I know what you mean. To me and you it would be a claustrophobic sort of life but the world needs their kind. They do all the graft for a community that we can't be bothered to do."

"It would drive me crazy. All that protocol, that politeness. Do they ever lose their temper with each other, do you think?" Sophie pondered.

"Oh, I dare say there's a fracas or two at the Committee meetings, wouldn't you think? They can't be that saintly, surely."

The silent pavements glistened with frost and lights from buildings reflected across the paving slabs, the Lloyds Building, the Bank of England, the dome of St Paul's silhouetted in the distance.

"It is a pretty special place, don't you think? The City," James said.

Sophie looked at him in amused surprise.

"You surprise me," she said. "Is that a touch of romance I see gleaming in your eye?" and she turned her face towards him laughing, not a mocking laugh but one of affection. He was not the love of her life but she truly loved him in her way. He saved her from being alone. Loneliness was the one thing that frightened her, terrified her. The thought of being alone and unloved. He adored her and she needed his adoration.

He grinned, hunching up his shoulders self-consciously, his collar up around his chin. There were changes coming. There were whispers and rumours; Chinese whispers maybe but they were rooted in fact. He could feel it in the winds that whipped around the side streets of the City and toyed playfully with the branches of the trees along the Embankment. The City was bracing itself for changes and

Caroline Jones Lewis

The Dream Robbers

he feared them. I have betrayed it, he wanted to tell her. I have betrayed this City. But not as badly as some. There were those that had ransacked its coffers to line their own, those that had made millions. There were City institutions that would bow their head in shame before many more months were passed. His involvement had only been recent, his profits only modest. Still he could not tell her. So he passed it off with a flippant response instead.
"Don't tell anyone," he quipped. "I have a reputation to maintain."

January 2008

The New Year brought renewed hope and a host of resolutions to the Bailey household.
"I'm going to ... umm, take more trouble with my homework, without grumbling," announced Hannah at the breakfast table on New Year's Day. "And ....save my pocket money instead of wasting it on things I don't need."
"Hmmm, right," Pete hummed, grinning wryly. "Jolly good." He winked knowingly at Emma. What's brought on this unexpected but welcome bout of good humour, he wondered.
"So what's yours, Joe?"
"Don't know," muttered Joe through a mouthful of bacon and mushrooms. "Haven't really thought about it.
Anyway, everyone breaks them by the end of the first week so there's no point really, is there?"
"Well, you could try," laughed his mother. "There must be something you think you should make an effort at improving."
"What, me? No, I'm perfect," he protested with a grin.
"Yeah - right," muttered Hannah good-humouredly.
"How about 'I promise to clean my football boots and put my dirty football kit in the washing bin so that Mum doesn't have to search for it and wash and dry it overnight before the next match?" suggested his father.

Caroline Jones Lewis

The Dream Robbers

"Oh alright," Joe mumbled sheepishly. "I'll try."
"Your turn, Izz," Emma challenged. All eyes turned to Isobel who sat daintily buttering her toast and smiling. She was thoughtful.
"Well, mine's easy," she answered. "Mine is to be a wonderful musician and make everything Mum and Dad are doing for me worthwhile."
Pete and Emma were silent, touched by the sentiment.
"Creep," muttered Joe, abruptly sticking the tip of his tongue out at his sister, then grinning his broadest, cheekiest grin and Hannah feigned retching into an imaginary bucket.
Isobel shrugged off their disdain with a grin, ever conscious that this was a moment of sea-change for her mother, whose dearest elder daughter would soon be launching out into the world on her own and that she, the mother, would miss her for every waking moment. And for her - a mixture of excitement and nervousness competed for dominance.
"So what about you two, then?" she challenged her parents. "Come on, you've put all of us on the spot. How about you?"
"Well, I'm going to get fit. Really fit. Not just slim. Fit." Emma volunteered staunchly, patting a nonexistent paunch.
"Oh, that old chestnut," Pete laughed. "How many weeks do you think it will last this year, kids? 6? 8?" and he and the children took bets while Emma, rising from her seat, puffed with fake indignation, grinning at what she knew to be the likely truth of their debate on her good intentions.
"Alright, smarty pants. You haven't told us yours yet," and she flipped Pete playfully as she reached for the coffee pot from the Aga. He thought for a moment, then spoke.
"Oh, I think I'll just take more care of my lovely wife and family," he replied.
Emma sat back down on her chair beside him. She leaned forward on her elbows and cupped her face in her hands.
"Not possible," she told him smiling. "That's just not possible. How could there be more?"
Isobel and Hannah raised their eyebrows at each other and

Caroline Jones Lewis
The Dream Robbers

grinned and Joe jumped from his seat, scraping the chair on the tiles of the floor with a screech.
"Fancy a game of footie, Hann?"
"OK."
"Me too," insisted Izzie.
And they disappeared into a frost kissed garden.

******

The year began in quiet disquiet with housing analysts predicting the further collapse of the UK housing market, already close but with those in the business struggling to keep the embers of the dying fire alight. Anxiety in the Bailey household was growing by the day. At the breakfast table Pete read from the Financial Times.
"Look," he exclaimed. "Look at these insurance companies fined for mis-selling. Thousands of inappropriate policies sold to people who are self-employed so aren't covered anyway. Is there no integrity left in any part of this country's economy," he grumbled. "For God's sake, every sector of business just seems set to rip off the consumer. When I think of the malice aimed at us in the property industry for simply trying to earn a decent living while this lot are all at it, it makes me fume. Not to mention what people say about estate agents. Thank God we don't have any of this insurance, Em. Tony does, though. He's been trying to get his money back but the insurance company won't part with it. They knew full well when they sold it to him that he wouldn't be covered and they're guilty but they still won't refund it. He's had to go to the financial ombudsman service and it will take months for them to deal with it, apparently. He could really do with that money right now, too. He's just been put on short time. With the new build market stalled there's not much work about for plasterers so he's really struggling."
Emma, too, was indignant.
"Oh, poor Tony. And Jen was telling me how much it had

Caroline Jones Lewis
The Dream Robbers

cost them to kit the twins out for senior school last autumn. I think they're still recovering. It's awful, isn't it? I suppose he thought he was being responsible taking out insurance in case of illness. Then to just find you've been taken for a ride - it's disgusting. It's theft really, isn't it? Taking money under false pretences. I agree - it does make you wonder if there is any part of the business sector that isn't corrupt these days. We estate agents aren't such a bad lot when you see what others have been up to."

"I know there are estate agents who rip people off. And property developers," conceded Pete. "The trouble is it means we all get tarred with the same brush. And all the time this is what's going on in the board rooms of big business."

They were sitting together at the desk in the study, running through their budget on the computer.

"Well, their fine is over a million each so that's another £1. Million or two for the insurers to pass onto the consumer somehow," muttered Pete. "A bit more to top up the cost of the premiums. Where the hell's it going to end?"

"Yes, well, at least it's been stopped now so that's ok. Let's get back to our own problem."

Emma changed the subject with subtle determination, mindful both of Pete's view of the fat cats at the top of the commercial heap and once more of his blood pressure. The difficulties already being inflicted on the business were enough of a weight for him to carry without him stressing over things he could not control.

"Look," she interjected, "I need to take Izz shopping on Saturday. She needs a few things for Sunday - when she goes to the Academy. Can you be home with Hannah and Joe? Why don't you spend some quality time with the kids."

"Yes, fine. I've got nothing on this weekend," he answered half-heartedly, as though he were not really listening. Then he snapped to and answered determinedly.

"Why don't we all go to Blue Water? Hannah and Joe and I

Caroline Jones Lewis
The Dream Robbers

could go to the cinema while you and Izz do your shopping. Then we could meet up afterwards and go for a pizza. I'm damned if we're going to stop enjoying everything. The rate they're growing up they'll be gone before we know it."
"Oh, darling, that would be lovely. Is there anything on worth seeing?"
"Don't know but I'll look on the internet and see what's on. That's a date then."

******

An air of excitement and tension buzzed in the Bailey household on the morning of Isobel's departure. The entire family piled into Pete's 4x4, along with Izzie's luggage and the necessities for survival insisted on by her mother. They set off for town in good humour. Though flushed with excitement, Isobel was quiet on the journey, apprehensive too of the new adventure on which she was embarking - without the most important people in her life around her day by day. A cocktail of emotions swirled in her head and butterflies fluttered in her stomach. Settling into the room she would share with her roommate, they all assisted in the unpacking of the monumental pile of possessions.
"Oh, Mum. Not my old hot water bottle?" protested Isobel, raising into full view the once pink and fluffy but now faded and dog-eared object of objection. Pete and the children erupted into howls of laughter.
"For goodness sake, there's everything but the kitchen sink in here," she continued, delving further into the offending box packed by her mother.
"You might be cold in bed," protested Emma in all seriousness before she too descended into giggles.
"These old buildings can be really draughty, you know - and they'll sure to turn the heating off at night," she continued, her attempt at justification only serving to amuse them more.
The moment of parting was emotional. Hugs and kisses.

Caroline Jones Lewis
The Dream Robbers

Hannah and Joe quiet. Emma fighting back tears of both pride and dread and Pete gruff with emotion. And Isobel, an Isobel suddenly wanting to hang on to her sister and brother, the in-fights and challenges between them of normal daily life insignificant in the magnitude of the moment. When only four people left for the journey home, they sat quietly, with little said between them until they entered through their own front door.

"Well, that's the first little fledgling taking her first step outside of the nest," said Pete, wrapping his arms around his near-tearful wife in the hallway. "And a truly good first step it is, too."

"I know," squeaked Emma. "But she's still my baby. And I miss her already."

"Come on, don't be sad. Let's be happy for Izz," and he hugged his wife close.

"You can talk," teased Emma. "I saw you trying to hide the tear in the eye," and they each grinned at the other.

"I wish Mum could have been here to see today," murmured Pete. "She really adored Izzie."

Pete's mother had died of cancer when Isobel was just a baby, a single mother after Pete's father had left when he was barely five years old, never to be seen again.

"Maybe she was with us," Emma comforted. "Do you think?"

"Don't know," Pete replied thoughtfully. "Jury's out on that one, Em."

Differing in their religious conviction, Pete could only offer tolerance of Emma's participation in church activities, an attendance that had continued from Sunday school to eucharist, his belief at the least agnostic, at most a total denial of any deity at all. They each fell into silent thought for a moment. Emma was first to break the mood.

"I just hope we can cope - financially, I mean. She'd be devastated if we had to take her out of the Academy now she's started."

"She would have been devastated if we'd told her she

Caroline Jones Lewis
The Dream Robbers

couldn't go at all. We're just going to have to find a way to keep going, aren't we? Others manage. So will we."
Emma nodded. Their eyes met and without another word spoken between them they acknowledged the challenges that lay ahead.

******

Sophie and James had returned from Brittany on New Year's Day to the continuing demise of the financial sector. Ensconced in James' parents' home near the French coastline, they had detached themselves from the growing economic crisis in a self-indulgent refusal to read the English newspapers or watch English TV, immersing themselves in all things French apart from the company. James' parents had little interest in the storm that was raging across the Atlantic and since their ample funds were deposited offshore in a Euro account, the plight of the pound sterling was of only passing concern. They had no inkling of James' current predicament and no idea of Sophie's impending calling to account, a matter Sophie had dismissed with a casual "well, we're all having to tighten our belts a little" in response to their only and brief enquiry into the fortunes of the British banking sector. Christmas had been a warm and mellow time of walks in the French countryside, strolls along the coastline, of good food and good wine and in social gatherings in front of log fires in the evening. It was with a sigh and reluctance on New Year's Day that Sophie contemplated her return to business.
"Aaagh," breathed James as he stretched lazily on the sofa in the evening. "Can't believe it's a return to the grind tomorrow, can you, old girl?" he mused with a yawn.
"No. I can hardly bear the thought, frankly. Can you?"
He shook his head and sighed. It would be back to the gruelling, back to the interrogations. Back to the reality he had striven over the festive season to block from his consciousness.

Caroline Jones Lewis
The Dream Robbers

"New Year resolutions?" he queried.
"Nope. You?"
"Nooo, don't think so. Take the year as it comes, I think, don't you? With troubled times ahead I think that will be enough to deal with. We could think about booking a holiday, though - something to look forward to. Brighter days. What do you think?"
Sophie agreed.
"Good idea. I'll get some brochures, shall I?" she asked.
"Where do you fancy? Mauritius? Miami?"
They busied themselves with diversions, neither wanting to confront or confide to each other the depth of the trials that lay ahead as they plunged back into the icy waters of the new year's dealings, as yet resisting all mention of the flood of retribution swelling around them.

******

The year continued with more dismal news and a prediction that the UK housing market was close to collapse. Interest rates had crept up, fuelled by the libor rate, the inter-bank lending rate that the banks kept stubbornly high. There was a spate of mortgage brokers charged with fraud and banned from practice and in the market-place an over-supply of newly completed flats stood empty and unsold. Gavin's business was at a standstill, a matter of considerable stress to himself and his wife Rosie.   With two young children still in junior school, it was fortunate that at least Rosie was in employment, but it was only part-time and it was only local. And local wages, as everyone knew, did not live up to the earning potential of those that commuted to the City. She had been lucky to get the job - a school secretary working hours that fitted with her family commitments and the school holidays, but the pay left a deal to be desired. Gavin had switched the focus of his business activity to life insurance and pensions, but neither were as lucrative as the mortgage market. Times were hard and threatening to get harder.

Caroline Jones Lewis

The Dream Robbers

In the disappointment of a blustery rain-dogged April, Emma received the news she had been hoping would not come, called to the office by their employer, the part time employees attending especially for the meeting. The two other branches closed for an hour for those in and on duty to attend, such was the magnitude of the news Max was to impart. Emma and her colleagues assembled expectantly in the board room on the first floor above the High Street shop. Max stood before the assembly doing his best to appear at ease. In his mid-forties, a slight man with sleeked back hair and dark pinstripe who spoke in clichés, he had started the business at the end of the recession in the 1990s and built it to its current level of three branches and 20 employees, full-time, part-time, some casual as and when the need arose. It gave him no pleasure to address them today and he cleared his throat nervously to make the announcement he knew that none of them wanted to hear and that he did not want to make - that times were tough and they must all cut their hours or risk the complete loss of their job.
"Good morning, everyone and thank you all for taking the time to come. As you all know, times in the industry are difficult and predicted to become more so. At the end of the day, like any business looking to survive, we have to cut our coat according our cloth, so to speak. So, going forward …."

Emma recounted to Pete later in the day. Sunday opening was suspended altogether. On Saturdays they would close at midday instead of 5 pm. And during the week the staff on duty in each branch at any one time would be cut from four to three. If things did not improve over the coming two months, it would be necessary for each branch to remain closed for a further day each week, rotating cover between them which would mean a further reduction in hours and accordingly to pay for each member of staff. They all of them knew there was no room for debate. They were fortunate, they agreed, that Max was spreading the economy around them all instead of announcing redundancies.   There was no dissent.

******

Still across the Atlantic the winds were getting stronger, blowing harder, the panic spreading wider as the housing market regressed further.   Repossessions rose on a daily basis with families turned onto the street and in distress, migrating from once comfortable owner-occupied neighbourhoods now increasingly boarded up and facing dereliction to downtown seedy rentals.   The most pitiful sight of all was the deserted garden swings swaying in the breeze, abandoned by tearful children headed for rundown streets as their playgrounds and shared bedrooms with their siblings instead of a room of their own.   The tears fell like the rainfall of a tropical monsoon.   There were calls for resignations but still the affluent at the top of the social tree clung to the branches, drawing their hefty bonuses with their minds and consciences closed to the devastation they had caused around them.   The winds that had begun as a whisper became a wail.   Change, change, change was their message.   New, new, new.   And they blew ever more eastwards, ever more strongly, gathering pace and intensity as they went.

In the presidential race, a battle for the Democratic nomination was building, a Hilary Clinton striving to be the first woman President of the Union against a Barrack Obama aiming to be the first black president in the White House.   His rallying cry of 'change' was finding resonance with a public disillusioned with the current administration.   They were challenging times that lay ahead.

In the West country of the British Isles, rain was deposited in a torrent, flooding homes and communities in the

Caroline Jones Lewis

The Dream Robbers

deluge. The cost to insurers was enormous, the misery to families more than some could bear. The politicians argued the cause and the solution, climate change a reality to one, a red herring to another. The year rolled on.

Caroline Jones Lewis

The Dream Robbers

Chapter 4 - Growing Unease

June 2008

By the time Izzie came home for the summer break, it was clear that her parents were facing a crisis. Her first two terms had passed quickly and excitingly despite the intermittent bouts of homesickness, with tales to tell on weekend visits home and relaxation from a frenzied schedule over the Whitsun break. Now that the summer sun was attempting to break through the heavy, cloud-laden skies her delight at being home for the school holidays was marred by a hint of tension within the wider family. Little was said to begin with but she noticed small things that indicated that all was not well. Within the household, too, there were things that had changed, small economies apparent in everyday life of things that had previously been taken for granted but now were missing. The fruit bowl on the kitchen table had always been brimming. Apples, oranges, grapes, pears and banana. Nectarines. Her mother loved nectarines. The fruit had always been fresh for it had disappeared with rapid regularity. Now it was bought in small measured quantities and restricted in its distribution. Bags of crisps were rationed, chocolate biscuits that had been freely accessible before were now hidden the children knew not where and brought out only when Emma allowed it - a restriction Joe was finding hard to bear. Visits to the pizza parlour were replaced with supermarket pizzas cooked in the oven and eaten at home. Mobiles phones that had been on contract were now replaced by pay-as-you-go models with a monthly allowance that made Hannah grumble.
"But, Mum, it's too stingy. I need longer call time. How can I keep up with what's going on if I can't call my friends?"
"Hannah, you see your friends every school day. You have no need to launch into hour long conversations with them the minute you've stepped off the school 'bus to go your

Caroline Jones Lewis
The Dream Robbers

separate ways for only an evening and with less than twenty four hours before you meet up again. For goodness sake, what can you possibly have to say that can't wait that long?"
"But Mum." An insistent Hannah. "We're on holiday. I don't see them every day so I need to call them."
"Exactly, Hannah. You're on holiday - with your family. With your sister who will be away again once term time starts. Time for you to spend together. You'll have plenty to catch up on with your friends when you go back to school, then, won't you? And if there's anything you need to say that is **so** urgent that it can't wait, then you can send a text. It's cheaper."
"Oh, I suppose now that we're **poor ....**" spat Hannah.
"Hannah, we're not poor," Emma countered with a sigh of exasperation. "But we're not rich either and it's high time you learned the facts of life where money is concerned, young lady."
Hannah stomped away to her room refusing to continue a debate that she was clearly losing. The door of her room slammed with a thud.
"That girl needs a talking to," protested Emma to her husband later in the day. "From you. She's getting unbearable."
"Alright. I'll speak to her - much good that it will do."
Izzie noticed that the cars stayed on the drive for all but vital journeys. With the rocketing price of fuel, their bikes had been retrieved from the back of the garage. They were given a vigorous cleaning and overhaul and declared fit to be the first choice of transport, an unfortunate measure while rain continued to lash the landscape on a daily basis making cycling prohibitive to those concerned with hairstyles and make-up and fashion. Hannah developed a new talent for inventiveness. The excuses she was forced to trot out for not cycling were a challenge to her ingenuity. When all else failed, she stayed home but in ill humour.

Amidst all these subtleties, however, Izzie perceived that the

Caroline Jones Lewis
The Dream Robbers

main focus of the tension seemed reserved for her Aunt Sophie, a state of rancour apparent between her father and her aunt as they sat around the kitchen table on a damp and dismal Sunday following a restrained roast lamb lunch. Aunt Sophie was trying to appear her usual carefree self but somehow on this day it failed to ring true. There was an artificial quality to the performance, a failure to convince her audience that all was well. Her laughter sounded brittle, a forced joie de vie that failed to fool even the children and Pete's only contribution to the proceedings was the occasional grunt or caustic remark in her direction accompanied by a frown or a grimace. Isobel was well aware of the worsening situation in the banking sector and the damage that had been inflicted on both of her parents' livelihoods, a matter that a younger Hannah chose to ignore and of which Joe in the main seemed blissfully unaware. The role played in the disaster by her Aunt and the bank she worked for was a natural source of acrimony between her Aunt and her parents - at least, in the main with her father. While her mother did her best to keep the peace. Furthermore, the strain on the family purse strings created by her attendance at the Academy was beginning to impress itself upon Izzie. Her parents made no mention of it to her directly, intent on keeping up morale for both themselves and the family but the obvious economies needed no explanation to three children of their intelligence. It was all beginning to look to Izzie like something approaching a nightmare.

As the days wore on, the tranquil and relaxing sojourn to home that Izzie had anticipated, punctuated by shopping trips and outings with her family, was slipping into a daily routine of near boredom. With Abi away in France with her family, Izzie spent her time reading magazines or playing card games with her brother and sister while trapped within the house by the weather. Even her Grandma and Granddad seemed to remain subdued on their less than frequent visits,

Caroline Jones Lewis

The Dream Robbers

restricting their journeys as the price of petrol scaled to ridiculous heights. How long, Izzie wondered. How long would her parents be able to continue to afford the fees at the Academy if this went on? She would just have to make the best of the time she had, she pondered - just in case it should come to an abrupt end.

******

For Sophie, life had descended into one long round of recrimination. It was clear at the bank that the axe was going to fall. It was just a matter of when. She had assessed her financial position which, in the short term, was of little concern.

It was the long term implications that were of importance. With her last bonus still sitting safely in an offshore bank, a mortgage free home and a nearly new car that was paid for, her exit package would afford her a reasonable standard of living for the next year or so. But what then? Even when all the furore had died down, when the crisis had blown over, what bank would ever employ her again? What financial institution would consider her a potential asset worthy of employment? In which case, what would she do with the rest of her life? She was tainted now - even socially she was becoming a pariah as former friendships fell away. It was clear a change of direction was to be forced upon her. But what and how were yet to be determined. It would come, she was sure - in a flash of inspiration a solution would present itself. She was sure that patience and determination were all that was required. Worse than that was the deterioration in her relationship with a family she had until now considered herself to have exceeded, left behind in their parochial little world while she had conquered the big City. It had soured as the consequences of her actions and those of her contemporaries in the entire banking world hit home and threatened their own lives and families. The

Caroline Jones Lewis

The Dream Robbers

survival of her brother-in-law's business was causing considerable anxiety to her sister and her niece's future at the Academy - now there too was a problem. Whatever else she thought of Pete, she had to admit that he had worked hard and responsibly at his business over the years. For the first time in her life, Sophie Gray was being troubled by a conscience she had never before recognised she had. Just a quiet niggling to begin with that was growing and which she had found impossible to chase away. Equally as bad was the knowledge that Robert's business was also suffering as his clients looked to economise. The first line of defence for his Client families facing hardship was to sell the children's' pony, to cut down on riding lessons and all things equestrian. Pete had taken pleasure, knowing the history and the fondness Sophie still harboured for Robert, in making it known to his sister-in-law. To date it was, for Sophie, the deepest cut of all, to have betrayed the man who had been, and remained, the constant if unreachable love of her life.

Back in the office Leo had launched at Sophie with a torrent of retribution. Sophie was saddened at that. She had always liked Leo. There was something so engaging about his youthful naivety, his hitherto dogged devotion to her as his source of inspiration. All that had now changed. Distressed by the news that Tess would be one of the first to face redundancy and no job to return to after the baby was born, the stress of their impending situation had taken its toll. Whether as a consequence of recent events or whether it would have happened anyway, Tess miscarried, plunging them both into an abyss of grieving. After discharge from hospital, weak and unhappy, she had withdrawn to the home of her parents for peace and recovery leaving Leo distraught and alone. Now the focus of his grief and anger, he reinforced to Sophie daily the contempt in which he now held her with glaring looks each time they met in the office or passed in the corridor. The puppy dog had turned on the

Caroline Jones Lewis
The Dream Robbers

hand that no longer fed him. Open hostility was barely veiled, too, amongst her other colleagues whose own jobs and homes were threatened now that the bank was faced with insolvency and with closure by its overseas parent company. The investment team that had once held the respect of all as the producers of the bank's soaring profitability had now been exposed as an imposter, a prankster, a confidence trickster that would bring them all to ruin. She ran the gauntlet as a daily routine.

James' position was even more worrying. He had at last confided to Sophie the investigation over insider dealings under which he was being pursued and admitted that it was entirely possible he could be found wanting. Why suddenly everyone was getting excited about the issue he failed to comprehend, he protested, since insider dealing had been a fact of his entire life in the markets - but there it was. She was so stunned as to be rendered speechless, the last reaction he would have expected in place of the torrent of anger he would have wagered on. When at last she did regain her tongue it was to ask him quietly and uncomprehendingly why.
"But why James? Why? We don't need any more money. We're fine already."
He had no answer. No real answer.
"I don't know, Soph. I don't really know why I did it. It was a spur of the moment thing."
It had come to his notice too late in the day that The Financial Services Authority were intent on cleaning up practices within the market, charged by the Treasury to stamp out malpractice in a financial sector that was increasingly falling into disrepute. To date there had been several successful prosecutions and there were still more pending. James was not a big player, indeed had only participated on the fringe of a network dealing inside information but he could still be found culpable. If things went against him, then the destruction of his career would be

Caroline Jones Lewis

The Dream Robbers

total. And worse - there was the potential for a spell in prison.

It was that very revelation that had paralysed Sophie's tongue, the very idea of James incarcerated, an image she could not bear to contemplate however foolish he had been. The effect on his parents would be devastating and more than he himself could contemplate. The shame for Sophie, he considered, would be beyond her endurance. She would not wait for him, he was sure. He would lose her to Robert Welling, of that he was convinced. He had always felt that she was only on loan to him, for as long as he could hold her. He had always believed that. But he had also believed that the longer he could hold on the better had been the chance that the Robert Welling option would be withdrawn. He had waited, hoped and wished for the announcement of the man's engagement, for the marriage to another beautiful and desirable female but it had not come. And now it was he himself that might be withdrawn. If he were not there, what then?

Sophie, it must be said, had at times contemplated the alternative life she might have led if she had chosen differently, if she had fought for Robert instead of flouncing away in an exhibition of pride to cover the sting of rejection. He had been willing to see it through, to stand his ground. We must wait, he had insisted, take our time and show them we are serious. She had hoped he would come after her and convince her to stay. She had more than half believed that he would, had more than half expected him to do so, waited for the ring of the telephone or the knock on the door. But she had been disappointed. She had walked away, impatient at his patience, angry at his forbearance. She had wanted him to rail against them, to defend her to the hilt. But he had simply told her to be patient and she had walked away smarting at the slight. And he had let her. Later she had wished that she had not, that she had stayed and talked it

Caroline Jones Lewis

The Dream Robbers

through like an adult. But later was too late and by that time
her pride would not allow her to retract so she had covered
her hurt with a show of defiance. I'll show them. I don't
need them - any of them. They'll see. Robert's mother
was now gone but his father would see, she fretted. When her
fall from grace became known, he would see - and see a side
of her she did not want seen. They had called her greedy.
A greedy little strumpet. Robert had told her that much.
"You can prove them wrong," he had insisted. "Show them
the best of you. They'll come round, you'll see."
But she had flounced away angrily.

She had not seen Robert for almost a year at that time. The
job at a bank in London had offered a welcome escape to the
City and she had taken it in a fit of determination. Their
paths had not crossed until a chance encounter at Tunbridge
Wells station on a visit to home, an awkward encounter but a
reminder of the feelings they still shared. But there had
been James by then, already a successful trader and a
presence that Sophie could not help but flaunt.
How his father would crow at her unveiling. How smug he
would be with their 'I told you so,' and now James too. Yet
even now, it rankled enough to fire her determination. Yes,
she would show them - all of them. She would overcome
this temporary setback and start again. But a hard lesson
had been learned and a question mark raised over her entire
future. What now? Where do I go from here? Where do
James and I go from here? If James was taken from her and
Robert was still there, still waiting - what then? Would she
have the courage to be honest about her feelings and go to
him? But could she really abandon James in his greatest
hour of need? She did not know for in her maturing years it
seemed that new emotions were outstripping the old. There
was a thing called loyalty. And then there was this new
thing called guilt that refused to let her go.

******

Caroline Jones Lewis

The Dream Robbers

Above the Atlantic and the Caribbean the winds circled and spiralled, bunched together into the greatest series of storms and hurricanes within record, heading towards the North American continent. They clipped its territory as they went making landfall whenever and wherever firm ground lay within their path. One after another they came, like a series of blows in a fist-fight that would leave the southern borders of the continent and its neighbours bruised and battered and punch-drunk, veering off course and out of control. In May, tropical storm Arthur had set the running unusually early making landfall in Belize, followed by Hurricane Bertha bringing rain and storm-force winds to Bermuda in early July. Tropical storm Cristobal followed on, licking the coastline of North Carolina, depositing more heavy rainfall before crossing the Gulf Stream and weakening in its path into Nova Scotia. Hurricane Dolly hit the Gulf of Mexico and tracked its way across Guatemala leaving costly damage in its wake. As August approached so too did Tropical Storms Edouard, and Fay, making landfall in Southern Texas and Florida. But the worst was still to come as the winds continued to blow.

September 2008

Despite all attempts by both US and UK governments, pouring tax payers' funds into the banking sector to shore up the markets and attempt to restore consumer confidence, stocks on Wall Street continued to plummet and banks continued to withhold the funds that were needed so desperately to support the economy. It was learned that two of the largest UK banks had been within hours of insolvency, of being unable to open for business until the Bank of England had stepped in. It seemed inconceivable and yet it was true. If that were not enough, the largest insurance organisation in the world was brought close to extinction,

Caroline Jones Lewis

The Dream Robbers

brought low by massive losses following disastrous involvement in the derivatives market. The news prompted mass anxiety, leaving their insured hanging on the end of telephone lines or scanning the company's website for news of whether their cover remained valid. Its worldwide interests spread like the tentacles of an octopus to so many corners of the world economy that its downfall had to be prevented for the sake of global security. So once more the US Federal Bank delved deep into its reserves of taxpayers' money for a bail out, the ordinary man and woman in the street once again coming to the stricken company's aid.

The collapse of Lehman Brothers, the fourth largest US investment bank, sent shock waves through the financial world. Founded in 1870 on the western side of the Atlantic, the self-same year as Northern Rock had been founded on the eastern, it had hitherto represented a constant in the banking community, a once constant that now was destroyed. When the bank filed for bankruptcy there were insufficient funds on its balance sheet even to meet the monthly bill for staff salaries. When called to account before the Senate Committee, its Chief Executive admitted to drawing bonuses in the millions of dollars whilst the bank's coffers - and the jobs of its employees - dwindled away. The anger on the streets was palpable. And while it had been deemed worthy to rescue Bear Stearns bank when faced with the same scenario, Lehman Brothers, it was decided, would be let go to the wall. It was a decision the consequences of which would be grave. When the American mortgage giants Fanny Mae and Fanny Mac tottered on the brink of disaster, they were deemed to be too vital to be allowed to fall and were pulled back from the very edge of the precipice by another loan from federal reserves.

In the City of London, bank after bank had now admitted massive losses in the US fiasco creating a deficiency of

Caroline Jones Lewis
The Dream Robbers

funds for loans and mortgages that looked set to continue for some time to come. There were talks of huge loans by the Government, of tax payer monies to be used to prop up the ailing financial sector and with the nationalisation of Northern Rock and the same potential fate lying in wait for several other financial institutions, the banks were queuing up to take advantage of the bail-out. It was unreal - just unreal to the man and woman in the street whose quality of life was being eroded daily by nothing they had done to cause such devastation.

"So why have all these banks nearly gone bust?" asked Andy. "I don't understand why it's affected all of them. One or two I could understand but it's all of them."

Faces turned towards Sophie for an answer. The family were assembled in Pete and Emma's garden for Joe's birthday lunch, Andy and Kate, Emma and family and their Aunt Sophie. James, as ever, had declined the invitation, preferring instead to join friends for a champagne lunch and racing at Sandown Park. The weather was heavy and close, the threat of thunder hanging appropriately in the air. Joe had abandoned them to their conversation now that the meal was over, leaving the adults seated around the table on the patio, while he and Hannah attacked the trampoline at the end of the lawn and Izzie had excused herself to take a call on her mobile 'phone.

"Well," began Sophie, shifting uncomfortably in her seat. "It's because of something called securitisation."

"Which means what exactly?" insisted Pete, determined to cause his sister-in-law the maximum discomfort possible, his week having been one of robbing Peter to pay Paul, juggling funds to meet the weekly pay packet and at the same time satisfying his creditors. He was in no charitable frame of mind where banks - and that meant Sophie - were concerned.

Sophie considered her answer carefully, how to make an explanation in words that the family, and her parents in particular, would understand but would avoid antagonising her brother-in-law further. In layman's language. She

Caroline Jones Lewis

The Dream Robbers

tried again.

"Well, what the banks do is to take out short term borrowing from other lenders, such as each other, to swell their pot of funds to make long-term loans to their customers. Mostly for mortgages, of course. The interest they receive on the long-term loans is set at a level to cover repayment of the short term borrowing they have taken out. The problem arises if their customers default on the mortgages so they don't receive the interest to make their own loan repayments to their own lender. Then they have to dip into their own capital reserves. If this happens too many times or over too long a period, their reserves become depleted until eventually they are gone. The bank is then insolvent."

"So basically they've all overtraded," Pete observed.

"Well, why did they?" Andy insisted. "Pete has to know where to draw the line in his business. The people who run the banks are supposed to be experts. If he can do it why can't they?"

"Greed," prompted Pete tetchily. "Let's not beat around the bush. It's greed. Wanting to make more money more quickly for themselves, for their bonuses."

"But also for their shareholders," defended Sophie. "Don't forget the banks are answerable to their shareholders."

"Well, that's where the whole thing's gone wrong, if you ask me," grumbled Andy. "Everything these days is for the benefit of the shareholders. There was a time when the customer came first."

Pete persisted in his questioning.

"But, Sophie, they use a rating system, don't they?" he asked.

"They do but the rating system is flawed, I suppose," admitted Sophie. "The higher the risk with the mortgage the higher the rate of interest and therefore the more profitable…"

"So the better the rating?" finished Pete. A rhetorical question to which he already knew the answer.

"Sort of. And it all became more complicated because a

Caroline Jones Lewis

The Dream Robbers

system was devised to sell the loans on.   Maturity transformation they call it.   The first lender sells the mortgage on and receives the redemption value up-front. So they receive the money they have loaned back before its term in return for a fee to the purchaser."

"Oh, it's all just ludicrous," puffed Pete.   "Who in God's name devised this system?"

"The rocket scientists of Wall Street, we call them.   They are.   Really."

Sophie shifted once more in her seat and looked out of the window, hoping to avoid any further explanation.

"So it literally *is* rocket science," quipped Pete.

Emma grimaced at her mother and cocked her head at her husband.

"I don't really understand it," she told him.   "I don't understand the point."

"It means that the banks get their money back more quickly," Pete explained.   "To top up their reserves again so they can lend even more - on more bad loans.   And so it goes on and that increases bank activity and therefore increases bonuses and share dividends and everyone gets their bonus or dividend quicker than if they had waited until redemption of the original loan, etc etc.   It's a bit like factoring except that presumably the buyer of the loan can't request repayment of the money they've paid for it if the loan goes bad?"

Sophie nodded wanting to avoid further explanation.

"Sort of," she agreed, hoping that having satisfied their curiosity the tone of the conversation would now turn to a different subject.   She wanted to bring this one to an end, too close to home for comfort.   She excused herself to the toilet.

"But that's just madness.   Doesn't it just mean that the risk is spread around and it's more risky for everyone involved?" asked Emma.

She grappled with the concept.

"Which is exactly what has happened," concluded Pete. "The risk was too great."

Caroline Jones Lewis

The Dream Robbers

Andy was irritated now, the damage being inflicted on his personal circumstances making itself continually apparent. For a normally temperate man the whole situation that had developed was ruffling his feathers more than was good for his health. Sophie returned and slid as inconspicuously as possible onto her seat but aware that Emma's eyes had latched onto her, aware that she and Pete would have put two and two together in respect of her own bank and involvement.

"I blame Maggie Thatcher for this whole thing of bigger, better, more," declared Andy, a lifelong Labour man. "She encouraged everyone to buy their own house. It became the be all and end all and some people really just can't afford it. They buy a house and they think it ends there. Well, it doesn't. There's all the running costs and the upkeep to think of. And then we all had to use our homes to fund our old age, to pay for nursing homes and such because the NHS was being cut back under the Tories. Under Thatcher. So people decided they had to get the biggest most expensive house they could so that later they had more equity behind them. Houses are no longer peoples' homes. They're an investment to fund old age. It was her that started all of that, too - her and the rest of the Tories. They were the ones who caused the recession in the 90s, all on their own. That Lamont character. They think everyone's forgotten - the Tories. Well, I haven't. A lot of people haven't. At least it wasn't the Government this time. It's those wretched banks."

He puffed with indignation.

"They've always cosied up to the boys in the City, the Tories.," he continued. "That's where New Labour went wrong, if you ask me. In order to get re-elected they thought they had to do the same and now look where it's got us."

"And Maggie encouraged everyone to buy shares," piped up Kate, an echo of her husband's political views. "And now look what's happened. The stock markets in a real mess

Caroline Jones Lewis

The Dream Robbers

and our pension and investments along with it."

"I don't think we can blame Maggie Thatcher for **all** of this," defended Pete, reluctant to relieve New Labour of all the blame as a dedicated Conservative supporter. "The Government are supposed to keep tabs on all this sort of thing. It's the job of the Treasury, the Chancellor. The Financial Services Authority. Organisations like that. They should have been more watchful."

"But the Tories were shouting as loud as anyone for deregulation of the banks. That bald headed chap - you know who I mean. It wasn't just the Government. It was the opposition as well."

"Well, I guess you've got a point," Pete felt reluctantly compelled to concede.

"The thing is - where's it all going to end?"

"It's affecting so many people now," sighed Emma. "I went into the gallery in the village the other day to get the 'photo framed. You know, Dad. The one of the retirement do."

Andy nodded.

"Michael was marking down some of his stock. You remember Michael, Pete. Crofter's Gallery? He lives next door to Gavin in our office. His wife's expecting another baby some time soon. He didn't say too much but business is obviously pretty bad. He was talking about closing earlier and not opening on Mondays, that sort of thing. Everyone's being affected now. No-one knows how bad it's going to get - where it's going to end."

With no ready answer to offer there was no response from anyone present. A silent tension hung in the air and a reluctance to look in Sophie's direction.

To Sophie's relief a sudden shower prompted the party to rush indoors, hurriedly gathering up the remnants of the lunch from the table, with good-humoured reference to the typical British summer. It broke the mood and changed the direction of conversation.

Caroline Jones Lewis
The Dream Robbers

"So there is a god," she thought to herself as she helped with the sudden move indoors. Joe and Hannah came rushing from the top of the garden to join them in the conservatory, squealing with laughter and soaked to the skin.
"Go and change out of those wet clothes, quickly," Emma instructed laughing.
"And don't leave them on the bedroom floor. Bring them down to the kitchen and put them in the washing machine," she added, anticipating soggy patches on the bedroom carpets.
Grasping a convenient break in the proceedings, Sophie took the opportunity of the moment to announce her need for departure.
"We're out to dinner with friends tonight," she explained. "It's an engagement bash at a club in town. You know how it is, Em. Shower and wash the hair, and all that. God knows what I'm going to wear. I haven't even given it a thought yet," she prattled on quickly, covering the awkwardness of her situation.
Of course, thought Emma. Just the perfect moment to run away, when the subject of the conversation is too close to home for your comfort.
Emma saw her sister out at the front door while the rest of the family settled themselves in the conservatory. The rain, now heavy, lashed the double-glazing. It soaked the leaves and blossoms of a cherry tree in the side border that only moments before had been bathed in sunlight . She watched the branches flailing in the gusting wind and the dismal light of yet another cloud-laden afternoon and sighed. Global warming I suppose, she thought despondently. Or climate change as the politicians now like to call it.
She returned to the family in the conservatory.
"Whatever's happened to our weather I really don't know," murmured Kate absent-mindedly, brushing droplets of rain water from her clothing.
"Oh, global warming, I expect," laughed Pete wryly.
"Everything's blamed on global warming these days."

Caroline Jones Lewis
The Dream Robbers

"Climate change," interrupted Emma. "They're calling it climate change now. Which is different to weather, we're told."

"I'm not convinced," said Andy stoutly. "I can remember when the girls were little being virtually washed out at Porthcawl in mid-July. Do you remember, Kate?"

"I certainly do. There were boy scouts camping up on the cliff top. Those poor lads. They had all their tents blown away by a gale force wind and it rained cats and dogs for the entire week. But the wind," she emphasised. "The wind was every bit as bad as the winds we're getting now. We just put it down to the British weather in those days."

"I just don't understand why the world's supposed to be warming up when we're all cold all the time."

"I agree, Dad," Emma chimed in. "I don't understand it either. The last two summers have been miserable."

******

October 2008

Across the Atlantic in the United Kingdom, crisis seeped insidiously into the town hall with little noise or warning. Potential losses of millions were revealed by one hundred UK councils who had invested funds in a failing Icelandic economy. As Iceland's major banks failed and were nationalised and trading in their stocks suspended, these funds were frozen, their ultimate return a matter of uncertainty. It was not the only catastrophe to be unveiled. Shock followed upon shock overnight as stocks went into free-fall around the globe, South Korea down 7.5%, Singapore stocks down by 8%, Australian stocks down 7% and in Tokyo the Nikkei fell by 11 points. The IMF issued warnings that countries must work together or face global bankruptcy. There seemed to be no end to the bad news. Traumatized traders sat before the screens of their computers watching the flickering and sliding figures come and go

Caroline Jones Lewis

The Dream Robbers

unable to prevent or influence the events that were unfolding.

******

Sophie, too, sitting alone, watched the news coming in. Her face was drawn with tension, her complexion pallid and the hint of shadows around moistened eyes that until now had rarely shed a tear except during a bout of self-serving tantrum. It was all out of control. Everything, the whole financial establishment, was out of control. And the end yet may not be in sight, wherever the end would be. The axe for her had fallen amidst mixed emotions. While she had known it was coming and understood the reason, it rankled that those above her who had taken the lion's share of the booty remained securely in place, stubbornly refusing to accept responsibility, avoiding apology or any act of contrition. She had just been a pawn in their greedy game. Sophie the golden girl, Sophie teacher's pet. There had not been a single word from one of them in support of her now that the truth was out. Why had she not seen it before? They had never regarded her with any serious respect or affection, a woman in a man's world, in their cosy boys' club. They had simply played on her love of money to fuel their own greed, actively encouraging the activities she had engaged in, creating perceived wealth for the bank to enhance their own position. It had looked good on the balance sheet to present to the shareholders. It had earned them money, bonuses, huge amounts that until now no-one had even envisaged on such a scale. She had been shocked when the true extent of their payouts had become known. Her earnings by comparison had been paltry. They had made hay whilst the sun shone, these high level City bankers whose names and faces were now emblazoned across not only the tabloid press eager for scalps but respected broadsheets and City publications. Well, the sun was not shining now. Gale force winds were blowing, ripping apart

Caroline Jones Lewis
The Dream Robbers

the illusion of wealth to expose the dearth of substance beneath. She and her contemporaries were the scapegoats, and the likes of Leo and his colleagues who had received no huge bonuses - indeed no bonuses at all - were faced with enormous personal loss and were bearing the brunt. With countless others they trailed helpless in the wake of the devastation she had helped to create. Now she understood the depth of the implications and she felt sickened at all that was happening. Now it was dogging her conscience. There had been voices raised in warning but no-one had heeded. In this respect the Government, it seemed, had not been governing, a Government intent on the course of deregulation, egged on by an opposition who had promised even more so should they be returned to power. So the government had not been governing, the regulator had not been regulating, the consciences of the industry had not been listening. And the bosses of the banks had taken full advantage of their operational freedom to further their own pursuit of wealth.

There was yet more to concern Sophie on a personal level. She was bordering on shock.
"It's Mum and Dad," she told James in the evening. "I advised them to invest their money in Iceland. The bank I told them to invest in has collapsed and their savings might be lost. All their savings. Everything. They may never get any of it back. At the least it's out of their reach for the foreseeable future. And it's my fault."
She had heard the odd whisper a day or so earlier and moved her own money to a safer-looking haven but the call she had intended to make to her father she had overlooked. Now was too late. Now the bank had frozen all movement of funds. For all her high-flying expertise, she had potentially reduced her own parents to penury. She berated herself for her lack of care on their behalf and determined to give them some money - at least until their own was hopefully released and repaid.

Caroline Jones Lewis
The Dream Robbers

"What do you want to do?" James asked her.
"I'll have to help them," she replied. "I'll just have to. I can't leave this one to Emma. This one's down to me. I'll have to lend them some money until they get theirs back. If they get it back, that is."
"Well, do whatever you have to," James told her. "The money's there. Just do it."
"Thank you, darling," she told him, grateful for his understanding. "I'll ring them as soon as I get a chance."
She would ring them - right now. But no, she decided. No, not now. She mustn't rush at it and get it wrong. This must be done logically making sure she transferred enough in one fell swoop to see them right. She mentally put things in order.
First thing in the morning she would go to the office and clear her desk and while there she would check her bank balance and all her liquid assets on the computer. Her company laptop had been impounded along with her files and as yet she had not replaced it with one of her own. The task still languished on her 'to do' list. She could use the office computer to check on her portfolio and then, later in the day, when she was sure of the funds she had available, she would telephone her mother. Better not speak to her father who, temperate as he normally was, would surely have a few rough words to say. As it turned out, it was a delay that she was to regret before 24 hours were through.

******

Andy Gray's heart attack came without warning, sneaking up like a thief in the night to overwhelm the creeping portliness of a body no longer lean from daily labour. On the previous morning, he had opened the letters in the mail with a growing trepidation. What today? He had thought. What next? Yet another letter had arrived from the gas board asking for money he had not and could not pay.

Caroline Jones Lewis
The Dream Robbers

"We shouldn't have cancelled the direct debit," he had observed to Kate. "When money became tight we should have cut out something else."

"Such as what?" Kate had challenged. "Our budget is down to the bare bones already. It's becoming a choice between eating and heating," and she giggled nervously at her poetic rhyming.

"I don't know but I'm sure there was something we could have done. Cut down on the food bill, or something. Gone to a cheaper supermarket, or something - like Lidl or Aldi. Other people are doing it."

He sighed.

"And we cancelled the one to British Telecom, too. That's another bill that will be coming in."

Andy thought he had steeled himself to whatever more was to be revealed, but in reality there was an inevitability about the events of the morning that had been growing since the day of his retirement. The stressful revelations of the last few months had taken their toll and the latest news about Iceland had been one shock too many to bear. With all their money invested there, the balance from the sale of the old house, their savings, now frozen and beyond reach for the foreseeable future if not lost forever, both he and Kate were at a loss to know what to do.

"We invested everything," he fretted. "Everything. Like Sophie advised us. And now it might all be gone for good. Scraping by on our state pension for the rest of our lives."

"Well, darling, perhaps we shouldn't get too pessimistic until we know all the facts," Kate had suggested, trying her best to remain optimistic however bad the news.

"Let's ring Sophie and find out the latest situation. Then we can decide what to do."

Andy had tried the call.

"Answer machine," he had sighed as he replaced the receiver and glanced at his watch. "They're probably out for the evening."

Caroline Jones Lewis
The Dream Robbers

"Well, why don't you leave her a message then?"
"You know how I hate those machines. I never know what to say. I'll wait and try her again in the morning."
"Are you sure," Kate had insisted. "If you left a message she'd know how worried we are and ring us as soon as she's in."
"Well, you ring then. You leave a message," said Andy.
Kate had considered.
"It would be better coming from you," she had insisted. "She'll take it more seriously. She just thinks I fuss too much, you know what she's like. She hates me fussing."
So it had been left until this morning for Andy to call his daughter, tossing and turning through the dark hours of night in worry, waiting for daylight to break to ring her before she left for her work. As soon as he had made the tea he would call, he told himself - just as soon as he had taken an early morning cup of tea to Kate.

He filled the kettle and switched it on at the socket. The pain sneaked up his arm and into his neck. Then it gripped his chest in a tight spasm. He paused and caught his breath to steady himself, sweating profusely and in a state of confusion. He wandered around the kitchen trying to remember what it was he had intended to do. The buzzing of the kettle jogged his memory and brought him back to the task at hand. It was when he reached for the cups in the cupboard on the wall that the first real pain caught him but the cause did not occur to him right away. He rubbed his chest, winded for a moment, putting the first cup down on the worktop to catch his breath. When he reached for a second, another wave of spasm caught him, this time stronger and his arm was aching, a pain shooting up his neck His head was throbbing and he felt unexpectedly sick. He shuffled to the chair and sat down abruptly, almost fell onto it, slumping across the table. The first inkling dawned that maybe something serious was happening, something more than just a tiredness wrought out of anxiety. He called his

Caroline Jones Lewis

The Dream Robbers

wife weakly.
"Kate. Kate," his voice falling almost to a whisper.

In the bedroom, Kate was wrapping her dressing gown around her, tying the belt around her waist and studying the face - now careworn - that stared back at her wide-eyed from the mirror. There were fine lines around her eyes now that had not been there until recently, creases across her forehead that she hid beneath a newly acquired fringe. She sighed a weary sigh for weary was what she felt, a weariness that had been growing over the days. When they were younger and money had been tight, with young children to feed and a mortgage to meet, there had always been the belief that they would manage, that over time things would improve. Andy could work overtime or look for a job with better money and prospects. Or she could work part time once the children were at school. They were young then. There had always been options. There had always been energy and they could work through it. They had lived responsibly always. Had tried to do all the right things to provide for a retirement that would not be a burden on their children. Now it was different. Now they were old, too old to cope with all these problems. She felt old. And there was no time left to make things better, no prospects or desire to work, no opportunity to replace their savings. All their options had been withdrawn by age. Yes, she felt weary. Just at the time when life should be easy. It was so unfair.

Andy had left her in bed, gone to make tea to bring to her in the bedroom but she had been too restless to stay there, too anxious and stressed from a night of disturbed sleep. So she had raised to follow him into the kitchen. It was then that she thought she heard something, someone calling her name, quietly, ghostly, strange sounding. But who? It was not Andy's voice and there was no-one else in the house. She craned her neck to listen. A voice, yes, but not Andy's voice.

Caroline Jones Lewis

The Dream Robbers

It must be him, she realised, but why so wan? Then it struck her and a sudden fear sent her turning on her heels and hurrying along the hallway to the kitchen. She found him slumped across the table, the kettle bubbling merrily and unheeded, puffing clouds of steam into the vacant space where Andy should have been . She knew instantly what was happening and she was afraid.

The paramedics worked steadily as the ambulance sped towards the hospital. Kate sat at his side, still in her dressing gown and slippers and the flowery pyjamas the children had bought her the previous Christmas. She held his hand, stroked his clammy forehead and urged him to hold on. By the time they reached the hospital Emma had arrived already, fumbling in her handbag in the car park for change for the parking machine. She saw the ambulance arrive and she ran towards A & E, saw her mother standing anxiously aside while the ambulance crew drew out the stretcher that carried her father. Her mother looked smaller and more frail than Emma had ever seen her.
"Mum," she called. "Mum," and she wrapped her arm around her mother's shoulder protectively, hugging her close, guiding her through the sliding doors behind the trolley that now carried her father and was surrounded by medical staff who left them stranded in their wake.

By lunchtime Andy Gray was still critical but stable, sleeping in ICU, wired up to this machine and that, oblivious for the time being of the drama that he had starred in. Kate sat quietly at his bedside. She was showered now and dressed in clothes that Pete had fetched for her, nourished by a bite or two of toast and a slurp of tea that the kitchen staff had fetched for her and that Emma had insisted she should eat and drink. Emma, pale without her make-up and her hair unkempt from lack of grooming, feeling grubby from the lack of showering in the jeans and sweater she had thrown on in her need for haste. She stayed determinedly

Caroline Jones Lewis
The Dream Robbers

with her mother as the day wore on. By the time that evening had come, she felt she had been holding her breath all day and with her father settled now in ICU the staff assured her she could relax briefly and go home for a comfort break, despite her reluctance to leave her mother alone.

"Mum, I just need to pop home now. Now that Dad's stable. Just to wash and change and see to the kids. Then I'll be back. Will you be alright if I go?"

"Yes, dear. Of course I will. You go and do what you have to. Take whatever time you need, Em. I'll be fine."

"No, really, Mum. I won't be long. And I'll try to call Sophie again while I'm home. She'll probably be home by now, I would think. She must have been travelling to work when I tried this morning and Pete couldn't get hold of her either but she should be there now. I won't be long, I promise."

Sophie was shocked, more shocked than she had ever been in her life and in view of the events of recent months that was saying a great deal. After clearing the drawers of her desk she had tried several times to call her mother but there had been no reply so she had abandoned the exercise and determined to call from home later in the day. When the call from Emma came she had paled at the news.

"I'll be down as soon as I can get there," she assured her sister.

"I should have called," she fretted to herself. "I should have called."

The following day Sophie sat alone with her father as the afternoon sun dipped lazily in the sky. Her mother and sister had left him in her care while they went outside for a brief breath of air. She clasped his hand in her own and kissed it, rubbed it against her cheek, a cheek damp with that unfamiliar moisture that once more was insisting on creeping from beneath her eyelids. The room was quiet but for the

Caroline Jones Lewis

The Dream Robbers

blip of the heart monitor and the loud thudding of her own heart.
"Don't die, Dad; please don't die," she urged him in a whisper. "I'm so sorry. I'm truly, truly sorry. I'll do everything I can to make it up to you, whatever it takes. But please - just don't die. Mum needs you. We all need you."
Memories of the father of her childhood swirled around in her consciousness. Nostalgic images of when he was younger and more vibrant. He looked old now. Tired and old. He seemed to have aged a decade in just a few months and she felt responsible. His retirement had not been as it should have. That guilt again. That damned guilt that was becoming her constant companion.
Her mother returned to the room clasping a plastic cup brimming with coffee.
"It's from the machine, dear, so I'm afraid it's not that special. Not like you're used to, I'm sure. But it's better than nothing. At least it's hot," and she handed it to her daughter.
"Thanks Mum."
Sophie took the cup and watched her mother walk to the window, looking out over a world below carrying on as normal, as though nothing had changed when for her it had changed beyond recognition. Her anxious mother, thought Sophie, bearing the crisis with her usual quiet calm. Her mother could become a widow. Such an emotive word, widow. An awful word. She had never thought of it before, one parent or the other left alone. Widow. Widower. Awful words, both of them.
Outside the window the radiance of a golden sunset lit the sky but in the fear of the moment it seemed to Sophie to take on a darker and more threatening hue, like an angry fire about to consume. She sipped at the coffee that she barely tasted. All was unreal, abnormal. And again she pleaded, silently within herself. "Please Dad, please don't die. Mum would be lost without you. We all would."

Caroline Jones Lewis
The Dream Robbers

As darkness fell, Andy Gray was squinting through bleary sedated eyes at his wife and two daughters gathered in quiet conversation around his bedside. The worst, it was hoped, was over. At least for now.

Once back home Emma prepared a meal in the kitchen.
"Can I do anything?" enquired Sophie.
"I think you've done quite enough already," blurted Pete angrily. "You and your cronies in the banking community." Sophie shrank from words that stung, like the sharp slap of a hand across the face.
"Did it never occur to you in that ivory tower of yours to watch out for them? Oh, no, of course it wouldn't have. You barely give them a second thought, do you, these parents who gave you everything through your childhood, who gave you the opportunities that you now flaunt in their face. You wouldn't have…."
"Pete - please. Not now," begged Emma sharply. "Please. We've had enough today. Leave it. Please. Leave it." Her hand trembled as she sliced through a tomato with a razor-sharp knife. She slashed the knife into the fruit recklessly and frighteningly close to her fingers. Pete stopped abruptly, fuming, his leg quivering and his face apoplectic with rage. He placed his arm protectively around his wife's shoulder as he noticed the tears that were welling in her eyes and he steadied the hand that wielded the knife so precariously.
"Sorry, love," he whispered. "Sorry. Couldn't help myself. I didn't mean to upset you. I don't think that tomato meant to either," and he planted a kiss gently on her cheek.
She attempted a smile but it was futile.
"I know how you feel, Pete, but we don't need to hear it right now. Let it go, love, please. And Mum will hear you. She doesn't need it either."

In the sitting room her mother sat in quiet relief, trusting that

Caroline Jones Lewis
The Dream Robbers

- at least for the present - the danger had passed. Joe and Hannah sat with her, like her guardian angels.
Would you like another cup of tea, Grandma? Are you tired? Here, have this cushion behind your back - you'll be more comfy, and in the hallway the telephone began to shrill. The family stiffened with tension. The hospital? Please God, no.
"It's alright," Emma attempted reassurance. "I'll go. That will probably be Izz. I left a message with her roommate. I'll get it. Soph, can you finish the salad. The chicken will be ready any minute."
"Pete, I'm sorry," Sophie attempted. "Really I am. I would never have hurt them like this. I tried to ring earlier to help. I did, truly. But no-one was there. There was no reply and then it was all too late. I just never dreamt that..." Sophie's voice trailed away. She knew her words were of little value, that her recognition of the damage caused was too little too late. She and her brother-in-law worked together, silently, an unspoken truce for the present acknowledged between them.
"Come if you want to, darling. He's stable now but, yes, come if you want to. I'm sure Grandma would appreciate it."
Emma's voice was soft and tired with emotion.

James accepted without question Sophie's news that she must stay, at least for the next few critical days. The axe for him was being sharpened daily and his day had been a nightmare, one that he had wanted to share, ready to unburden himself to her the moment he walked in through the door. But her message on his mobile had put paid to all that.
"And at least if I'm here I can take Mum to the hospital in the night, if she's needed. God forbid," her message had ended. He had awaited her call with trepidation, with foreboding of more disturbing news. The news that Mr Gray was stable - at least for now - was a relief.

Caroline Jones Lewis
The Dream Robbers

"Of course you must stay. Let me know how he is in the morning."

"I will do." She sought to change the subject. "What will you do with yourself for the evening?"

"Oh, not a lot. Might go for a glass or two at the wine bar before I go home. There's sure to be someone there we know. Read a bit maybe. Watch TV for a while."

"There's food in the freezer. Some of that salmon you enjoyed so much. And there's sushi in the 'fridge I bought earlier."

"Don't worry about me, darling. I'll pick up a takeaway probably. Just you worry about your father. And ring me if you need me. I will come if you need me, you know that don't you?"

"Of course I do," she assured him.

Best not, thought Sophie. Not in the current climate. And there was another reason. Right now she longed to see Robert. She longed for the comfort of his face, of his voice. How selfish of me, she thought, how selfish to burden him with this when he has his own worries to cope with. How typically selfish of me. My family are so right about me, my selfishness. And this need I have for Robert, at the same time as I need to hold on to James. I shouldn't do this, making use of them both. But the longing remained.

"Miss you," said James softly, wishing that she missed him enough to insist that he went to her. "Let me know - if you need me."

"I will," came the reply and the line clicked dead.

James felt bleak. A chill draught licked around his neck despite the clement weather and a sharp breeze of fear caught his heart. His life was changing direction, blown off course like the winds encircling the globe. His life was slipping out of his control and he was afraid of where it might be heading. He would not go to the wine bar. He had lied to Sophie. The place that had once been a favourite retreat was turning hostile. He felt it when he walked in the

Caroline Jones Lewis
The Dream Robbers

door, felt the eyes that followed him boring into the back of his head, the whispers that curled around his ears like the wisps of smoke from a dying bonfire. Former friends and colleagues were avoiding his gaze, pretending they had not seen him arrive where formerly they would have called a cheery welcome. Evenings without Sophie would be lonely and bleak.

Over the next few days the dust began to settle in the Bailey household. Izzie came home to visit her Granddad and to hug her Grandma. Pete and Sophie maintained a truce and Emma strove to hold her family together. With Andy's slow improvement, life developed into a routine. The anxieties that had been building for each component of the family became a mutual discussion, the full extent of damage being inflicted within the family unfolding with each story told.
"If I have to leave the Academy," Izzie ventured. "If you really need me to leave …"
"We're not there yet, Izz," insisted her father. "It isn't for you to worry about right now. You just make the most of the opportunity you've been given."
"But I do understand, Dad," she insisted. "It will be really hard but I'd just have to try another way of getting there. I could go on Britain's Got Talent, or something" she ventured, trying to sound enthusiastic.
"Over my dead body," breathed Emma.
"Don't worry about it," Pete assured her. "Where there's a will there's a way. Your mother and I will work it out somehow," though right now he was not sure how. Sophie sat once more with her father at his bedside as another dusk was falling. She was planning to return to London the following day now that he was settled but found herself strangely reluctant to leave him, afraid to leave him for fear if she took her eyes off him for just one moment, she may never see him alive again. This father she had so dismissed as parochial and banal had taken on an importance of

Caroline Jones Lewis
The Dream Robbers

gargantuan proportions. He had slept an hour or so and she had offered to stay while her mother took the opportunity to slip out to the shops. Emma came to take her and the two of them had left Andy in Sophie's care .

"We won't be long, dear," Kate assured her. "Just a quick trip to Tesco and home to put the shopping away and freshen up. Then we'll be back."

"It's alright, Mum. Take your time," Sophie replied. "I'll stay with him."

She was glad of a chance to be with her father alone, just the two of them. Perhaps a chance if he woke to tell him things she should have told him before. Through eyes still heavy from drugs and from sleeping, Andy watched his younger daughter reading a magazine in the chair beside his bed.

She sensed his eyes upon her in that strange, familiar way that people do and she looked up, smiling gently, pleased to see him waking.

"Hi, Dad. How are you feeling?"

"I'm alright. Just tired, that's all. I'll be as good as new in no time."

His voice was weak and tremulous and it frightened her, still fearful that he might have a relapse any moment.

"You mustn't rush it, you know. Just remember what the doctor told you yesterday."

"Oh, I will. Your mother will see to that, don't you worry."

She nodded her agreement grinning weakly, and paused a little.

Then "I'm going back to town tomorrow," she said. "Lots to do," she explained.

"Aye, OK," and he closed his eyes, resting his head back on the pillow.

"Your mother tells me you've lost your job."

Sophie shrugged her shoulders.

"Well, it's my own fault, I suppose. I'm really sorry that the things I've done have caused you and Mum so much worry."

Andy squeezed open his eyes to regard his daughter,. He

Caroline Jones Lewis
The Dream Robbers

slid his hand across the bedclothes and slipped it into hers, quiescent on the bedspread.

"Ah, well. Water under the bridge, heh? We'll just have to work things out somehow. What are you going to do now then?"

"I've no idea."

She tried to make light of it but in reality her heart was heavy.

"Chance to do something new, I think."

"It's not all your fault, you know, Soph. Those bosses of yours. Why weren't they keeping an eye on things?"

Sophie said nothing.

"I'll bet they've still got their jobs."

She nodded.

"You bet right," she replied quietly.

"There's too much put on young people these days. Too many young people running too many things in this world we live in. I know you think the likes of me are old dodderers and all that. The wrinklies."

He paused for a moment, breathless.

"But there's no substitute for experience," he continued. " You can't put old heads on young shoulders, that's what I say. We've lived more, us oldies. Seen more of life. We know more of the pitfalls, though I must admit I've never seen anything the likes of this before. It's a catastrophe. A real mess. What's happening now is far worse than anything that happened in the 90s."

He paused, catching his breath yet again.

"Careful, Dad. Don't overdo it now. You're talking too much, you old gossip," and she grinned nervously.

"Nor you," he lectured. "Don't you overdo it. Rushing back into the thick of things. Take your time and sort out something good for your life. Something ….. Well, something a bit less pressurised. More fun."

He paused again, steadying his breathing.

"You're still young, Sophie. You've time to rethink your life. You've made some money - enough to give you a

The Dream Robbers
Caroline Jones Lewis

decent life. More than we had at your age. But it isn't everything, is it? That's where it's all gone wrong. People out for nothing but money and more money. It isn't what life's really about. First and foremost, it's about family. And we're here for you. We're your family."

He paused again, breathing hard.

"Do you fancy a cup of tea?" she asked, anxious to quieten her father.

"Aye, that would be grand."

"I'll ask the sister if I can make you one. She's a bit of a dragon - have you noticed? But I expect she'll let me."

The news of Sophie's job loss was treated with simple acceptance by her sister and brother-in-law. For Pete Bailey it was an incomplete justice. As far as he was concerned, her bosses should be under arrest for gross malpractice. But he held his tongue. Sophie resolved her mother's anxiety with the immediate transfer of funds already planned. With all bills paid and foreseeable solvency, the imminent threat to her parents' financial stability was lifted.

Pete and Emma's dilemma was a little harder to address but in Isobel's absence on a visit to see Abi, Sophie broached the subject.

"I can pay Izzie's fees- for the rest of this academic year - at least," she offered, trying carefully not to dent the Bailey pride.

"Well, that would be a help and thanks for the offer but it isn't really the answer. Not if she's to stay the full course, which is what we intend her to do," Pete insisted. "That would be just trying to plug a leaking pipe with a sticking plaster. We need to find a way of cutting back as painlessly as possible and at the same time realise some of our assets. Trouble is, all the assets we have are now devalued - or unsaleable. There's no finance available for anything. It isn't just mortgages. If we tried to sell any of the vehicles –

Caroline Jones Lewis

The Dream Robbers

I mean the big stuff, the plant - no-one has the cash to buy and the banks aren't lending. So they're only worth half what they were six months ago, a fraction of what we paid for them. They've had all this tax payers' money, these banks and they're hanging onto it for their own purpose. Trying now to justify it in the name of responsibility. A bit late in the day, I must say. Do they think we have no brains? Born yesterday, that's what they think. We all know they're replenishing their balance sheet at the taxpayers' expense."

Sophie considered another approach but with care. She couldn't offer Pete a loan herself. He would never accept it - not from anyone but least of all from her. She had made an offer and not unexpectedly he had turned it down. It was difficult to know what else she could do. Perhaps a word with Emma on her own, she mused.

"Sad to say," he was continuing, "the time has come for redundancies. Much as I hate to do it to the men - I have no other choice. We've tried short time. It hasn't been enough. But who? They've all got families, mortgages. There's nothing to choose between them. It will have to be based solely on who has the least skills and who can be managed most without."

He made the decision with a heavy heart.

Emma was crestfallen. She knew full well he was right but it was the last thing either of them had wanted to happen. "It's the same for everyone," she sighed. "I was talking to Michael Croft when I picked up the 'photos the other day. He looked so worried. He tried to make light of things but I think he's really struggling. Things are getting worse for him too. I think their new baby's due any time."

******

On the eve of her return to London, Sophie shared a late supper with her mother at the dining table in the Gray's

Caroline Jones Lewis
The Dream Robbers

bungalow. They talked gently of Andy's recovery and the measures Kate must take to keep him in good health.

"Well, I know he'll be in good hands, don't I, Mum? But if you need me at any time, please let me know. I'll come if you need me."

"Thank you, dear, but I'll try not to bother you. You have things of your own to sort out right now, don't you? It would be nice to see you a bit more, though. I know your Dad would really like that, too."

Sophie paused, then taking a deep breath tried to put into words what she wanted to say to her mother.

"I know I've been a disappointment to you, Mum. I'm sorry. I'll try to be a better daughter in the future. But I can't be Emma. I'm just not like her."

Kate looked at her daughter aghast.

"Of course you're not like Emma," she protested. "No-one wants you to be. And you're not a disappointment, Sophie. Not at all."

She took her daughter's hand.

"Why on earth would you think that?" she went on. "We're so proud of what you've achieved for yourself."

"But I think you disapprove of the way James and I live."

"No, dear. It isn't that. It's just that your Dad and I have always felt that ..."

She paused, choosing her words carefully, not wishing to waste this precious moment of understanding.

"Well, that you've, sort of, looked down on us. And that hurts. Because we've always loved you and tried to do our best for you. That's all."

"And I haven't given you the grandchildren you would have liked. Like Emma."

Kate shook her head vehemently.

"You mustn't think that," the insisted. "Yes, we would have loved more grandchildren. But no-one should have children to please other people. Only if it's what they truly want for themselves. Children are a huge commitment. It's your decision whether or not you want children and we

Caroline Jones Lewis

The Dream Robbers

respect that. But you would make a wonderful mother and we know the rewards that children can bring."
Sophie scoffed.
"A wonderful mother. What - selfish me?" she retorted.
"You wouldn't be selfish with your own children," Kate argued. "But you'd be a different kind of mother to Emma. More …"
Again she paused, thought for a second.
"Oh, what's the word?" she breathed. "Spontaneous," she continued. "That's it. Spontaneous. And fun. Emma plans everything carefully. Maps life out for years ahead. Perhaps because she learned that from your Dad and me. You would never be like that. You'd be different, that's all. And different isn't wrong, is it? It's just different. My own mother taught me that. She was different. Defied convention. She never seemed to plan anything. Life just happened to her. And that made her great fun in some ways. She made me laugh a lot when I was little."
She smiled in reminiscence and Sophie saw the love and happiness that glowed in her mother's eyes at the memories.
"But life was sometimes rather uncertain," Kate continued. "Especially where money was concerned. You could never really depend on anything to last. One day we'd be having treats and eating luxuries. Chocolate and ice cream and the like. They were luxuries in those days. Then she'd be worrying about where the next meal was coming from. Perhaps that's why your Dad and I have always been so careful. And Emma follows suit. She doesn't like uncertainty, she likes everything organised. She even tries to organise me at times," and she laughed, stopping short of saying how irritating she sometimes found that to be.
She looked at her daughter, a daughter not known for tears of regret but now struggling to keep her emotions at bay.
"I'm surprised. I've always felt unable to live up to Emma," spluttered Sophie.
Kate pressed Sophie's hand fondly.
"Emma's not perfect, Sophie. No more than the rest of us,"

The Dream Robbers

Caroline Jones Lewis

she told her.
"Is anybody? But I never knew you felt this way. You and Emma always seemed so close - until recently, that is."

They talked on into the early hours and when Sophie kissed her mother goodbye in the morning and waved cheerily from the car as she drove away, they both treasured a lasting change for the better in their relationship.

Caroline Jones Lewis

The Dream Robbers

Chapter 5 - Fallout

In the village, Michael Croft worked diligently in his workshop behind the gallery at the craft he loved. He had bought the shop out of his inheritance when his widowed mother had died two years previously. He lived with his wife Helen in what had been his mother's cottage, the house in which he had spent his childhood and which she had left to him in her will. A small house set in a cottage garden, both he and Helen loved it despite the many lumps and bumps in its structure and the creaky stair halfway up the staircase. Buying the business had been an occasion of joy for Michael, a sensitive man of delicate disposition who had found working in the City environment beyond his ambition or aspiration. He had loathed the tedium of commuting, disliked the greed-driven goals of his colleagues - a square peg trying against all odds to fit into a round hole for the sake of a regular salary - and failing miserably. Life had been a continuous and nerve-ridden struggle against a depressive urge to flee. The change of lifestyle his much-loved mother's demise had made possible had brought a source of great joy amidst the sadness of her loss and it was no chore to him to spend his time in his workshop working on the mouldings selected with his help and care by his customers to frame their precious paintings and memorabilia. He loved the feel of the mouldings in his hands, the tactile feel of the wood beneath his long and sensitive fingers, the creation of the finished article, a blend of contrasts and colours that made it a work of art, the modern and contemporary and the old and antique with its fake patina. It was not so much a job for Michael as a labour of love.

Michael and Helen had moved from their adequate but unenviable rented flat in town into the cottage along with their baby daughter who had been the last source of great joy to his frail and fading mother.

Caroline Jones Lewis

The Dream Robbers

Helen, in contrast to Michael's nervous nature, was the epitome of calm and organisation. The moment he had met her on a balmy summer's day in a friend's garden, amid the chatter of good company around the lunch table and the scent of honeysuckle in the air, Michael had known in an instant that he would love her, this tall, slim woman with warm, sparkling eyes and a gentle smile that radiated calm and confidence. And Helen had known in an instant that she would love this man, with his tall, lean, bearded frame and gentle eyes that betrayed an air of vulnerability. They had each recognised they would love the other for a lifetime with barely a word as yet spoken and little more than a handshake between them.

To the delight of the friends who had brought about their meeting, there could have been no other outcome to that first encounter than marriage and a family. The loss of Michael's mother, while a source of grief to them both, had also been the source of financial security. At a time when Helen was faced with the prospect of returning to her work as a teacher, inheritance had provided the means to be a stay-at-home mother to care for baby Polly. Now heavily pregnant with their second child, she radiated contentment. It was therefore a disappointment to them both that, as the money supply became tighter, the business began to fail. For Michael's corporate clients, adjusting their overheads to meet the challenges of the economic downturn meant that framing the company memorabilia sank to the bottom of the agenda - or fell off the agenda altogether.

"People are just holding back on spending on things that aren't essential," he had told Helen. "Framing photographs or reframing pieces of art that are looking a bit shabby isn't vital to their existence, is it? The work just isn't coming in at the moment."

"What about the corporate clients?" Helen asked him. "Is there any chance there of them filling in some of the gap?"

"I spoke to Wheelers the other day," Michael replied.

Caroline Jones Lewis

The Dream Robbers

"They said pretty much the same thing. Business is tight so they've cut their budget for non-essentials."
"Well, yes, it's understandable," Helen agreed. "But it's just bad timing for us, isn't it? If we'd recovered completely from the set up costs, buying the stock and advertising and such, we'd have a bit more put by for a rainy day. It's just started raining too soon, that's all. But I expect we'll get by. We'll just have to economise on a few things."

When Michael's account began regularly to slip over his overdraft limit, letters from the bank began to mount in a discarded heap shoved discreetly into the desk drawer, out of sight but never out of mind. They loomed unseen above his head like a large black cloud that followed his every footstep. As takings had fallen but the family bills had continued to land unrelenting on the doormat, it had become his habit to pay more and more on his credit cards, of which he had had two but the offer of a third had been snatched up without a second thought as the balance of the first two had approached their limit. Helen, whilst aware there was a problem, remained blissfully unaware of the scale of that problem as Michael protected her from the extent of their increasing debt. She had reached the stage of her pregnancy that made extra effort with a toddler more of a chore than a pleasure. Her trips into the village and to the shop had become increasingly infrequent so of the mounting paperwork from their creditors she remained deliberately uninformed. When Michael left the shop of an evening, turning the key on the problem it was rapidly representing, he strove to shut out the economic realities the moment he stepped over the threshold of home. He refused steadfastly to waste precious time with his darling daughter and the wife he so loved fretting over his mounting debts. Polly, the light of his life, would bounce energetically to greet him at the end of each working day. His eyes lit up at the sight of her, at the sound of her voice. His heart warmed at the very

The Dream Robbers
Caroline Jones Lewis

thought of her.
"Daddy, Daddy. Come and look. I drawed you a picture."
He needed no second invitation.

As the days rolled on towards the birth of their baby, Helen became increasingly aware that things were going wrong, of her unease at Michael's erratic behaviour, of the brittleness of his tone and laughter. It was clear to her that he was in a nervous state. Whenever she broached the subject of the business with her husband, he diverted the conversation somehow and quite obviously was reluctant to give her a straightforward response to the gently probing questions she posed and needed answered. How is the business doing? Are we in real trouble?
"Oh, well, things are still a bit slow - you know how it is at the moment. But it will pick up, I expect - especially coming up to Christmas. Now young lady," turning to Polly. "What have you drawn me today then? A crocodile - Oh, my goodness. How fierce is that."

When gradually more cheques began to bounce and rising charges to appear on the bank statement, the warning bells really began to ring more loudly for Helen. It was fortunate, she thought, that the statements came to home for otherwise she would know nothing. With his ability to shut out what he did not want to confront Michael had simply avoided all reference to the topic intent on pushing the problem aside. Helen knew that the time had come to insist on some straight talking. But she knew, too, that she must handle it carefully, not to force Michael into a corner of self-defence. It was not his fault. It was the financial climate, those wretched banks and the damage they had done to the economy. She knew that. Job losses were being announced daily, losses in their thousands by businesses forced into administration as frightened consumers continued to draw in their belts. Not just new concerns but long-standing businesses that had been well run and hitherto

Caroline Jones Lewis

The Dream Robbers

successful. But Michael would not see it that way. Michael being Michael would blame himself for any and every failure, for causing worry to his family. She was considering how best to make an approach to the subject when matters were taken out of her hands.

The first blood loss frightened her and she lay on the bed speaking to her friend and neighbour on her mobile.
"Are you sure it's OK, Rosie? I need to see a doctor and I'm not sure how long I'll be."
"Of course it's alright. Polly's always happy here with our two. She can sleep here if needs be. Gavin will be home shortly to give me a hand. He's short of appointments these days since the mortgage market has collapsed so he's usually around in the evenings. You need to look after yourself, Helen - and the baby. I'll pop round and fetch her straight away. You ought to ring Michael. I don't like you being on your own."
Next Helen called her midwife and was told to contact the maternity hospital immediately.
"They'll want you to go in, Helen," her midwife advised her. "Can you go straight away? Will Michael be able to look after Polly?"
"We'll do whatever we have to," Helen assured her.
"Good. Then I'll be there to see you as soon as I can. And stay on the bed - until the ambulance comes. Don't move around the house. Just stay put."
So she rang the hospital who told her she must come in carefully and without delay. Then it was Michael's turn. Her hand trembled as she pressed the buttons on the keypad, doing her best to quell the panic that was rising inside her. For someone even as calm as Helen this was hard to cope with without giving in to her fears. She kept her voice as steady as she could manage.
"Hi, darling. Look, I've not been well today and the hospital want me to go in for a check up. They're sending an ambulance. Can you come - to the hospital?"

Caroline Jones Lewis

The Dream Robbers

As she awaited the ambulance she prayed. Fervently she prayed. Please God. Please don't let me lose our precious baby.

******

Hurricane Gustav began in the latter part of August and tracked westwards into the Caribbean Sea. Crossing Haiti it left a trail of devastation and a death toll in the 80s. Not content with its deadly tally it continued on to Cuba, causing catastrophic damage before emerging into the Gulf of Mexico. Making landfall on Lousianna before absorption by a cold front over the Ozarks, it took 138 lives and left in excess of $8 billion in damages in its wake. Close on its heels came Hurricane Hanna, meandering around the Bahamas, then moving northerly along the east coast of the United States until moving offshore in Massachusetts. Hanna claimed over 500 lives before blowing itself back out into the Atlantic. Then came Ike, tracking south of the Cape Verde Islands before ripping across Great Inagua Island and Grand Turk Island damaging or destroying 80% of the buildings and claiming another 75 lives.

Barrack Obama claimed the Democratic nomination in the Presidential race leaving a bruised Hilary Clinton to acknowledge defeat. The little known Senator from Illinois, son of a black immigrant father from Kenya and a white mother married to a lawyer who herself was the descendent of a family enslaved, took the nomination with overwhelming conviction. Change remained on course as the rallying cry for the day.

******

The whole world seemed out of control, and with it Sophie's entire life was crumbling into ruins. She could see no hope

Caroline Jones Lewis

The Dream Robbers

of working ever again in an industry that was all that she knew. The world she had known had disappeared for ever in the few short days since she had cleared her desk and left the building. But it was not only her world. The worlds of thousands, millions, were now at stake. The job loss tally was rising daily and set to rise further. Fear stalked the square mile as never before. It was felt in the frightened heartbeat of the City and smelled in the clammy air that wafted through the streets and alleyways.

With the closure of the bank, Leo Trask found himself without prospects or money and his redundancy money - small as it has been since he had only recently joined the staff - soon ebbed away. Creditors began closing in. Credit card bills that in his earlier optimism he had recklessly allowed to rise to their limit were now an ever-present threat and telephone bills from over-indulgent use of his mobile and the inevitable domestic charges for energy and utilities all represented a nightmare scenario. As payments were missed on his credit cards, the telephone calls became constant and insistent, some verging on the abusive, and the warning letters fell through his letterbox like confetti in a churchyard on a Saturday morning in spring. He missed Tess and her down-to-earth practicality but most of all he missed her comfort. He missed working, too, the need to fulfil a role in a society from which he now felt estranged. He scanned the local newspaper for jobs but any jobs for which he would even vaguely have qualified were now conspicuous by their absence in an industry rent apart. At the agencies, he joined the ranks of others from his erstwhile profession seeking more of the same, clerks and secretaries, personal and business bankers - all now surplus to requirements. His search brought no success. The shedding continued and the ranks of the discarded continued to swell.

When the letter came from the building society following the

Caroline Jones Lewis
The Dream Robbers

first missed mortgage repayment, he bought himself a bottle of whisky and drank himself into oblivion - the first time of many. In his fall to rock bottom, there was still a way to go.

And James? For James, investigations were now proceeding towards their inevitable conclusion.

******

Helen Croft received the news calmly as was ever her disposition. The scan had shown the placenta dangerously placed beneath the baby making a stay in hospital essential until delivery by caesarean section when the time was right. "If we can just wait a week or two more to allow baby a little more growing time, then everything should be fine," her consultant assured her. Their baby, she determined, was to be delivered safe and sound.

Michael fretted with concern and an even greater conviction that she must not be bothered with the problems of the business. He had become almost immune to the frequent calls from the credit card companies, promising payments he knew full well he would be unable to make just to get them temporarily off his back, sending out cheques he knew full well the bank would not honour.

The threatening letters that arrived almost daily were stuffed determinedly into the desk drawer in the office but when the letter came from the bank demanding immediate repayment of the overdraft, he was close to collapse. He recognised the address on the flap of the envelope as he turned it in his hand to slit it open. His hand trembled and at first he was tempted to stuff it into the drawer unopened. Then decided against it, decided that it was better he knew its contents than spend his entire day worrying about what it might say. He tore it open and read the letter with verging disbelief. 14 days, it said. How could he possibly repay the overdraft in

Caroline Jones Lewis

The Dream Robbers

14 days?

Panic gripped him fiercely. Then came his anger. Anger at these banks whose actions had caused the whole decline in the first place. How dare they, he fumed. How dare they treat people like this - baled out by the very taxpayers they were now threatening to destroy for he knew from the media reports that he was not alone in his plight. He tried hard to blot out his anger and panic as he collected Polly later from their neighbours, taking her first to visit Mummy in hospital, then home to bed. He wished he could turn off his brain, his thought processes, but it was not possible. His brain just kept whirring on, fretting, worrying, fearful of the future and unable to find a solution to a problem that dogged his every step and hung above his head like a huge black cloud that moved as he moved. It dogged his every footstep and threatened at any moment to engulf him in a torrential downpour that would sweep away the stability of his entire world. He wished he had Helen's calm composure but however hard he tried to mimic it, calm eluded him. The pressure was building daily and it was inevitable given his persona that eventually he would crack under the strain.

******

The day her father was to be discharged from hospital, Sophie drove to her parents' bungalow to see him safely settled back home. She sat at the table in the small, neat kitchen with her sister, awaiting their father's arrival by ambulance as their mother watched anxiously through the net curtains draped at the sitting room window.

"How are things with you? With the business," ventured Sophie.

"Not good. But Pete's come up with a temporary solution. He's put two of the properties at The Tythings into auction. He's put a reserve of £300,000. If we can get upwards of that for each of them, it will recover some of the build costs

Caroline Jones Lewis

The Dream Robbers

and free up some capital to tide us over for a time. It's way below the selling price he'd intended but we have no choice. It's all about survival while the market is down."

She sighed and Sophie noticed for the first time a change in her sister's demeanour. Emma, normally optimistic and energised, was more subdued than Sophie had ever seen her. "He's trying to let two of the others but everyone's doing it now," Emma continued. "The lettings market is saturated, especially with buy-to-let properties."

Emma sipped at her mug of coffee.

"It's hard not to feel bitter in the light of all that's been done. But at least we're mortgage free ourselves. We won't lose our own home. We're luckier than most. Because the forecast is for worse to come."

She paused, aware of her sister's complicity in the unfolding chaos and not wanting to confront the issue head on. There was a time and a place and to Emma this was neither but it would come, especially if Pete had his way. It would come. At least Sophie had bridged the gap in her parents' funds for the time being and Emma was grateful for that. Sophie was silent in response with nothing to say in a defence she felt sure she would be called upon to express at some point. The silence hung pointedly between them.

"How about you? What's happening with you and James?" Emma ventured at length.

Sophie sighed. Until now she had said nothing of James' situation but unable to contain herself any longer, she related the whole sorry saga. She knew in an instant she had misjudged the moment.

I should have waited, she acknowledged to herself. I should have taken the cue from Emma's body language. Why do I do this? Why do I always get it wrong?

Emma raised her eyebrows in exasperation.

"So….." she began hotly, her hackles rising. "So not content with the wreckage you've created in *your* quest for more more more money, James has actually been indulging in illegal practices to make an even greater pile. Fantastic.

Caroline Jones Lewis

The Dream Robbers

You two - who have so looked down on us poor stupid, honest, hardworking people in our clean little world while you two superior beings - as you seem to consider yourselves - ruled the world from your lofty heights in London and lorded it around us.   So this is what is all boils down to. Corruption.   My God, Sophie, this really takes the biscuit. I don't know how you can sit there and calmly admit it without even the slightest hint of an apology.   And as for your bank.   All the banks.   Well ... not a word of apology from any single one of them.   Do they understand what they have done?   What **you** have done?   Do you?"
She rose agitated from her seat and paced the room as she spoke, slapping her mug down on the worktop and releasing her angry torrent at her sister who sat head in hands before her.
"Please, Em.   Please don't.   I'm sorry.   I didn't know what James was doing, really I didn't.   I would never condone anything like that."
"Sorry," blurted Emma angrily.   "You're sorry!   Sorry doesn't even begin to cover it.   It doesn't even come close, Sophie.   What you did may not be illegal but it was irresponsible.   That doesn't make you any better.   You were just as greedy.   Do you understand what the likes of you have done to people like us?   If we don't sell these houses at auction we're finished.   Pete's company is finished.   All he's worked for for years and years.   Gone - and the men's' livelihoods with it.   We know how they feel, Soph, because we're like them.   We have children to provide for, children whose needs have to be met.   Isobel's fees at the Academy - her career, her entire future at risk. Hannah looking to go to university in a few years' time. We have responsibilities and we work hard to fulfil them. As do the men.   One of them is already fearful of their home being repossessed and there's nothing we can do to help him. Nothing.   However responsible we feel.   He has a wife and six month old baby for provide for.   You wouldn't understand that.   You've never wanted children.   Why?

Caroline Jones Lewis

The Dream Robbers

Because you're too damned selfish. Too wrapped up in living the high life."

She paused for a moment, lost for more words to express her feelings, but then continued more quietly and contemplative. "And we're not alone, are we? Our plight is repeated over and over across the country. Families like us who are facing hardship because of people like you. Not just this country even - most of the western world. And then there's Mum and Dad, too and people like them. Pensioners. They've worked hard all their lives and put money into pensions that are now worth a fraction of their previous value. And as if what you have done isn't bad enough at least it **was** legal. Maybe that **is** something to your credit. What James has done, this criminal, corrupt ……"

She ran out of words and breath once more.

"Oh, for God's sake. Sorry just isn't enough," was all she could manage.

She stopped in her tracks, breathless and hot with anger after her tirade, at the sight of her mother standing in the kitchen doorway whose attention was drawn by the raised voice of her eldest daughter, a daughter whose voice was rarely raised in anger. Distressed at the sight of her two daughters in conflict she begged an explanation.

"What is it?" she began. "Why are you arguing like this? I hate to see you two at loggerheads with each other. What is this about? You could cut the air with a knife in this room. I don't want your father distressed when he's home. We have enough to deal with."

"You tell her," fumed Emma glaring at her sister. "You tell her, because I can't bring myself to."

As Sophie stared blankly down at the table, struggling to find the words she needed to say, a ring of the doorbell distracted their mother's attention. Andy Gray had arrived home.

Sophie stood in the little kitchen diner while her mother and sister settled her father home. She stared out of the patio doors onto the pristine little garden, the neatness of a

Caroline Jones Lewis

The Dream Robbers

bowling green lawn and the flower beds that were usually immaculately tended but that now, since Andy's illness, were beginning to show the first signs of neglect, the first clusters of tender weeds dotted here and there between fading blooms hanging on their stems. It was a garden her father normally tended meticulously. Small and neat and wholesome. That was her parents, everything about them and everything they owned. And in her arrogance she had belittled it - until now. Small it maybe but it was also respectable. Right now she felt big and ugly and ashamed.

******

As the autumn evenings darkened earlier and earlier, the winds howled in every nook and cranny and whistled down every chimney. Change, change, change they demanded. Change. With the falling of the last leaves came the falling of empire upon empire, a chain store here, a retail outlet there, forced into administration with no-one to save them and the loss of more jobs and livelihoods following suit. The values of properties plummeted further, the pound sank more and more against the euro with the share value of organisation after organisation sinking to all time lows. But the housing market was not the only one that was now threatened with meltdown. In Detroit, USA the motor giants were facing crisis as the lack of credit funds hit their market. The ripples of destruction were widening further. With the year drawing ever nearer to closure, the winds became colder, more biting with a sting in every tail.

******

Michael Croft reached breaking point, an event as inevitable as night following day. After three weeks of coping with Helen in hospital and with the pressures of the business and their finances building, the imminent birth of a new son or

Caroline Jones Lewis
The Dream Robbers

daughter was a potent reminder of the responsibilities he bore. Polly was now staying with Rosie and Gavin at night, returning daily after a trip with her father to visit her mother in the hospital. It would continue until Helen returned home.

"Just 'til our new baby comes, Daddy?" Polly asked her father.

"Yes, sweetheart. Just until your new baby brother or sister is born and comes home with Mummy," he promised. "Then we'll all be home together."

"With my new baby," she responded proudly.

The caesarean section was booked for Friday morning at 10 am.

The evening before surgery, Michael left his wife's bedside to take Polly back to their neighbours, then returned home to find another letter from the bank on the doormat. Once again the familiar address on the flap of the envelope gave him warning. He had pleaded with the bank for more time to pay but to no avail. The threat of court action remained their only response. On his mobile phone, which he had left in the car during his visit to the hospital, the list of missed calls from the credit card companies was six calls long. In his agitated state and without his wife to support him, he moved around the house not knowing quite what he was doing or why. Tomorrow, he fretted, his child would be born to a father no longer capable of providing for even its basic needs. After court action, when then? If the business failed completely he still couldn't pay them. There would be courts. There could be bailiffs. Unable to calm himself and restless with anxious energy, he visited the shop to check for any messages and retrieved the mail from the mailbox. It was a journey he later regretted he had made. The letter from a debt collector on behalf of a creditor struck fear through his very heart.

"We have checked with the Land Registry," it told him "who confirm that …."

Caroline Jones Lewis
The Dream Robbers

They were threatening to take their home, he panicked - the house that had he had grown up in, that had been the home of his mother, of his father, that his parents had worked all their lives to pay for and had left to him and his family to become their home. He had heard of such cases on the TV and radio and now it could happen to him and his family. He would have let them down, all of them, his wife and his children, and the parents who had worked all their lives to give him everything they had. Returning home in the agony and despair of his own self-reproach he sat on the bed almost paralysed with fear, an avalanche of tears clouding his eyes and mucous seeping from his nostrils. He wiped it away on the back of his hand like a hapless street urchin oblivious of his appearance. He could not think straight, could not motivate himself to seek a solution. His eyes fell on the bedside table where Helen's book lay just as she had left it before her hasty rush to hospital. It was an anthology of poetry, a favoured dog-eared volume that was a constant companion at her bedside and it lay open at the poem she had been reading, an old, weathered leather bookmark resting on the spine so that the lines she had last read leapt to greet him. The words of Yeats impressed themselves upon him, more than apt for the moment.

> *'Had I the heavens embroidered cloths*
> *Enwrought with golden and silver light*
> *The blue and the dim and the dark sloths*
> *Of night and light and half-light.*
> *I would spread the cloths under your feet:*
> *But I, being poor, have only my dreams;*
> *I have spread my dreams under your feet;*
> *Tread softly for you walk upon my dreams'*

The words so timeless in their poignancy juddered in his troubled mind. She had always walked softly and encouraged, his Helen. Nurtured, helped him to build and turn his dream into reality just as he had done with hers. It

Caroline Jones Lewis
The Dream Robbers

was these others that had destroyed it. Others who cared nothing for the likes of himself. Cared nothing for the hopes and dreams of those they held in their power so in their greed they had trampled the dreams of those others under foot. It was almost too much to bear, too much to confront, to even glimpse in his mind's eye the rubble of their devastation. He was close to breaking, close to falling over the edge into an abyss. Until now it was his love for Helen and Polly that had kept him holding on but the strain was threatening to break him. How much more could he absorb? How much longer could he hold on? At this moment he felt there was no more strength within him, nothing left in him to fight on. And yet – just when he thought that despair would drown him completely, when a breakdown seemed about to overwhelm him - something sparked within him, a spark that set alight a spirit deep inside. His stress converted into anger, his anger venting into fury, like a gale whipping a landscape so that he thrashed around the house seeking direction for the nervous energy that was now building.

******

On the outskirts of his village, a large detached property stood in darkness behind tall closed wrought iron gates that opened onto a long landscaped driveway. The country property of a City banker, it was used as a weekend retreat, a holiday home for the banker and his wife and their two married children and grandchildren. Just a modest cottage, the banker called it, seven bedrooms and a conservatory at the rear with a swimming pool and terrace and views to die for. Just a modest little get away for the occasional sojourn on home territory, when the weather was not inviting enough to tempt them to their holiday home in the mountains of Majorca. They were seen around the village on occasion, pleasant enough people, the villagers thought, but aloof from village life. They bought the odd bottle of wine or

Caroline Jones Lewis

The Dream Robbers

patronised the greengrocer and butcher but with a possibly and unintentional air of superiority, particularly the man himself. It smacked to the villagers of condescension.

Earlier in the day, the banker and his wife, under siege by the press at their prestigious London property, determined to slip quietly away under cover of darkness for the sanctity of the country retreat of which, it was hoped, the press were so far unaware. Majorca had been ruled out, the need to run the gauntlet at an airport departure lounge an uncomfortable proposition and the likelihood of further harassment at an already known destination making it as unattractive an option as staying where they were. A feeding frenzy by the media had followed the disclosure of enormous losses by his bank on badly selected investments, despite which, it had also leaked out, he and his cohorts had paid themselves bonuses in the millions of pounds sterling. And not only the US subprime market was deemed the culprit for the name and investments of a man called Madoff were also beginning to attract attention, another chapter about to commence in the financial drama.

"Do you have any comment to make, sir, on the bank's disclosure of its huge losses?"

"Do you intend to resign, sir? Have the Board requested your resignation?"

"Do you intend to make an apology to the British public?"
The telephoto lenses and probing questions of the media dogged his every footstep but to date the banker had declined to comment on each and every occasion.

"Bloody parasites," he had complained to his wife who was more traumatised than he was by the unwelcome intrusion and more ashamed and embarrassed by the revelations. The children and grandchildren had wisely stayed away.

"Mum, why don't you come to us for a few days?" they had offered but loyalty demanded she should stay with her husband. At the altar she had promised for better or for worse so stay she must.

Caroline Jones Lewis
The Dream Robbers

"We could slip across the channel at the weekend," he had proposed. "Take Eurostar from Ashford to, say … Paris? Don't you think?"
"It's bound to be better than this," his wife had agreed, staring disconsolately from behind the drapes at the bedroom window onto the huddle of reporters encamped in the street below.
"The house will be cold," she mused. "It's too late to ring Peggy and ask her to switch on the heating. And we'd better pick up some food on the way. There won't be anything in."
From the back entrance of the house they had slipped out to their large garage in a block at the rear and absconded in her less conspicuous BMW, leaving the Jag discreetly closeted in the garage, sneaking away like thieves in the night to their weekend country retreat. It was against this country retreat that Michael Croft was about to vent his mounting anger.

******

Unable to settle now that a giant rage had woken inside him and with his wrath building to a frenzy, Michael Croft rattled around in his empty house. His brain was misfiring on all cylinders and lurching into overdrive and he hatched a plot to take revenge. At a little after midnight, he turned the car key in the ignition and headed as quietly as the engine would allow towards the banker's weekend retreat. In the boot of the car was a half full can of petrol retrieved by torchlight from the garden shed. The petrol used to fuel the lawn mower slopped and slurped in its innards as the car lurched into action, an old rag used for the cleaning of the mower and a box of matches snatched in haste from a kitchen drawer by its side. He drove determinedly down the lane from the cottage to the country road that led out of the village, surrounded by silent darkness apart from a glow in the bedroom window of Ruby Blethery's cottage and the headlights of the car. In the sweep of their beam across the

Caroline Jones Lewis
The Dream Robbers

stony surface, leaves skittered ahead of him and the branches of the trees along the hedgerows thrashed and swayed and bent double, blown by a cold northerly that had been growing in pace all evening. A fox caught unawares in the beam from the headlights paused momentarily, fixing him with an accusing stare, its eyes glowing fierce and seemingly straight into his own.

"What are you up to, Michael Croft? What are you doing?" they seemed to ask him.

Michael dismissed the notion as the fox darted through the hedge, the white tip of its brush disappearing through the bracken into the darkness beyond.

When he reached the entrance to the country property, Michael pulled up before the elegant gates that had loosened in the increasing wind. One of them was swinging to and fro with an eerie whine, like a scene from a horror movie. Then it crashed with a clang as it hit the central peg in the ground. It had not occurred to Michael how he might enter the property. In his hypertensive state he had given it no thought. But the sight of the gates wide open only served to enforce his conviction that fate was on his side, that justice should be his. He collected his tools of destruction from the boot of the car and strode purposefully to the front door into the shelter of the wooden porch way, muttering as he went, his hair flared by the violence of the wind and his eyes bright with a fury verging on the loss of all reason,. He poured petrol through the letterbox and around the wooden structure of the porch, then onto the rag which he stuffed halfway through the opening. He struck a match but it flickered then died, extinguished by an overwhelming draught before it could reach its quarry.

"Damn," he snapped. "Damn you. Damn all of you. Greedy bastards. Greedy. You won't get away with it. You won't. You're destroying everything I have. Why should you have all this? Why should you get away with it? I won't let you. Burn, damn you. Burn."

Caroline Jones Lewis
The Dream Robbers

He struck another match, this time shielding it from the wind with his hand, and he lit the end of the petrol-soaked rag that hung limp from the letterbox. It flared into flame as the petrol caught alight and he raised the flap of the letterbox so that the blazing rag slid quietly inside the door onto the pool of petrol beneath.

"Let's see how *you* feel when you come and find what's left of your precious little country retreat," he muttered.

"Some of us will be lucky to keep one home let alone more because of you greedy bastards. It's time you had your annus horibilis."

The puddle of petrol on the floor inside ignited with a whoosh that caused him to start and flames licked up a curtain caught in a tieback behind the doorway. They spread across a rug on the polished wooden floorboards, the edge of which had become saturated with the petrol and a thin draught between the floorboards fed the flames sending them higher. The fire spread more quickly than he had envisaged, licking up the inside of the door where petrol had dripped down the paintwork and the feet of an antique wooden coat stand that lived beside the curtain began to glow in the pool of liquid that had seeped across the floorboards towards it. The burning petrol flared over to the carpet that led up the stairs urging the flames upward towards the staircase.

Michael turned and raced back up the driveway, lanky and awkward, unnerved now, his feet twisting this way and that as he stumbled on the gravel and suddenly shaken and surprised by the rapidity with which the fire took hold.
The sense of injustice that had fired his conviction, bubbling and spitting inside him like lava in a volcano about to erupt, subsided with unexpected speed as the consequences of his actions began to sink home, to snap him out of his temporary insanity. What if the property were not empty after all? What if there were someone in there? What if they did not hear the fire start? If they were burned in their beds? His

Caroline Jones Lewis
The Dream Robbers

fury was turning to panic and he watched the flames light up the lower floor of the building from his standpoint at the opening of the gateway. The heat in the hallway blew out the windows of the half-glazed front door and with nothing between them and the gusting wind, the flames fanned higher, the painted timber of the wooden porch starting to crackle merrily. The light from the blaze lit up the immediate skyline now, silhouetting the barren skeletal trees in the garden and the shrubs that formed the hedge and lined the flower beds. Michael turned and fled.

Back at home he replaced the petrol can in the shed and closed and padlocked the door. He let himself in through the back door and stood in the kitchen trembling. Oh, God, he muttered. Oh, God. It was all he could think of, all he could say to himself in the silence of the empty house. The whiff of petrol fumes from a spill on his sleeve caught his attention and he tore off his coat and threw it aside. As his temper cooled, the magnitude of his actions and the implications of the fire hit home further. How could he alert the fire brigade without revealing his involvement? But how could he dare not? It was surely too late now. The fire had already taken hold before he left. Now after the drive home the whole place must surely be well alight. The questions raced around inside his head in a jumble, demanding answers he was unable to give. The property had looked deserted but how could he be sure? Of course there was no-one in there, he argued with himself. No-one had raised and he had hardly been quiet. No light had appeared at any of the windows. There had been no movement. And didn't they have a dog? He was sure he'd seen them with a dog in the village. It would have barked. Surely they had a dog? Or was that just the banker's daughter and not the banker himself? He couldn't remember. It was a while since the family had been to the village. They had come into the shop late one Saturday afternoon when he was about to close and lingered, talking

Caroline Jones Lewis
The Dream Robbers

amongst themselves as they examined his goods and from which he gleaned they were looking for a birthday gift for aunty someone or other. He had asked if he could help but had been summarily dismissed by the man. They had left to the sound of the man's voice declaring arrogantly there was nothing of interest and Michael had watched them leave and collect the dog tethered to the lamppost outside. He had remembered the incident clearly, stung by the man's insult but softened somewhat at the gentle smile of the wife who had thanked him and apologised for keeping him late. Remembering now transformed them once more into real people and the fear that he may have harmed them - or worse - made him tremble. The smell of petrol on his skin flared his nostrils and he fled to the bathroom and showered frantically, trying to calm himself in the warmth of the water. When he stepped out into the steam-filled room and wrapped himself in his dressing gown, half frozen with fear and in shock, the shrill of the telephone in the hallway below called for his attention. In an instant his mind switched to his wife in hospital.
"Helen," he thought. "It must be Helen. The baby."
He raced barefoot to answer the call.
"Mr Croft," a voice began. "This is Sister Andrews at the hospital. Your wife has gone into early labour. We need to carry out a caesarean immediately. She asks for you to come."
"I'll be there," he gasped. "Tell her I'm coming. As quickly as I can."
He was grateful for the diversion and in a single moment the fire and its consequences were snapped from his mind.

At the earliest respectable hour, Michael rang Rosie to give her the news.
"We have a son," he told her ecstatically and related the emergency of the night with brevity.
"I'll pick Polly up at 10 o'clock, if that's alright with you. Please don't tell her about her new brother. I'd like to …."

Caroline Jones Lewis

The Dream Robbers

"Of course I won't. We'll see you then. Congratulations Michael. I'm so glad everything is alright. Give my love to Helen, won't you? Tell her I'll see her later."
And as she would tell the police later, no, no, we heard nothing - but then that house is a little out of the way. I doubt anyone in the village would have heard anything. Next door? No reply? Oh well, no. There wouldn't be. They won't be able to help you at all. They were both at the hospital all night. Helen was giving birth to their new baby. She has a boy. They're so thrilled. It was an emergency caesar. We had Polly here with us - their little girl. Their house was empty all night so they won't be able to tell you anything.

******

In the cold light of dawn, the banker and his wife stared bleakly at the smouldering ruins of their country retreat, a steaming mess from which the smoke was still rising, and water still dripping. A tall slim man puffing contemplative on a panatela, he surveyed the scene that had greeted them. It was one of organised chaos. A fire tender remained parked on the driveway, firemen trudged their wellingtoned feet across saturated flower beds, stepping over hoses coiled in abandoned heaps like a clutch of lifeless serpents and the pool at the rear was a mess of charcoal splattered water.
"We were lucky," exclaimed the banker. "If we hadn't stopped at the services for food and then been held up by that accident on the M40, we could have been in there. We could have been murdered in our beds. Bloody thugs whoever they are."
His wife shivered despite the heat emanating from the smouldering ruin.
"Maybe that's what they intended," she said flatly. "They hate us, don't they? Because of what the banks have done. Because of what you have done. They hate us."
"Who's 'they', for God's sake," enquired her husband

Caroline Jones Lewis
The Dream Robbers

impatiently.
"Everyone," she replied. "Everyone. The public. The press. You don't seem to realise. You just don't ….."
"Don't be ridiculous, woman. For God's sake calm down. You're being paranoid. Neurotic. Nothing justifies doing this."
But the banker knew well enough. There had been death threats. 'Phone calls he had dismissed as cranks and not told his wife about but that now he realised he must take seriously. He had asked the police not to tell her, convinced them that they were empty words. But now he knew.

To one side of them stood their ageing housekeeper Peggy, aghast at what had greeted her when she walked down the drive to attend to her duties. Once her initial relief had subsided that no-one had been in the house and that no-one had been hurt, the effect on her own situation had struck full force. A pensioner with no source of income other than that the state afforded her, she relied on the additional money from this work to make her life even bearable. She had been ecstatic when they had appointed her despite her dislike of the man. *She* was alright, the wife. And it was the wife that really she would deal with. She had been thrilled that at last, after being forcibly retired by her former employer, life would be more bearable. But they would not need her now. Not while the house was in a state of disrepair. And afterwards? Would they want her back or replace her with someone younger? So there would be no money to supplement her pension. She led a measured existence in a little flat belonging to a housing association, counting out the apples in the greengrocers, half an apple for each day of the week, measuring the tea carefully for each pot that she brewed, taking each day the required number of slices of bread from the freezer so that the loaf would last until her next pension and homemade soup was her fall back on the days that the cupboard was otherwise bare. Without the income from her job with the banker, there would be no extra

Caroline Jones Lewis

The Dream Robbers

money to cover the cost of heating and homemade soup would become her staple diet. He would not pay her. Not him.

"Tight as the duck's proverbial," she had told her close friend Ruby.

Ruby was the village gossip, the font of all local knowledge who worked at the village post office spreading the word on every subject under the sun that she could glean from the village grapevine; a colourful widow whose conversation was as inventive as her flamboyant dress and who had lived alone for some years since the loss of her dearest darling Frank.

"All their money," Peggy had told her, "an e's tight as a duck's ass. Even with 'er," she continued. "'is missus. I've heard 'im telling' 'er - she can't 'ave this or she can't 'ave that, an' in front of me an' all. 'e doesn't give a damn. Proper embarrassed she was, I can tell you.."

"Well, that's it with the likes of them, Peg," Ruby had answered. "The more they've got the more they want and the tighter they are with it. You know what the bible says - the love of money, and all that."

On this morning, Peggy's spirits sank to rock bottom and she turned to leave.

"I'll be off then," she told them.

"Fine," came his reply. "We'll be in touch but of course there'll be no point in you coming for some time. I'll pay you 'till the end of the month. I'll send it on."

"I'll see he sends it, Peggy," the banker's wife assured her. "We'll be in touch - as soon as we need you again," and she touched Peggy's arm gently, aware how much the loss of the extra money meant to Peggy. She watched her walk disconsolately away.

"Come on," the banker addressed his wife. "We might as

Caroline Jones Lewis
The Dream Robbers

well head off for Paris straight away. No point in staying here," and he gave the police his mobile number before he too marched away. Something in the moment triggered a rare bout of rebellion in the banker's wife.

"No. I don't think so," she said bluntly. "I'm going to ring Claire. I think I'll go and stay with her and the children for a while. They did tell me I could go so I think I'll take them up on the offer."

The banker puffed in exasperation.

"What do you mean - stay with Claire? I'm just expected to trot along as well, I suppose? They won't like it if the press come trailing after us to camp outside their front gate."

"They won't follow *me*," she insisted. "It's *you* they're interested in, not the rest of us."

"Oh." He was taken aback. "So you mean you're going on your own, then? What about me?"

"What about you?. You're not keen on spending too much time with the children, are you? You'll be far better going to Majorca, or something. Go and play golf for a week or two."

"What - on my own?"

"Why not on your own. You usually clear off with your golfing buddies and leave me by the pool anyway."

"That isn't the point. We always go to Majorca together."

We always go everywhere together, she thought - and it's always where you want and what you want to do.

"Well not this time," she insisted. "This time I want to go to Claire's. So you do as you please, dear. You always do anyway, don't you?"

She sighed inwardly. Where had it all gone wrong, she wondered. Where was the man she had married? The man she would have followed to the ends of the earth, and he for her? Not here, she pondered. Not here and now. He had been so different then, a caring husband and father in the days when they had little in the way of property or money but had been a happy family. Somehow things had changed over the last decade. The higher he had climbed on the

Caroline Jones Lewis

The Dream Robbers

career ladder the more ambitious he had become and the more importance money had held. At least, not the money, she thought. It was the power that money gave him, the esteem in which he had increasingly been held by the wider world. And as his own profile had been raised the less importance she and the family had held, it had seemed to her. She dismissed the thought from her mind, took her mobile from her handbag and rang for a taxi. Then she rang their daughter.

"You're not bringing Shylock, are you?" asked Claire. "I don't think we could cope with the media circus, Mum. We have to think of the children."

"No, dear. I'm coming on my own," she replied, making no attempt to reprimand her daughter for the disparaging reference to her father.

Within minutes her taxi arrived and retrieving her bag from the boot of the car she waved an au revoir, leaving him standing there staring disbelieving after her.

"Oh, and I might as well take the food," she added. "You won't want to take it to Majorca with you, will you?."

He puffed again with exasperation - but said nothing.

The glow of the taxi's rear brake lights had barely died as it disappeared from the driveway before the banker rang his mistress. Not for the first time in recent days, his call was met without response, just the buzz of a ringtone that remained unanswered. He tried her mobile with the same result. His calls had always been answered without delay until now. He flipped his mobile closed with a grunt of impatience. She was just making a point, he assured himself, annoyed by his lack of contact during the recent difficult days and with his wife's constant company in the glare of the press. He had no office to ring from now, no private domain over which he reigned supreme. His life had changed beyond his wildest nightmare, a future blown away like the leaves ripped from the branches of the autumn trees and no-one he could blame apart from himself. He

Caroline Jones Lewis

The Dream Robbers

shrugged his thoughts away. She would come round in a day or two, he decided; no doubt of that. He would send her something by way of apology. A gift. Diamond earrings perhaps. Or a bracelet. She loved the money. She loved the presents. She would come round.

******

A knock on the door took Peggy by surprise. She had returned to the flat in a state of despair, the spectres of the 1990s hardship looming large for a second time. She had lost her house during that recession, redundancy from the factory office followed by a period of unemployment that had left her helpless to prevent it happening. Once her livelihood had gone and the comradeship that had in those days been her support system, with no other job on the horizon it was inevitable. She had loved her little house. It had been with a great sense of achievement she had bought it on the advice and support of her colleagues and moved in with their celebratory cards and flowers. And she had never forgiven "those bloody Tories," she told Ruby. "They made the recession happen and the likes of me lost everything."
But she had coped with it in time.

Peggy had been married once but not for very long. He - the husband - had run off with a colleague from the office where he worked, a silly tarty piece well past her prime, in Peggy's opinion, all bright red nail polish and stilettos with skirt's half way up her backside and plunging necklines to emphasise her ample bosom. It had been almost a relief to Peggy. She had never really enjoyed married life, especially the sex, even with a man 15 years her senior who she thought would be less demanding. She had been quite presentable when they first met, in a quaint sort of way, in her neat little suits and twin sets and pearls or georgette blouses with peter pan collars, pin tucks and little pearl

Caroline Jones Lewis

The Dream Robbers

buttons up the front and on the cuffs of the sleeves. Not see through, of course. Never see through blouses like the trollops that waited alongside her at the 'bus stop. She had worn court shoes in those days though not high as she almost matched his five foot nine in height without their help and, though slimmer than of late, stoutness had always been threateningly near. Her hair had been slightly longer in length than the utilitarian style she had latterly adopted, softening a face that could appear solemn and a personality to whom humour was not a readily available asset. But the fripperies of life had never really impressed her. She had tried make-up for a while to please the man but it was abandoned fairly quickly as indeed he had abandoned her. She had wondered sometimes how she had come to be married at all, a sentiment echoed by her husband as he had walked out of the door. On reflection she had decided that perhaps his ability to treat life lightly had appealed to the sense of responsibility that caring for an ailing parent had instilled in her before their death. And ultimately it had seemed to her they had been two people simply thrown together temporarily by the winds of life until falling apart again quite naturally as the winds subsided. He had helped her through the process of grieving and finding a new purpose to life - and then moved on.

The divorce had ended her brief status as a Mrs and her only other family in the world were a widowed aunt in London with two children, Peggy's cousins. The eldest cousin, a son, had emigrated to some far flung corner of the world some years past and Peggy had not heard from him for years. The youngest, a daughter, had married well and moved in social circles far elevated from Peggy's modest life. The only contact between them for years had been the exchange of Christmas cards that were little more than the acknowledgement of each other's existence. She would have liked a sibling or two, Peggy, a sister to share things with or a brother who perhaps would have been protective of

Caroline Jones Lewis

The Dream Robbers

her. But it was not to be and she had wasted little time contemplating the 'if onlies' of life. She had been content to build a life on her own. Buying that little house had been a landmark. Losing it had been a source great of pain. She had never forgotten the Court hearing, swallowing hard to keep her emotions in check, her ears harangued by the distraught sobbing of another woman about to lose her home. Herself - she felt numb as the Judge approved the repossession order. He was a kind man who had explored all the alternatives but could see none, he had told her. It was true. There were none. She had tried so hard to get another job but her advancing age had been against her and with no prospects in sight at the time of the hearing the outcome had been inevitable.

On the last day, while she had awaited the arrival of the bailiff, she had stood in the back garden she had so enjoyed, breathing in for the last time the scent of the Philadelphus she had planted so lovingly and tended with loving care. The house was empty at that moment, bereft of all the knick knacks that had made it her home. Rehoused by the Council days before, Peggy's belongings had been removed to the spartan, expressionless flat they had found her on a Council estate that was less than salubrious. She had cleaned the little house from top to bottom for the last time, pride disallowing anything less than an immaculate handing over for its next occupants to enjoy. She hoped they would cherish it as she had done. Then fighting back the tears, she had walked from the garden through the kitchen and handed over the keys, had left through the tidy hallway, through the polished front door, taking the last few steps down the front pathway and closing the white painted front gate behind her. Without glancing back and with a breaking heart, she had walked briskly away. Fear of homelessness would never leave her from that time on. She had given in to her pain only once, an occasion that afterwards she had come to regard as a source of shame.

Caroline Jones Lewis
The Dream Robbers

There had been a rare encounter with her local MP, an unexpected crossing of their paths as she had trudged towards home from the local labour exchange on a wet and windy autumn day. She had taken a favoured route out of town, quiet and tranquil, a wide tree-lined street of large Victorian properties converted into offices for the professions, accountants and lawyers and amongst them the local party office. He had emerged from his car outside the office returning from an engagement. This sudden and abrupt convergence of their paths had pierced the veneer of calm acceptance she had wrapped around herself in recent months. She was all but brushed aside by his entourage paving his way into the building just as her life and home had been brushed aside in life by the policies of his governing party and the devastation caused. The irony did not escape her while of course the damage he and his party had caused to her life escaped him entirely. As she watched the man and his entourage disappear into the building, the quiet hurt and anger she had locked away inside herself bubbled and spat in his wake and finding herself alone in the street, disregarded in the descending gloom of dusk, her pain had erupted and she had given vent to her emotions in an uncontrollable and uncharacteristic outpouring. In her shopping bag she carried a can of paint bought that very afternoon to brighten up the dreary flat that was now home. Determined to make the best of her surroundings for as long as she must, she had chosen the paint to spruce up the dismal kitchen, to transform it from a grubby and cheerless magnolia with a crisp calm blue that would look clean and fresh against white tiling she had scrubbed free of grime. Propping her shopping bag on the wall of the party headquarters, she had prised off the lid with her front door key and tossed the paint across the gleaming black bonnet of his polished car. Then dropping the tin and the lid into the gutter she had walked steadily away. It had been nothing short of a miracle that just at that moment there had been no-one about to see her commit the crime, no-one to notice

Caroline Jones Lewis
The Dream Robbers

the insignificant unremarkable woman who strode
purposefully towards home. Later, she had remonstrated
with herself. It had been a foolish gesture.
"A criminal thing," she told herself. "I'm a criminal."
She had waited for days for the knock on the door, expecting
a visit from the local constabulary which mercifully had not
come, only a report in the local paper with a photograph of a
shocked politician standing by his vandalised car. No
CCTV to catch her on camera. No public spirited member
of the public to make a citizen's arrest. There had been no
come back. She had realised in a flash of practicality that it
had been a pointless gesture that in the end had cost only her,
both financially and in emotional angst. Her coat had been
ruined by a splash of paint on the front and of course she
would have to buy more paint for the kitchen. Having
replaced the paint and decorated her kitchen and consigning
the coat to the dustbin, she put the entire matter into that
compartment at the back of her mind reserved for 'things
best forgotten". Like the marriage. Like the day she left
her little house and garden. No-one would ever know, she
had decided. No-one. She had locked the compartment
and thrown away the key.

Despite all she had rebuilt a life for herself, finding work
albeit less well-paid and of more menial content. But at
least she would survive.
"I lived on that Council estate for nearly a year," she told
Ruby. "It was like living on another planet. Nothing but
unmarried mothers living on benefit. Rent free. One girl
'ad three children by three separate fathers. Scandalous, it
is. Scandalous. But it's the norm to them. I was a
dinosaur, an old relic an' they took the mickey all the time."
Ruby tut-tutted sympathetically.
"You poor soul, Peg," she said.
 "Their kids yelled insults at me through the letter box. Then
one day I was ganged up on. These three pimply youths,

Caroline Jones Lewis
The Dream Robbers

jeerin' an' tauntin', jabbin' at me with their fingers and shovin' me between 'em. They pushed me from one to the other. It was frightenin'. I've always carried a 'brollie with me since then, just in case. A good'efty one that belonged to my mother. I could give someone an 'efty wallop with that if needs be."
"Did you report them to the police?" asked Ruby.
"No. I was too scared. Anyway, it would probably 'ave made 'em worse."
Then a sympathetic colleague had introduced her to a housing association, she went on, who had offered her the little flat she now lived in. It was small and out of town which meant the cost of 'bus fares but the compact sitting room had french doors that opened onto a little courtyard. She could keep pots with plants in and hang out her washing, and beyond the fence at the bottom of the courtyard the land dropped away down a gentle hillside looking out across the weald. The bedroom window looked out across the same landscape and from the moment she walked in she had known she had to live there. She had accepted help with gratitude and breathed a sigh of relief at leaving the Council estate behind her. She had shut the memory of those days, too, behind another closed door in her mind, swallowed the past with dignity only now to find herself faced once more with hardship because of someone else's actions, someone else's greed and irresponsibility. It was hard to bear. If she failed to pay her rent, what then? Another Council estate?

At the knock on the door she pushed away a cup of tea only half drank and gone cold, made as an automatic gesture when reaching home, the great British panacea, but that really she did not want or need. Her visitor, whoever it may be, would find her in quiet despair. She raised from her seat and trundled to the front door to answer the call. The sight of the banker's wife took her by surprise.
"Oh," she began, then paused not knowing quite what to say.

Caroline Jones Lewis

The Dream Robbers

Then "come in," she invited, struggling to regain her composure and waving her arm self-consciously, aware of the difference in their social standing, the elegant and groomed visitor from a mansion stepping into the miniscule hallway of her tiny home.   She felt shabby and poor.
"I won't keep you, Peggy," the banker's wife promised.   "I have a taxi waiting.   I'm going to my daughter's for a few days.   I just wanted to give you this.   I thought there may be expenses we hadn't settled and I didn't want you to be out of pocket," and she made to press a banknote into Peggy's hand.   But feeling a cheapskate in light of the distress on Peggy's face, she delved into her handbag for her purse and took out a second £50. note which she folded inside the first. She thrust the two notes into Peggy's hand.
"Don't worry about any change.   We can always settle that later - when you come back," she emphasised.
Peggy was speechless.
"I …." don't know what to say, she wanted to tell her, and "thank you," but her voice failed her.   The lump that had swollen in her throat just would not let the words through. She swallowed, trying to clear it but it persisted.
The banker's wife touched her hand gently, an emotional pause.
"He isn't really a bad man, you know," she ventured.   "He didn't mean to be unkind.   It's just that ….   Well, he has a lot on his mind at the moment."
Oh, yes, thought Peggy.   I know that.   I saw 'im, she wanted to say.   I saw 'im on the telly, chased by all those reporters.   It's 'is fault that someone hates 'im so much they've done this.
She did not condone the action but she understood it.   "It's me that will suffer," she wanted to protest.   "Again."   But she held her tongue.
"Take care of yourself, Peggy.   You have my telephone number if you need me.   Call me if you need anything, won't you.   I do mean it."
Peggy nodded, the gratitude she was feeling etched across

Caroline Jones Lewis
The Dream Robbers

her face. And then the wife was gone and Peggy closed the door.

Peggy took the crumpled notes from her hand and placed them on the kitchen table, stroking them flat and tidy. It was a kind gesture, she recognised it. Some may think it patronising but she knew this woman. She was a kind person and Peggy had always liked her. Not the husband. No, she didn't like him. But this woman - yes, she liked her. And she knew it was not intended to be patronising, not offered as charity. And even if it was, in her present state of mind she didn't care. She was grateful and the kindness lifted her spirit, fired her with renewed determination to struggle on.
"It's a loan," she decided. "To 'elp me manage. It's just a loan."
She would make herself a fresh cup of tea, a nice hot one, maybe have a biscuit or two. She only had six left in the barrel to last her until her pension was due but now she could allow herself two. She would walk into the village and buy a local newspaper to read on the 'bus into town. There would be cleaning jobs, she was sure, both advertised in the paper and at the job centre in town. By the end of the day she would get herself back on her feet in some way. She would not let them beat her. Especially the likes of that bloody man the banker. No. She would not give in.

******

"Now," demanded Helen gently, taking her husband's hand in her own and meeting his gaze eyeball to eyeball.
"Michael, are you going to tell me about the business?"
Polly stood by the side of the bed, her finger clenched firmly in the grip of her baby brother's hand.
"Eam John," she said. "Eam."
Michael disengaged himself from his wife's stare.
"Liam," he corrected Polly. "His name's Liam.

Caroline Jones Lewis
The Dream Robbers

She looked up into her father's face.
"Say the L - like this," and he rolled his tongue in an exaggerated gesture. "Llliam".
"Llliam," she copied carefully and grinned at her success. "Liam."
Michael turned to his wife smiling.
"I didn't want to worry you," he began.
"I know. But I'm a big girl, you know, and I need to know what's going on," she answered. "And then we can talk about a solution."
"I've let you down," Michael said blankly.
"No, Michael," she insisted softly. "The timing's been all wrong for us, that's all. We'll find a way. We have to so we will. But it's our problem, not just yours. That's what families are about, isn't it?"
"But to fail ….. We had such high hopes. It hurts to let people down like this."
"You haven't failed," she insisted. "You haven't let anyone down. Other people have failed us. Their greed has failed us. But it's only about money, Michael. We'll survive it. It isn't like … Well, the failures I've seen - in my work. A child let down. A child society has failed to protect. Abuse that people like me that should have seen it and stepped in. That's real failure. That's what hurts me. Every time it happens to a child somewhere, I hurt. A real pain."
She looked down at her baby son, tiny and vulnerable in her arms, and his big sister proud and trusting.
"This is just money, Michael," she said, "and we'll survive it somehow."
"I was afraid they'd take the house. My parents' house that they worked a lifetime to pay for. This letter, it said …"
Helen shook her head.
"You should have told me," she insisted gently. "And they won't take the house. Believe me. They won't. We'll sort it."
Michael, too, looked at his gentle but determined wife,

Caroline Jones Lewis

The Dream Robbers

propped up in her bed against a heap of pillows, his new baby son comfortably sleeping in the crook of her arm, his daughter at their side already protective of her new baby brother.
"I'm blessed," he thought. "Despite all this money stuff, I'm so blessed."

When Rosie visited the hospital later in the day and related the details of the fire and the enquiries of the police, Michael forced himself - as casually as he could manage - to ask the question that was praying on his mind.
"Was anyone hurt?" he ventured, his breathing restricted, his chest constricted with anxiety and his fingers metaphorically crossed behind his back. Rosie kissed the tiny fingers of the perfect newborn she was nursing and answered casually.
"No, thank goodness. The place was empty apparently. Well, they're hardly ever there, are they? You know what they're like. I think they rather regard it as slumming when they come here, think themselves above the likes of us. I don't know why they keep the place on really. They won't lose out, of course. Gavin says the insurance company will stand the cost of rebuilding, so they'll have lost nothing. Oh, look, he's peering up at his big sister. He knows his sister already," and bored with what was already yesterday's news in the village, she changed the subject deftly back to one of far greater interest.
"Oh, bless him. Look at your brother, Polly. Isn't he beautiful? He looks just like you, Michael," and the subject of the fire was lost in favour of the fascination of Baby Liam.

For Michael it was the answer he had been praying for. He felt weak with relief. He dared to breathe again. Thank God, he thought. Thank God. What would I have done if the answer had been yes? How would I have lived with myself? Much as he resented the banker's apparent immunity from justice and his lack of morality, he would never have intended him physical harm, even less so to his

Caroline Jones Lewis
The Dream Robbers

family. But the irony of it all did not evade him. All that angst. All that risk he had put himself through, the risk of discovery and the consequences to himself and his family. And it would cost these people nothing. Just a time of inconvenience, if that, while the insurance company restored their property to better than before. While he could go to prison leaving his family to cope without him and with the shame. It could even mean that his own insurance premiums might well increase as a consequence. What a pointless gesture. What a fool I am. And he vowed that God and police incompetence willing, his actions in the night would be a secret he would carry with him to his grave. Helen must never know. They must never know, his wonderful family. They must never know. Just he and a fox - the only living creature to share in the confidence. He pushed the memory of the night's activity to the back of his mind and closed a door in his subconscious. He found himself a stronger man than he had been 24 hours earlier. Nothing would be that bad ever again. Not as long as he had Helen and his children. He looked down once more on his newborn son, his little daughter at the baby's side, and thanked a God he had never before been sure he believed in.

******

With a heavy police presence in the village and the subject of the fire on everyone's lips, Pete and Emma were no exception. They discussed the matter at the dinner table.
"Your Tony did some work for that man, didn't he?" recalled Emma.
Pete nodded.
"And was diddled over the bill, if you remember. All the millions that man has and he has to cheat my brother out of a few measly pounds for a bit of plastering. Makes you sick doesn't it? No wonder someone's had it in for him."
"It was arson then?"
"So I believe. That's why the police are questioning

The Dream Robbers
Caroline Jones Lewis

everyone."

"What's arson?" asked Joe.

"Arson is when someone starts a fire deliberately," Emma explained.

"Why? Why is that man so bad that someone would do that?"

It was Hannah now. Pete tried a brief explanation of the events in the City and the banker's role in the present state of collapse of the economy, the damage it had caused to people's lives and livelihood.

"Not that that makes it right," he stressed. "It was still a bad thing to do. A criminal act."

"Oh," said Hannah, apparently unimpressed. "So really someone's jealous because he's made a lot of money."

"Not exactly," Pete ventured thoughtfully, feeling that somehow Hannah had missed the point he had tried to make. "It's the way he made all that money that matters."

"Well, I don't care that he made loads of money," Hannah retorted. "I'm going to make loads of money one day."

Pete sighed and Emma's heart sank. Oh, God, she thought. She really is like Sophie.

******

It was the sons of Bernard Madoff who turned him in to the US authorities following his confession to them that he had committed fraud. Bernard Madoff had graduated from college in 1960, married his childhood sweetheart and worked at her father's firm of accountants. He moved gradually into the world of investment operating under the radar of the regulator, first in New York and then moving to Florida. Promising an astonishing 18% return, he attracted the wealthy and famous and by 1990 was dealing in large pools of money under a strict policy of secrecy imposed on his clients. By 2008 a large proportion of Geneva fund management was invested with his firm until its collapse and exposure as a 16 billion dollar fraud. Broke and disgraced,

Caroline Jones Lewis

The Dream Robbers

there was nothing left of the millions he had conned from his victims, both institutions and individuals alike. Those unwise enough to be his investors were left with no hope of recovery. They had taken too little care checking out his promised yield, the potential he had assured them was realistic. For realistic it could never have been. Individuals formerly worth millions found themselves ruined and penniless, institutions found their reserves, already depleted by unwise investment in the US housing market, depleted even further. One investor ruined to the point of no return resorted to suicide. From a lavish lifestyle lived on other peoples' money, Bernard Madoff was on his way to goal.

******

In the United States of America, President Elect Barack Obama accepted election success with humility and determination. His call for change had been the ultimate rallying cry. But change indeed had come, for who would have thought - ever in a million years - that a black man would be voted into the White House. In his acceptance speech he made it plain to the American people that his success was also theirs.

"Because of what we have done on this day, in this election, change has come to America."

Amongst the crowd of his supporters the Reverend Jesse Jackson stood listening intently, tears streaming down a face that had waited so long for this day, this man who had been present at the speech by Martin Luther King - "I have a dream that my four little children will one day live in a nation where they will not be judged by the colour of their skin but by the content of their character." The dream then had not survived then, destroyed by assassination. But now, now the day was here. There was much to do to heal a broken world, to repair a wrecked economy, to restore a reputation throughout a world that increasingly

Caroline Jones Lewis
The Dream Robbers

viewed the US as a pariah. It was a high mountain that he was faced with climbing but climb it he intended to do.

Caroline Jones Lewis

The Dream Robbers

Chapter 6 - The Road To Redemption

Sophie Gray had worked out her next course of action. She had checked all her liquid assets and ascertained the exact level of available funds. Without reference to James who, like herself, she considered owed a debt to many but in the first instance to her family, she transferred a chunk of money from their joint account to add to the funds of her own she still had on deposit. All in all, she had sufficient available funds if need be to bid at the auction as high as the reserve. Once there, she could let the property go to another bidder but if necessary could go ahead and buy on her own. Just as long as Pete received his reserve price the mission would be accomplished. On the morning of the auction, with her strategy clear in her mind and with James in France alone to break the news of his potential incarceration to his parents, she set off from the City for the auction rooms in Royal Tunbridge Wells. She had told no-one of her intentions. Relations with her sister and brother-in-law right now were, to say the least, frosty though their parents had taken pains to keep in touch with her. Sophie had not called Emma since their last disastrous encounter and she had not yet plucked up the courage to attempt reconciliation. The days of childhood pranks and scrapes were over, the days of a sister rescuing her renegade sibling out of duty of care. This was a grown up thing and needed a grown up resolution. It was now up to her to make amends. First she must attempt damage limitation.

"How's Dad?"

She had asked the question in a 'phone call to her mother the previous evening.

"He's doing alright. The doctor's pleased with his progress. He just needs to take things easy and not get overwrought about things. And they've suggested losing a bit of weight might help, of course. He pulled a face when I told him he's going on a strict diet."

"I'm sorry, Mum. Sorry things have come to this."

Caroline Jones Lewis
The Dream Robbers

"Don't keep apologising, Sophie. What's done is done. It's not all down to you personally, is it? You're just one of many. Now. When are we going to see you? We're here for you, you know. With all this that's going on with James."

There was a new warmth between Sophie and her parents now that everything was out in the open. What Sophie acknowledged to herself as her earlier arrogance was now replaced by a degree of respect for the family she had formerly derided. It was only with Emma that the coldness continued, a reluctance to forgive she had never expected from a sister who, for all of Sophie's life, had been forbearing and forgiving. She hoped that once her act of redemption was complete and became known there would be a gradual thaw, a recognition that she had acknowledged her failings and attempted to mend her ways. She enquired tentatively at what she needed to know.

"So the auction's tomorrow then. Is Pete going?"

"I don't think so. The auctioneer will keep him informed. He says he can't bear to be there. Anyway I think he has things to do at the office. He's meeting his brother, I believe. Something about lending him a van."

"Tony? The one with the twins?"

"Yes. Tony. I think his van's packed up and the way things are - well, you know. He's had hardly any work for months now and his wife's waiting to hear if she's being made redundant. The shop she works for has just gone into administration. So he can't afford to repair his van. Pete has one standing idle in the yard since he laid off some of the men so he's going to lend him that one for the time being. Might as well. He can't use it himself right now."

"Oh dear. Tony's in trouble too then."

"I'm afraid so. I think they're hanging on to their house by their fingernails. There are a lot of people hit hard in the construction industry. Anyway, Emma thinks Pete is better kept occupied elsewhere rather than at the auction. She's concerned about what all this is doing to his blood pressure."

Caroline Jones Lewis
The Dream Robbers

"I didn't know it was a problem?"

"Well, not a serious one I don't think, but he does have to just keep an eye on it. With all this stress - we don't want him keeling over next, do we?"

"No, absolutely not. And how's Em?"

"She's keeping cheerful. You know Emma. They neither of them give in to things. As long as they can sell these properties things will work out, at least for the time being. Her hours have been cut at the estate agents again, though. She's on a three day week now instead of four."

"And the kids? Are they OK?"

"Yes, they're fine. Hannah will be taking the first of her GCSE mocks after the holiday so she's studying hard at the moment. They take some early these days, don't they? It's different from your day."

"Oh, yes, of course. It's exam time. Does she know what she wants to do?"

"Something to use her languages, she says. You know she has a talent for language. She speaks French and Spanish like a native. Now she wants to learn Mandarin. Looking towards China for the future, I think."

"She's probably right there. That sleeping giant has well and truly woken. So they're going to need the money for uni as well, then."

"Yes, I would think so. It looks that way anyway. But not just yet. They still have a few years yet. Still, you know what Pete and Emma are like. They always like to plan ahead for these things and at the moment all their planning has gone right out of the window. Let's hope the future looks brighter next year, dear."

" Yes, let's hope so. The Government is at least trying to ease the situation, albeit slowly."

"Yes, I know. Hopefully things will get better soon. But it does worry me all this debt the country's going to be saddled with for the future. That will mean tax rises on top of all people have had to put up with already. I just don't know where this is all going to lead. It worries me sometimes the

Caroline Jones Lewis
The Dream Robbers

sort of world the grandchildren will have to live in."
She sighed wistfully. Sophie was silent.
"I can't think that far ahead, though. Your Dad keeps telling me not to worry about it, that things always work out in the long run. He says we'd better just concentrate on the present and I know he's right. So much has happened in such a short time - your Dad being ill, and everything. We have enough to think about right now."
"Fingers crossed for tomorrow, then, Mum."
"Yes, dear. Fingers crossed. Come and see us soon, won't you? Don't let these things keep you away. I want to see you and Emma friends again - sooner rather than later. So does your Dad. It doesn't do to let these things fester."
It seemed to Sophie that since her father's illness there was a new strength about her mother, who had quite naturally assumed a new status within the family. And it suited her, she thought.

The drive to Tunbridge Wells was straight forward and Sophie arrived in plenty of time before the auction, parking in a car park close to the Common. She strolled along the High Street to a once-favoured coffee shop and relished the warmth inside on this frosty morning. She sipped a latte as the minutes ticked by on the clock on the wall and stared down into the milky liquid deep in thought. It was like being in a time warp, sitting in this coffee shop that had been a regular haunt with some of her old school friends during the holidays and congregating around a seat on the Common before catching the 'bus home. The name was different, the décor changed but in her memory it amounted to the same. When they were older there were the nightclubs, raucous Saturday nights with rowdy teenagers spilling out onto the pavement before being whisked off home by weary parents doing the taxi run. Or in her case, sister Emma searching for her amongst the rabble, anxious to get her home all in one piece and with no potentially disastrous incident. She

Caroline Jones Lewis

The Dream Robbers

smiled fondly at the memory. Emma - her constant guardian Emma. She owed her so much. God knows how or where she might have ended up if not for Emma. It had been Emma who intervened when Sophie had been tempted to join the pill popping brigade, Emma who had been there to yank her away by the elbow when, inebriated and reckless, smarting at the break-up with Robert, she had been hell-bent on a promiscuous binge with any ready and willing spotty youth who had thought he was on to a promise, who saw her as easy prey with all the implications that could have held. Always Emma to pull her back from the edge of the abyss. And she had never properly acknowledged that debt, neither to Emma nor to her long-suffering parents. It was time. More than time; it was overdue.

The High Street seemed timeless, unchanging; just a few names here and there that were new but mostly little had changed. If one dress shop had disappeared into oblivion it had been replaced by another selling much the same style of merchandise and as one estate agent went under another rose to take its place, so the landscape had remained virtually constant. After the urgent bustle of the City and the nerve-ridden events of recent weeks it was soothing and familiar, comforting just watching a more tranquil and genteel world go by like an old and valued newsreel.

"Sophie? Sophie Gray? Yes, it is you. Good heavens, I haven't seen you for years. How are you?"

Sophie looked up abruptly, shaken out of her reverie by the voice of a young woman standing before her, heavily pregnant, her hand resting on the handle of a pushchair in which a toddler sat chewing on the soggy ear of a fluffy brown rabbit with a blue waistcoat. Sophie stared blankly, grappling in her memory for a name, for recognition but her memory failed her.

"Karen," the woman explained. "Karen Thomas that was. Sixth form. Remember?"

"Oh, of course. Yes, of course I remember you," Sophie

Caroline Jones Lewis
The Dream Robbers

gasped. "I'm so sorry, I didn't recognise you. You look so ..." She paused, considering her words.

"Pregnant?" Karen offered and they laughed.

"Different was what I was thinking, actually" Sophie corrected. "Different. But happy. Blooming in fact."

"Well, yes - I would I suppose. My life's somewhat different these days. But happy. Yes I'm very happy. And this is Ben," she added, indicating the child now staring up at Sophie from the pushchair. "What about you?" she went on. "You look marvellous. You don't have children, I would guess?"

Karen took in the designer clothing, the manicured nails, and the chic hairstyle.

"No, I don't have children. I'm not married though I do have a partner. A significant other, as the saying goes. We live in London, I work in the City. "

Worked, she thought to herself. Worked - but no longer. Past tense. But she made no effort to correct her statement.

"Oh, really. You didn't marry Robert Welling, then?"

Sophie grinned weakly.

"No I didn't marry Robert."

"I'm surprised," Karen continued. "We all thought you would. Become the lady of the manor, so to speak. You seemed so right together."

"Yes, I think a lot of people thought that," including us, thought Sophie wryly. "But it just didn't happen. I live with James. He works in the City too."

She stopped short of an explanation as to what she did in the City, of what either of them did in the City, no longer proud of either of their achievements. Professional anonymity came as a relief in the present climate and Karen showed little interest in the matter of Sophie's career. The two women chatted amiably for a short time before Karen excused herself. Her husband, Karen told her, was in the motor trade which was suffering because of this credit crunch business and their hopes for the future were on hold until the economic climate looked a little brighter, a house

Caroline Jones Lewis
The Dream Robbers

move to something larger and roomier with another baby on the way.

"It's really tough right now," she went on. "We really relied on his commission to get by but - well, you know how things are. Such bad timing, with me being pregnant and another mouth to feed. But we'll get by somehow. We have to, don't we?"

Sophie nodded wistfully.

"Yes, I suppose you do."

"Well, better get on," Karen concluded, hurriedly checking her watch. "I'm on my way to a hospital appointment. Ante natal. I'm due any time now so I'm hoping it will all be over within the next week. I'm at the stage where I really want it over. I'm longing to look down and see my feet again. We just popped in for a cup of tea, didn't we, Ben? The 'bus from the village only runs hourly so I had a while to wait and I hate hanging round at the hospital. That hospital smell - you know," and she grimaced. "I'm really glad I did, otherwise I might not have seen you. It was lovely bumping into you like this - seeing you again after all this time."

"Yes, you too, Karen," Sophie agreed, feeling a genuine pleasure at the meeting. "hope all goes well …" and she indicated the large bump that was soon to become another baby.

"Do you know the sex?"

"No. We decided we'd rather wait and have the surprise. It's part of the pleasure after the pain," and she grimaced at the thought of the giving birth part of the process.

"And I see Peter Rabbit's still a favourite," said Sophie, pointing to the soggy-eared waist coated rabbit now resting in the lap of a drowsy thumb-sucking Ben.

"Oh, yes. All the old favourites. Pooh Bear and Tigger, of course. We're regular visitors to Pooh Corner and the Hundred Acre Wood. Pooh sticks at the bridge and all that."

And Piglet, thought Sophie. Don't forget Piglet, the special

Caroline Jones Lewis
The Dream Robbers

significance of Piglet uppermost in her mind here in Robert's world, Robert's domain.

"Oh, yes. I remember us doing all those things when I was little," Sophie acknowledged. "It was quite magical, wasn't it?" and she caught herself indulging in a moment of unsolicited nostalgia. Pooh and Piglet, only in her case, Robert and Sophie.

"Yes, me too. I loved it. And Ben loves it, too." Karen was talking, interrupting Sophie's thoughts and reluctantly Sophie pulled herself back to the present.

"Well, good luck with the baby."

"Thanks. We're hoping for a girl, of course. A pigeon pair. Then I think we'll call it a day. We wouldn't mind more, either of us, but children are so expensive. And the way things are financially - who knows how bad things are going to get before they get better. Wave 'bye'bye to Sophie, Ben. 'Bye Sophie. See you again some time, I hope?"

It was a question to which Sophie gave no firm reply.

"Me too. 'Bye Karen."

Sophie watched them leave, wondering how different a person she might have been had she stayed locally, not worked in the City. How different her life would be now if she had stayed and fought for Robert. Robert would have wanted children, she was sure. His parents would undoubtedly have hoped for a son and heir. Would she have been willing to have children? Given her selfish streak would she have made a good mother as her own mother insisted? She would never know now, it seemed. Robert, she thought. Her thoughts always came back to Robert. The moment she crossed the M25 it was back to Robert, like crossing a natural divide, like crossing the Rubicon. So close and yet so far away. She planned to call on him after the auction hopefully with mission accomplished and she wondered what difficulties he was facing with his business. Part of her was reluctant to know but the other part knew that she must. Now that the process

Caroline Jones Lewis
The Dream Robbers

had started, there was a need in her to face all the consequences of her erstwhile life and career in a cathartic urge to somehow redress the balance, though what she could do in the case of the wider world she had no idea. Where had all this come from, all this great outpouring of conscience that she needed to indulge? All this self-reflection was unnerving. She stared thoughtfully down into the empty cup before her. She did not regret the good life she had had as a result of working in the City. It was just that now it all seemed tarnished, that it had always been too good to last because it was built on precarious foundations. Since leaving her job she had been forced back out into a world she had forgotten existed during those working years, outside of the cocoon she had lived in, the City and its business. She had been privileged in that world and along with others she had squandered that privilege and abused it in self-serving. Reminded of her reason for being here and suddenly aware that time was ticking by, she gathered up her bag and her coat and hurriedly moved on.

The auction rooms were only sparsely occupied as even for properties at auction activity remained sluggish. She took a seat at the back near the door, attempting anonymity, an inconspicuous presence that her very appearance would deny. The bidding for the first properties, a spate of repossessions, was slow and she feared the result that Pete was aiming for might not be achieved. They went for a fraction of the price they would have attracted only a few months before. But when the first property at The Tythings came under the hammer, the bidding was more brisk and it easily achieved its reserve, reaching a heady £350,000. before the gavel came down with a resounding thud. Its buyers, a couple in their late thirties who had been fortunate enough to sell their previous property before the market had crashed, left to deal with the paperwork in a state of euphoria. They had lived for some months with their two

Caroline Jones Lewis

The Dream Robbers

children in rented accommodation. To have their own property once more, and one that was such a dream and undoubtedly a bargain, would be such a joy. Some of the lucky ones, thought Sophie. The lucky ones for whom time and fortune had dealt a good hand. Life was all about timing and gratefully there were a few that were lucky, the exceptions to the prevailing rule - at least there were some winners. She watched them disappear into the office with mixed emotions. She was glad for them, for their good fortune, but sad for Pete that he had had to let the property go for way below its originally intended sale price, cutting his losses in the interest of survival.

The start of bidding for the second house brought her back to the purpose of the moment. Bidding began at £200,000. but was slower to rise. When it stalled at £240,000. she pitched in with an increase to £250. A rival bidder went to £260, then she to £270 and he to £280. She raised another ten thousand in the hope that he would go to £300K but the property had less garden than the one he had previously bid for and was on a plot less desirable and secluded. The bid price had now breached his self-imposed ceiling dictated by the funds he could realistically raise. He withdrew. With a shake of his head to the auctioneer he left her with a bid of £290,000. The bidding stalled. It was not enough. Not enough, still below the reserve and Sophie glanced anxiously around the sale room in the hope of a new bidder but there was none. All could be in vain. She held her breath as the auctioneer tried to rally further bidding without success. In an act of discretion, the auctioneer took her bid and sold at ten thousand below the reserve. It was close enough and he knew that Mr Bailey would be satisfied. With a tap of the gavel, Sophie found herself the new owner of a four bed roomed home in the Kentish countryside that she had no idea what she would do with and was unsure she would be able to rent out. But it mattered not a jot. She gave a sigh of relief. She had done what she had set out to do and Pete and

Caroline Jones Lewis
The Dream Robbers

Emma would live to fight another day. After completing all the paperwork and the transfer of funds, she left for the next item on her agenda.

Robert saw her car approaching down the drive from his viewpoint at the study window. It was an unexpected visit, a weekday visit when she should have been working up in town. Her car swung around to the stable block and ground to a halt. Watching her alight he detected less of a spring in the step than usual, and guessed without any prompting that things in her life were not plain sailing. City bankers, he thought wryly. Investment bankers to boot. Well, no. Life would not be. He went to the door to greet her there rather than leave her walk around the stables to find him as she would normally have done. He beckoned her into the house.

"Is it OK - for me to come in - this way instead of around the tradesman's entrance?" she queried hesitantly, attempting flippancy but glancing ahead into the hallway.

"It's fine," he grinned. "Dad's away, not that you were ever afraid of him, if I recall."

Not afraid exactly, she thought - but wary in latter days, certainly wary. And today of all days she did not want to confront Brian Welling, today when she had come to confide to Robert her fall from grace. She relaxed a little, returning his grin with a smile of her own.

"Come on, I'll make you a cup of tea in the kitchen and there's some sponge cake somewhere that Betty made at the weekend."

"Still your trusted housekeeper then? She must be really ancient by now."

"Of course she's still our housekeeper. Dad would never get rid of her. She was so good to us when Mum died. Betty will only go when Betty decides it herself. I suppose the day will come when she decides it's all too much but she's not there yet. A sturdy lady is Betty."

"I remember," grinned Sophie, a memory of Betty chasing

Caroline Jones Lewis

The Dream Robbers

them both from the kitchen, brandishing a broom to safeguard the freshly made scones they were about to pilfer, still clear in her mind. In the large comfortable farmhouse kitchen where Sophie had always felt so at home in younger days she looked around her, taking in so much that was familiar and the little changes that were not.

"Doesn't change much," she ventured. "It's still that warm, homely place I used to love."

"What is it with the British and their kitchens," Robert asked. "They say the best parties are always held in the kitchen. Everyone certainly seems to migrate to the kitchen when they visit us."

He filled the kettle and set it on the Aga, taking down cups and saucers from the dresser and plates for the cake which he found in a cake tin on the worktop.

"So what brings you down to the sticks during the working week?"

He was curious and Sophie's subdued entrance had re-enforced his first impression that something was wrong. He turned to face her, leaning back against the dresser, arms folded, as she sat now at the large kitchen table. He recognised the reluctance to speak that was always a warning sign.

"Come on, Piglet. Something's amiss."

"Actually, I came down on business," she began, shrugging her shoulders, not lying but reluctant to launch into the truth, the whole truth and nothing but the truth.

"Really. What business can an international investment banker have in darkest Kent?"

"I wasn't on bank business," she admitted. "Personal business."

"Ah. Don't tell me. You're buying a retreat - a little place in the country. Taking advantage of the economic climate. Piglet returns," he joked - but unconvinced by her show of bravado.

Sophie made a wan smile, trying to join in the joke but failing.

Caroline Jones Lewis
The Dream Robbers

"Not quite," she replied. "There is a property involved but it isn't quite like that. I've bought one of Pete's houses," she confided.

Robert's expression was one of amazement.

"What? Are you kidding me?"

"No," and Sophie shook her head adamantly, then laughed self-consciously.

"Well, you do surprise me. I always thought you were rather scathing of your brother-in-law's properties."

"Well, they're OK as far as they go. They're built well enough. Just not my cup of tea - for me to live in, I mean."

"Then why, Soph? An investment?"

Sophie explained her reasons, leaving out as best she could her contribution to the current credit wilderness.

"An act of philanthropy, Sophia Gray? Not like you, I have to say. Is this a new Sophie that we're seeing?"

Having begun her story, Sophie found herself pouring out the entire chronicle, chapter and verse, sparing nothing including James' current predicament though she had not intended to go quite that far. It all came tumbling out before she could stop herself. She never could hold back with Robert, had always poured her heart out once she began in a way she had never done with James. With James there was always that small part of herself that she liked to keep private, little secrets that she hugged to herself like secret treasures. Nothing important - except for Robert - but she just liked it that way.

With Robert the truth and the whole truth eventually came tumbling out of its own accord.

"I always knew he was a bad lot," Robert judged vehemently, not commenting on Sophie's failings but ready to condemn James without hesitation.

"He isn't. Really he isn't. It was stupid of him to get involved and he's really sorry that he did."

"Only because he's been found out. He'd have gone on

Caroline Jones Lewis

The Dream Robbers

doing it if he hadn't been. Come on, Sophie. Admit it. You've both of you always wanted more than your fair share of life's goody bag. I wish to God you had never gone up to the City. I wish you had stayed and fought for a future for us together."

"I might have done if you'd come after me," she blurted.

"Come after you?" Robert challenged. "Sophie, I told you plain enough how I felt about you, that I would stand my ground with my parents and win them round. You flounced off like a spoiled child. It was for you to behave like a grown up and come back and talk to me, not for me to come running after you like a puppy dog."

He paused, flushed with emotion. Then continued slowly, more gently.

"It isn't too late, you know. Even now. We could start again. You must know I still love you."

He paused again, waiting for her response. Please say you still love me, he urged silently. Please. When the tears came he pulled her to him and held her close, kissing the top of her head, breathing in the sweet scent of her hair, then kissed her neck and then her mouth. She kissed him back through her tears, passionately, longingly before she gently pushed him away. He looked at her his heart racing. She was vulnerable and he didn't want to take advantage of that however much he wanted her. If she came back it had to be for the right reason. So he watched her as she brushed her tears away. It was a rare thing, to see Sophie Gray cry.

"How could I possibly leave James now?" she sighed. "He needs me now like I've needed him all these years. I don't think I could do it to him."

Robert looked at her enquiring, then softened.

"Loyalty as well as guilt," he smiled. "Well, I can't fault you for that. So you are a grown up after all. A new Sophie Gray."

Honour amongst thieves, he thought but he said no more. Instead he took her hand and kissed it affectionately.

"I just wish things had been different. I just wish you'd

Caroline Jones Lewis
The Dream Robbers

come back to me. You know I'm here. I'll always be here
- any time you want to come to me. I can't tell you what
you should do where James is concerned. That's between
you and James and your conscience. But I'll always be here
- waiting. Hoping."

For Robert it was agony to see her go. He watched her walk
back to her car, this new Sophie with a conscience and
loyalty and all the finer feelings. He liked the new Sophie
even more than the old and it was hard to let her walk away.
He had been so close to winning her in this moment. So
close and yet still she remained at a distance. He would
wait. For time may yet be on his side.

Driving back to London, she too agonised over her situation.
It was true. She could not leave James just when he needed
her most. But being close to Robert again - it had been
blissful and she wanted more. They had crossed the line
today, that unspoken barrier previously acknowledged.
What now? How could they go back from here? But how
to go forward? She could not think straight at this moment.
Could not square her conscience with one option nor quite
reconcile herself to the other. The confusing emotions her
fall from grace in the business world had evoked had spilled
over into a private life previously clear cut and
uncomplicated. She had belonged in the City - with James.
Now she no longer belonged in the City. The City was
cutting their ties and she no longer knew quite where she
belonged. But with whom did she belong? Did she still
belong with James?

******

James accepted her actions at the auction without a protest.
After a stormy meeting with his parents, he was well aware
of the depth of condemnation he was faced with and the need
to make amends to those that he could. His involvement

Caroline Jones Lewis
The Dream Robbers

had been minimal but had he got away with it, he knew full well he would have done it again, knowing that it was wrong. His parents had accepted no excuses. He was now expecting a formal charge any day and a date for trial some time early in 2009. There would be little in the way of celebration over the coming Christmas and New Year. Suspended from business and with little to occupy their waking hours, both he and Sophie found their time together unusually strained. He found it difficult to fill the waking hours, pacing the flat at times like a caged and frustrated animal. They each took to being out of the flat for stretches of the day, creating activity elsewhere whether it was necessary or not.

For Sophie it was easier. She still had some hopes of job prospects, though the many agencies with which she had registered were coming up with nothing positive in the way of interest. The perhaps and maybes they were presenting she suspected to be exaggerated on their part and they led to nothing concrete. There had been a time when the agencies would have been ringing her, trying to head-hunt her for eager clients. Those times were gone, unlikely ever to return. Still, it had filled in time attending their offices armed with a CV that until now would have been regarded as impressive. In addition, she had taken to putting her affairs in order. She made a visit to her solicitor to review her will, suggesting to James that perhaps he should do the same though he was reluctant to face anything that smacked of practical reality. To him it implied what Sophie was clearly thinking. That with his possible removal from society, albeit on a temporary basis, it was necessary, she considered, to have their affairs ship shape. The purchase of No. 8 The Tythings had altered her situation somewhat since it was in her name alone and not jointly owned with James. She needed to decide its future should she unexpectedly demise. Then of course she had the property itself, a project with which to busy herself, planning furnishings and the garden in

Caroline Jones Lewis

The Dream Robbers

order to rent out this newly acquired asset. It was a good project for absorbing her time while she rethought a future career. Or perhaps it was meant to be, she thought. Perhaps that was her new career. Property investment and from here, property development, even if not for herself for James. It would resolve a difficulty for him as whatever the outcome of his present predicament, there would be no reference to recommend him to work for someone new. She involved herself in the project with alacrity with this thought in mind. After one such day spent studying swatches of furnishing fabrics and carpet samples, she headed on foot in the darkness of early evening towards home.

James, too, had not been entirely idle. He had visited his office to make sure his files were all in order for others to administer. Shouldering harsh words from the employer from whom he had received summary dismissal - 'bringing the firm into disrepute' and 'betraying the trust of your colleagues' but a few - and with looks of contempt from colleagues who had earlier held him in high esteem, he was despondent as he walked for the last time from the building that had been the centre of his financial universe. In his mind's eye he saw his colleagues at the windows watching his departure, with heads shaking and tongues clucking with disapproval. He imagined their eyes boring into his back as he made his exit in disgrace. Taking the tube to Hyde Park, he had walked through the park for over an hour, bordering the Serpentine with the collar of his coat turned up against a biting wind. It was difficult to avoid contemplating his fall from grace though he regarded it as a pointless exercise. What was done was done and the punishment would come all of its own accord and all too soon. There was no point indulging in self-recrimination, he reasoned. Crying over spilled milk. But still he found it impossible to avoid. Why had he been so stupid? He had earned good money without breaking the rules, more than enough for a good life.

Caroline Jones Lewis

The Dream Robbers

While he knew how Sophie loved money and all that it could buy her, he could place no blame at her feet. She had never asked for more, never been dissatisfied with their lifestyle as it had been before his descent into dishonesty. She would never have endorsed resorting to blatant illegality. It had been his own greed, his own need to impress with fancy living that had been his downfall, the desire to move in those circles where money was the key to all. Now, to his great regret, there was only shame not least of all for the parents who had given him their all.

He watched mothers kneeling with their toddlers to feed the ducks, breaking chunks of dry bread they had carried in plastic bags from their kitchens, mothers from the poorer parts of town dressed in well-worn clothing while their children wore new and bright and clean. These were people who once he would have viewed from a standpoint of superiority, viewed as losers. Now they held a legitimacy that he envied, like the parents to whom he owed everything and had ultimately let down, like his in-laws who had now been elevated to a moral standpoint above his own. Unlike others who steadfastly clung to denial of their wrong-doing, he accepted his guilt and felt grubby, dirtied by his own actions. The ducks quacked their appreciation of the food that sustained them in the sparseness of the winter grazing, like the sparseness of funds that was causing such hardship in the wreckage of the economy. After hours of unavoidable self-recrimination he, too, set off in the falling dusk for home.

******

As Sophie rounded the corner at the end of her street, Leo Trask was approaching from the opposite direction. He was unkempt, unshaven, his clothes dishevelled as though he had slept in them in all the elements, layer upon layer of grubbiness piled up around his chin against the cold. His

Caroline Jones Lewis

The Dream Robbers

hair, grown longer than usual and dampened by a fine drizzle, had curled into an unkempt mess. The street light on the very corner from which she approached was unlit so adding to the gloom of early evening. It had flickered in its death throes for the previous few evenings until now it had finally expired, leaving the street dismal in a damp mistiness. Another street lamp behind Leo glowed into the darkness casting his form into a long shadow like a spectre of times past. Sophie hardly recognised him at first, thought him to be a vagrant, an alcoholic or drug addict, especially in the dim light of the evening. She was almost upon him before she realised who the shuffling heap of unhealthy garments concealed. His continuing descent into penury had been accompanied by a continued descent into an alcoholic state of semi-awareness, of life carrying on around him without his participation. Now in a state of almost permanent inebriation, he had abandoned all but the most rudimentary attempts at hygiene, at order in his life, stumbling from his unmade bed each midday to make the journey to the off-licence down the street and back again for another bout of drinking fired by self-pity. To add to this parlous state, he was suffering from a bout of the 'flu like virus that was sweeping the country, coughing and sneezing through the dismal hours of night and neglecting any attempt to maintain a reasonable diet by day to help his constitution combat the illness. On this evening he had once again crawled from the pit of his bed, unkempt and feverish, to sate his craving for more whisky. At the sight of her and in his already disturbed state he became agitated, more animated, his bloodshot eyes stretching wide and wild and he shouted at her as he came closer, hurrying to catch her before she could vanish behind the safety of her own front door. She was shocked at the sight of him, shocked at what he had reduced himself to.

"Leo - what have you done to yourself?" she began in disbelief. "I hardly recognised you."

"Me. Done to myself," he screeched. "You, you mean.

Caroline Jones Lewis

The Dream Robbers

You're to blame for all this," he yelled. "You and your .....
bloody greedy colleagues. You and .... all those other
bastards at the bank. It's your fault. It's all your bloody
fault."

His speech was erratic and slightly slurred.

"That's ridiculous," she protested. "You've done this to
yourself. Look at you, the state of you. If everyone
behaved like this just because..."

"Just because what? Because ..... you've destroyed ......
everything ..... everything in my life that ...... mattered," he
intervened. "My whole life is ...... ruined because of you.
My life. Tess's life. We've lost everything. Our baby.
Everything ..." and he made to step towards her, raising his
fist angrily, then burst into a bout of coughing that stopped
him in him tracks.

"Leo, you're ill. Have you seen a doctor," and she raised
her arm to touch his sleeve with her hand.

He brushed her away.

"Ill," he exclaimed. "I'm not ill. I'm just .." and again
came the coughing. Again the anger and again he waved
her hand away.

"Leo," she began. "Please. Stop it. Pull yourself
together. This isn't helping anyone - least of all yourself.
You're young. You'll recover. You need a doctor to start
with. Why don't you..."

"Oh, really. Well, why should you care, you, you .... bitch.
You in your .... smart flat, with your big bank balance.
Would you say that if you were about to lose your home?
All you've worked for? Why should you care about all the
people you've hurt. "

His speech became faster, more heated.

"You've destroyed lives. Do you know that? Entire lives,
you've destroyed. You've stolen my life, my dreams.
Tess's life. Our life. Our dreams. And .... I want it back.
I want my life back. I want my dreams back."

He was becoming blind with rage, distraught with anguish

Caroline Jones Lewis
The Dream Robbers

and on fire with a temperature in his dehydrated state. He wobbled dangerously and unable to reason with him she was anxious to be rid of this threat to her safety.

"Leo, go away. Please. Go away. Get out of my way," she demanded, raising her voice as forcefully as she could muster without resorting to shouting, not wanting to draw attention from any of the surrounding apartments that may be inhabited.

"Oh, yes. Go away," he echoed. "Turn away. That's you, isn't it. Go away so I don't have to see what I've done to you - that's you, isn't it?. Well, fuck you, Miss Sophie fucking Gray. Fuck you," he jeered, gesticulating wildly and he continued to block her way to the entrance to her flat. She faced him a little nervously now, her usual bravado already depleted by recent events but still reluctant to accept the role of victim. His manner was increasingly threatening, a potential to erupt into a violence that she imagined to be simmering just beneath the surface. They were the same two people as they had been only a few months ago, working together at the bank, Sophie the Golden Girl and Leo, the would-be protégé. Only they weren't the same people. They were different people now. And while she was striving even unconsciously to become a better person from the change that had been forced upon her, Leo had been changed for the worse by what she and her contemporaries had inflicted upon his life. She backed away, not only from Leo but from the recognition of her own role in his transformation. She saw a Frankenstein that she had helped to create, not knowing what to say to him either to calm him or in her own defence since right now she felt she had none.

As he lunged unsteadily towards her, not really intending to be threatening, only accusing, but unaware of the sight he presented, Sophie looked around her uneasily, hoping for the intervention of some good Samaritan passing by. The only person around was a plump elderly lady shuffling along the

Caroline Jones Lewis
The Dream Robbers

pavement opposite, myopically studying a shopping list, silently mouthing the words written in front of her and obviously oblivious to events around her, unable to hear the heated, raised voices across the street over the buzzing of the battery in her hearing aid. There was no assistance coming from that quarter. At this time of the evening on a working day in the City there was little movement on this desirably quiet and calm street where she lived. Leo was rambling and abusive as his anger gathered momentum and his temperature soared, reluctant to release the focus of the distress that he had hugged to himself for so long and that now he held captive before him. Unable to reach her front door and unwilling to remain his hostage, Sophie could bear no more. She turned and fled, rushing back the way she had come, tearing headlong towards the junction only yards away. Unheeding of anything around her, she launched blindly across the road heading for the opposite pavement in the hope of leaving Leo standing alone and unsteadily behind her. But safety was beyond her reach. In the dismal light and the mistiness of the damp evening, the driver of the approaching taxi turned the wheel of his cab as he prepared to take the corner into her street. He did his best to stop the moment he saw her step off the pavement. His brakes screeched as he slammed his foot down hard on the brake pedal, mouthing an oath in a desperate attempt to avoid her.

"Jesus Christ" he breathed. "Jesus Christ."

The impact would not have injured her so badly had she not landed against the unlit lamppost, rolling off the bonnet of the taxi and slumping to the ground with her head crushed against the lamppost like a broken doll. The vehicle ground to a halt and its driver flung open the door and leapt from his seat to reach her. The blood drained from the face of his passenger who leapt like an automaton from the seat in the rear to reach her, galvanised by shock and panic. He cupped her face in his hands, calling, pleading.

"Sophie. Sophie. For God's sake - speak to me, Soph."

Caroline Jones Lewis

The Dream Robbers

James knelt by the side of her crumpled body, wanting to clasp her to him but afraid to touch her for fear of causing more damage. So he clasped her hand in his own, the warm, limp fingers unresponsive to his touch.
"Somebody do something," he screeched. "Do something."

There were sounds of doors opening now, of running, of feet hurrying towards her, people kneeling, talking, and the sound of a voice speaking hurriedly into a mobile 'phone. Ambulance, it said. Ambulance is coming. Leo watched from the opposite corner, silent now in shock at the sight of Sophie lying there, her head crocked against the base of the lamppost and a trickle of blood seeping from beneath the hair that concealed the wound. It was a seminal moment in his life, one that he would remember for his entire lifetime. It snapped him from his morass of inebriation and sickness and self-pity, led him to a gradual acceptance of responsibility, of each individual for their own actions and the recognition of the impact that those actions had on others, for no-one in the world acts alone. If only I hadn't, he would recall later. If only I hadn't been drinking. If only I hadn't been on my way to the off licence at that precise moment. If I hadn't been so threatening towards her. Alas pointless speculation. It prompted a renaissance of his own life, of the life and the person that had been lost in the slough of his own self-pity. His once adoration of all that Sophie Gray had stood for had turned sour in the revelations of recent months. But he too had been a party to the same ambitions, the same ideology. And this was where it had all led. No job. No Tess. No baby. And a crumpled body in an East End side street. A sobering thought. He left the scene struggling to confront the consequence of his behaviour head on, sobered by what he, too, had caused to happen, his contribution to the final deed. He would become wiser than he had been only moments earlier.

It was the turn of Andy Gray to sit at his daughter's bedside

Caroline Jones Lewis

The Dream Robbers

as she had done by his own, flanked by his wife and his other daughter with her husband. James could not be there. He was once more being interviewed at the police station, whisked away protesting only moments after the ambulance had taken Sophie away. The paramedics had worked hard at the scene, working desperately to save her. They had asked him to follow on, not wanting him in the ambulance to get in their way and he had agreed, hurrying back towards the flat to pick up the car keys. He had telephoned Sophie's parents on his mobile as he hurried but he had never reached the car. The detectives were already waiting, pressing the security button at the entrance to the dark and empty flat above. They refused to accept any excuse or delay and bundled him into the police car to be taken to the station. His continued distress and protestations were finally accepted as genuine and once he had convinced them of the honesty of the circumstances and pleaded for time, they had done their best to get him there in a police car but it was of little importance. Sophie remained unconscious and the news was not good. The blank, pale faces that turned towards him as he entered the room gave him the bad news without a single word being uttered. The doctors had declared Sophie brain dead and were requesting permission to switch off the life support.

The family had awaited James' arrival. The decision, they told the doctors, must be his. He crumpled at the news, sobbing. No. No. Please, God, no. Emma rose from her chair at the bedside that held the lifeless body of her sister and went to comfort him as best she could. For James, she had long since recognised, had loved her sister in a way that her sister had been unable to return. While the rest of the family remained in blissful ignorance, Emma knew. For her sister it had always been Robert Welling, a fact that James had known and chosen to ignore. In this moment, when he of all people had the worst decision of his life to make, she felt for him more than she could ever say. Sophie

Caroline Jones Lewis
The Dream Robbers

had not suffered, the doctor assured the family. She had been rendered unconsciousness on impact, never knowing what had hit her. It was a small comfort - but indeed only a very small one.

At length they left him with her, Sophie and James, just the two of them together, the rest of the family sitting in the corridor numb with shock and awaiting the inevitable. He held her hand and told her how he loved her, that he was sorry he had let her down.

"I hope you can hear me, Soph," he told her, but all the time knowing that the doctors would hold out no hope. She was brain dead, they had told him. There is nothing left now. She is no longer there. But he could not bear to believe it, so he talked to her anyway, hoping beyond hope that she would hear. It was the early hours of morning before he found the strength to agree to the doctors' request. Together they held her hands, he and her family, they stroked her hair and told her they loved her as the machine fell silent and died.

Caroline Jones Lewis

The Dream Robbers

Chapter 7 – Unfamiliar

The funeral was a quiet affair. Mostly family, half a dozen or so of her former colleagues, and a few close friends. They had never had many friends, she and James. Engrossed in their own life they had found little need of others but those friends they did have that had not deserted them in their recent descent into notoriety, were there. And of course James, a devastated, perplexed James flanked by his parents supportive either side of him. Why had she done this? Why had she run out into the road like that, not looking, not taking care? Why hadn't she seen the taxi? Why? Why? Why? He felt angry with her. He felt angry at himself for not being there to stop her, to pull her back onto the safety of the pavement. But most of all he felt lost without her and fearful of a life alone without her love and comfort in the uncertainty of his future. For she had loved him, he knew. Not perhaps as she had loved Robert Welling, not perhaps as he loved her, but she had loved him nevertheless in her own way. And now she and that love were gone and he was desolate.

Robert Welling came. He had known the news was unwelcome the moment he had seen the look on the face of Sophie's sister. She had stood by the open door of her car parked on his driveway, her husband leaping out in support of her from the driver's side to guide his wife gently by the arm. He had known it must be Sophie. There was no other reason for them to come. Even so, the news had hit him like a sledgehammer, a body blow that left him reeling. They had sat in his kitchen sipping tea, the great British panacea in the British tradition. Why is it, he had wondered? Why do we always make tea? How can it possibly help - a cup of hot water infused with the leaves of a plant, a dash of cow juice and a spoonful of sugar? But they did it anyway. And now he had come to see her buried in the little churchyard in her sister's village, standing at the back

Caroline Jones Lewis
The Dream Robbers

behind her silent family.

They stood around the graveside in quiet grieving, watching her coffin lowered into the cold unwelcoming earth. After the committal, Robert turned to walk away. James caught at his sleeve and Robert turned to face him, the two men who had loved her. James extended his arm in a gesture of shared grieving to shake Robert's hand.
"James," began Robert. "I'm so sorry." He could think of nothing else to say. He couldn't say she should have been with me. If she had been with me she might still be alive. Because she hadn't been. He couldn't say it was me who really loved her, not you. For that was not true. The sight of the man was enough to tell him. James had loved her too. There was no doubt.
"Yes," James answered. "Yes, I'm sorry too. You loved her," he offered.
"We both loved her," came the reply. Robert clasped the hand that was held out to him and they parted, if not friends, neither as rivals for her memory.
"Are you coming back to the house, Robert?" Emma asked him.
"No, thank you all the same," he answered. "I think I need to be on my own. This is for you - your family. And for James."

Back at the stables Robert saddled up his favourite mount and rode out across the fields to the copse on the hilltop. He tethered his horse to a great horse chestnut where they had come so often, in those young heady days when they had first discovered love and joy and the urgency of the physical. It was here they had first made love on a hot day of summer, passionate and urgent on the lush grass beneath the branches of the tree, then sat and gazed out in contentment across the weald ahead. Every couple, he guessed, had their own special place. Like their own special song. This had been theirs and they had returned eagerly and often. It had been

Caroline Jones Lewis
The Dream Robbers

an ardent affair always, a passion that had never dimmed with the repeating. Since their parting he had returned regularly. In the early days it was in suffering, hoping against hope she would return, then as time passed by, just wishing that things had been different. Now that was all over. The wishing was at an end. The uncertainty was at an end. She would not come back. He would never see her again. Never. And he still could not believe it. He was numb now but the hurt would come, he knew. A crushing hurt that would engulf him in huge agonising waves. His father's words of the night before echoed in his mind.
"After the heartache has died you'll have a new life. Do you think we didn't know, your mother and me, that she was still the only one you wanted? The one you still waited for? Do you think we never regretted our interference? Of course we did. To the day she died all your mother wanted was your happiness. She would have given anything to make things come right for you. But in the end it was up to Sophie. And she chose to stay where she was.
"It hurts now, son," his father counselled. "But now it's truly over. And when the pain subsides, you'll be free to find love again. In time. It will take time. But you will find love again."
Maybe, he thought. Maybe he would find love again. Yes, it was true. It was over now. All those years of wondering. Of whether one day she would come back to him, whether one day they would be together. She was gone forever. Not from his heart. Never from his heart. But from his head. The door had closed. One day, perhaps, when the pain of grieving had subsided, there would be another love. But of one thing he was certain. It would take time. A long, long time. Robert sat alone in their special place and with deep heartrending sobs he cried.

******

Caroline Jones Lewis

The Dream Robbers

Leo was not there. Leo was on a train to Oxford to see his Tess who had written a heartfelt appeal.

> *Dear Leo.*
>
> *Now that I have been away from you a little while, I've had time to think about all that has happened to us. We have both felt the pain of losing our baby, both said and done things that we regret, and though I told you last time we spoke that I never wanted to see you again it isn't true, Leo because I miss you, more than I can say and I love you still. But I also know that I do not want the things that you were striving for. I do not share the ambitions of the people who live and work in the City, the need to make money and to own fancy houses and cars and lead the sort of life they lead. All I ever wanted was for us to be happy and for that I don't need all those material things. Here, away from all that I have found a kind of peace. If you still love me, and can see a future with me outside of London and the rat-race and all those things that mattered to you back then, well I am here.*
>
> *Mum and Dad have encouraged me to write to you I have started this letter over and over again. The bin is almost full with screwed up pieces of paper. What I want to say is - if you want to come to Oxford and talk about a future together, then please ring me. And if you do not, then I hope you find what you are looking for and find happiness in whatever way you need.*
> *Love always.*
> *Tess xx*

It had taken courage for her to write the last part, afraid of the rejection it may prompt, but she had made herself write it anyway. It was true. She did wish him happiness in whatever route he chose to take in life - but she hoped more than anything that it would be with her, that he would find the strength to leave the City and the past behind.

Caroline Jones Lewis

The Dream Robbers

Leo had no need to think about his answer. He had longed to see her, to talk to her, to resolve the problems between them. He knew now that Tess was more important to him than anything else ever could be. All those things that had mattered before - without her they meant nothing.

He had thought, too, about Sophie. Over and over he had thought about Sophie, about her crumpled body lying in the street, that dark stain of blood on the paving slab seeping from beneath her hair. He had guessed she was dead. Somehow she had looked dead though he had no idea why he thought so. And then it was confirmed to him for he had returned to the scene. Compelled to return by some driving force inside him. What was it they said about murderers - always returning to the scene of the crime? He had seen the flowers left on the pavement, propped against the lamppost that had inadvertently become her killer, vibrant amongst the deadness of the sodden leaves blown from the chestnut tree down the street. Dead like his dreams and the dreams of so many others. He had seen the markings on the road where the taxi had swerved in an attempt to avoid her, the murder weapon that he had helped to create. After it had happened, he had fled back to the sanctity of the house, the alcohol he had gone to buy forgotten in the trauma of the moment. He had sat at the kitchen table in a state of disbelief. Life had become increasingly unreal since he had lost his job but this was the zenith. Or was it that life had now become real, that all that had gone before had simply been an illusion. Like the profits the banks had supposedly made and against which their executives had drawn their massive bonuses - all an illusion. He could not tell, could not fathom the truth of it all in his confusion. His whole body had become racked with guilt now. Where once he had blamed Sophie for everything and indeed blame there was to bear, he now recognised that the blame was also his. He knew why Tess had left him. It was not just losing the baby. He had not made her happy. His ambition to make money, to emulate a

Caroline Jones Lewis

The Dream Robbers

lifestyle she had never wanted, had caused her distress, then driven her away in grief and despair. In his naivety he had believed it would make him somebody, a man of substance when in fact it simply made him as greedy as others in a society that measured people by their wealth, by the value of their property, the make and model of a car or the prestige of a postcode. All it seemed now was a bad dream, a nightmare - a million miles away. From the darkness of his thoughts came the first glimmer of light towards a future. He knew that the time had come to pull himself together, to cease to see himself as a victim and to begin another part of his journey through life, albeit in a different direction. There were other jobs out there, other ways of living a different kind of life. He would earn less money and they may lose the house despite the Government's efforts to help people to avoid repossession. Perhaps he could rent it and find himself a single room somewhere while he looked for a job. But whatever was the answer it was down to him to find it. As one door closes so another one opens, he told himself - and all that. One dream may be as dead as the leaves blown down from the trees but there were always others, like the new leaves that would burst forth in the spring. So he had set to.

The days following Sophie's death were spent in cleaning up his life, himself, with a shower, a shave and a haircut, some polish on his shoes and an iron for the clothes he freshly laundered. As the fever of his flu subsided and the alcohol cleared from his system the Leo Trask that he knew he should be began to emerge. He set to on the house, set about cleaning as Tess would have done had she been there. If they lost the house then it would be lost in neat and tidy condition and he must face his creditors with honesty and self-respect. Little by little he pulled himself back from the abyss. When Tess's letter had arrived, he had needed no persuading. He had called her on her mobile and this time she had answered on the second ring.

Caroline Jones Lewis

The Dream Robbers

He looked around the neat little sitting room before leaving to catch his train. It was tidy now and smelling of polish, the rankness of the previous weeks consigned to the past. Even the windows were gleaming in the morning light. He felt a sudden sadness as he looked around, that soon it might be gone, taken away from them, their first little home, swept away by a torrent of events beyond his control. But he also felt a strange relief that the agony was almost over. Now he was hopeful of a new life ahead. He closed the front door behind him and set off on his mission.

******

The contents of Sophie's will came as a shock to a family ignorant of her final acts of contrition. In the quietness of the Baileys' sitting room the day after the funeral, her solicitor read her last will and testament to a family still numb with shock and grief. With the paperwork from the auction still incomplete, the identities of the new owners of Nos 6 and 8 The Tythings had been unknown to them until the moment of the reading. To find that Sophie had been one of them took everyone by surprise – except for James who had revealed nothing. He had stayed with his parents in town the previous evening and intended to leave for France with them later in the day. His attendance at the reading at all was a matter of nothing more than deference to her family and protocol performed in a state of suspended animation. He was operating quite simply on automatic pilot, programmed on his behalf by parents concerned for his state of mind.

The flat, it was confirmed, had been jointly owned by herself and James, as did the funds that remained, though dwindling, in their joint bank account into which her final months of salary had been paid. All of this now reverted to James alone, along with the proceeds of a generous life assurance policy. James accepted without emotion the news that he was

Caroline Jones Lewis
The Dream Robbers

provided for for years ahead. Late in the day he too was discovering that money was not the be all and end all. The flat they had so loved together he no longer considered home, unable to stay there without her. He had taken her clothes from the closet, held them close to him. He could still smell her when he opened the door. He had buried his face in their softness and their scent. To begin with it had been a comfort but so quickly became a source of pain. He could not sit at the table by the picture window where so many contented weekend mornings had begun, the orange juice and the pot of freshly perked coffee on the table before them, a pile of warm croissants on a plate beside the butter and the jam, while the two of them rummaged lazily through the Sunday papers or gazed out absent-mindedly across the river lit by a morning sunlight. He could not sleep in the bed where they had made love, sometimes gentle but always passionate. The smell of her lingered on the pillows, her cosmetics taunted him from the shelf beneath the mirror. It was unbearable. So he had booked himself into a hotel until the funeral and made arrangements afterwards to return to France with his parents. The police had no objection, they told him, once his contact details were confirmed.

No. 8 The Tythings - in a bout of conscience-driven generosity - Sophie had bequeathed in the event of her death to her sister, secure in the knowledge that her sister would use it wisely to provide not only for her own family but for their parents too. Emma was speechless.
"Did you know - that she was the buyer?" Emma asked Pete later.
Pete shook his head.
"I would have told you, darling. I would have known once the paperwork came through."
They were both amazed.
"She tried to make amends," he acknowledged. "At least to us - to her family. Buying No 8 like that. And now she's left it to you. Can you believe that?"

Caroline Jones Lewis
The Dream Robbers

"I'd rather have my sister back," was Emma's tearful response. "Last time we spoke I was angry with her. We argued. I was so angry about what James had done and what she had done to Mum and Dad and I really lost my temper with her. We never resolved it before she died. She must have died thinking that I hated her."

"Of course she didn't," insisted Pete gently. "She knew you loved her, always had done. Look at all the scrapes you got her out of as children. When you were teenagers. You've told me yourself. Darling, a row is just a row. It doesn't replace everything that's gone before. It doesn't mean that you hate someone that you've cared for all your life because of it. Sophie would have known that. And anyway, she obviously realised the unhappiness she had caused you. Otherwise she wouldn't have done what she did to make amends. Stop punishing yourself, love. The guilt's more mine than it ever could be yours."

He put his arms around his wife protectively and tried to reassure her but he was not sure he had succeeded. He was astounded himself that his formerly self-indulgent sister-in-law had planned to redeem herself in such an overwhelming gesture and critical as he had been of her when she were still alive, he was as rocked by her sudden and sad demise as the rest of the family. The children were almost inconsolable. To them their Aunt Sophie had been a glamorous and successful lady, mainly unaware as they were of the criticisms of her that their parents and grandparents had shared before she died. Only Isobel had an inkling and even she did not regard their differences as anything more than slight. It took a deal of care and attention to guide them through the processes of both shock and grieving, an effort to pick up the threads of living in the midst of death. But it had to be done. Isobel returned to the Academy only briefly to collect the things she needed and was granted compassionate absence to support her family. Hannah sought comfort in the arms of her father, spending tearful hours cuddled up to him on the sofa, a subdued Hannah that

Caroline Jones Lewis

The Dream Robbers

gave both Pete and Emma considerable cause for concern. Joe was simply quiet and private and they were unsure as to the depth of feeling he was holding inside.

Then again it was Emma that Pete had mostly to worry about. As the numbness and shock of Sophie's death began to subside, Emma felt a scream rising inside her which she tried painstakingly to quell but it broke suddenly and without warning. She had existed in a dreamlike state, feeling her way through a strange and unfamiliar world that had changed beyond recognition. It was a simple everyday happening that broke her trance and opened the floodgates to a tirade of suppressed emotion.

Clearing away the dishes after tea one evening, she was wiping clean the table. At its centre was a cruet that had been a present from Sophie many years before, a modest gift bought on one of her holidays abroad before the rise in fortune that had come with her work at the bank and her life with James and at a time when their relationship had been on a high. Two figures, a man and a woman, in national dress, that had reminded her of Pete and Emma, her newly married sister and brother-in-law, she had joked with them. The man the salt of the earth and the woman the spice in his life. Taking the pepper pot across to the sink to wipe away an unexplained stickiness, for no reason she was aware Emma dropped it onto the hard tiled floor. It smashed into a myriad of pieces, irreparable and irreplaceable, spilling its contents in a pile. Emma crumpled. Tears flooded into her eyes and she let out a wail that sent Pete rushing across the room to take her in his arms. She screamed and sobbed and beat her clenched fists against his chest so hard he felt bruised. He was afraid for her, afraid that his Emma would never be quite the same again. It was several minutes before her distress subsided and the faces of three anxious children who, having heard their mother's wail, appeared before him as they all stood in the kitchen doorway.

Caroline Jones Lewis
The Dream Robbers

"It's all right," his expression tried to reassure them. "Go back to what you were doing. It will be alright."

******

As December rolled on Emma stood in the queue in the village post office, a pile of Christmas cards for posting wedged in the crook of her arm. She was forcing herself to go through the motions of planning for a Christmas that no-one anticipated with joy. For the sake of the children, she told herself. For the sake of the children. Ahead of her an elderly lady was taking her time with her own mail, indulging in local gossip with Ruby, as was Ruby's pastime. Indeed it was regarded in the village as her raison d'etre.
"It's such a worry for her, poor Peggy," she was whispering. "Without the money from housekeeping for that banker and his family, she's really struggling to manage. I've told her she should go to the Social and apply for extra money but she's too proud. You know what she's like," and she shrugged her shoulders in an exaggerated gesture.
"Charity she calls it," she went on. "And on top of that she lost her purse the other day. Or had it stolen, she's not sure which. Can you believe it? Some people seem to get it all, don't they, dear? And they do say things come in threes. Goodness knows what else might happen to her."
Emma's ears pricked up at the name. She had visited Peggy quite recently at the request of the vicar.
"She's going through hard times," he had explained. "I have tried to offer her help but she's very proud, Emma. She almost evicted me from the house. An offer of help might come better from you. You know - a woman's touch?"
Emma had tried and Peggy had been polite, even allowing Emma into her neat little sitting room.
"It isn't charity, Peggy," she had insisted. "It's help from people who care about you."
But it had made no difference. Peggy had remained firm.

Caroline Jones Lewis
The Dream Robbers

There were those that showed her little acts of kindness that she was able to overlook, to pretend had not happened, like the butcher's boy who would weigh her sausages and tell her the price, then slide another sausage into the bag as he wrapped them, without a word or a look in her direction; or the greengrocer who would weigh her goods and deduct a few pence so that 58p. would become 50 or £1.10p become one pound. With these little acts of kindness she could pretend. But blatant charity was quite another matter.
"I don't need no pity," she had insisted bristling perceptibly with indignation. "I'm not a charity case," and Emma too had been sent on her way.
"Oh, poor Peggy," commiserated the customer. "On top of everything. This one's for New Zealand and then these two to France," she went on sliding her mail across the counter.
"Did they ever catch the culprit who caused the fire?" the topic of conversation switching to and fro.
"I don't think so. I've not heard anything. And who on earth would do that around these parts, for goodness sake? Nobody. Must have been someone from out of town, I reckon. Someone with a grudge. Well, it's not surprising really is it after what he's been up to with our money. Taxpayer's money. Getting all that pension. I ask you. It's obscene."
"Disgusting," agreed her customer. "He should be made to give it back, every penny."
" Not that I agree with violence, mind you," Ruby went on. "Not at all. It could have been very, very nasty."

Emma gazed out of the window, losing interest in their conversation and mentally trying to recall to mind the shopping list she had written and then forgotten to bring. The organisation that had always been her hallmark had slipped perceptibly since Sophie's death. She memorised it left on the table in the kitchen with the pen at its side ready to jot down anything else she needed that came into mind. Milk. Yes, milk was definitely on the list. Something for

Caroline Jones Lewis

The Dream Robbers

the school lunch boxes. Apples and crisps. And the
doodles all around the edge of the paper, large black jagged
lines that these days were all she could manage to draw.
What would a psychiatrist say about that, she wondered.
Her inability to draw. A habitual doodler now unable to
doodle. Across the road, a large 'Closing Down Sale' sign
was emblazoned across the window of Michael Croft's
gallery.
Oh, dear, she thought. Poor Michael. I wonder how they
are going to cope, and a new baby and a toddler to support.
Oh, dear.
"Yes, dear," called Ruby, now free of her previous customer.
"What can I do for you?"

Emma concluded her business at the counter, then left the
post office and crossed the road to Michael's shop. She felt
she must say something, must do anything she could to help.
The bell over the door tinkled as she entered, and Michael
came from his workshop at the rear, smiling as he recognised
his visitor.
"Hello, Emma. How nice to see you. What can I do for
you?"
"Oh, I'm just browsing, Michael. I thought you may have
something I could buy for a Christmas present or two. I'm
so sorry you're closing down. I remember how excited you
both were when you opened the shop. It's such a shame."
He looks tired, she thought. Careworn. It seemed that so
many people around her had that same look these days, not
least of all her own husband.
Michael nodded and grinned wryly.
"Yes. Isn't it. Helen says it was just the wrong time for us
but it shouldn't have been really. It would have worked - if
it hadn't been for the recession and these wretched bankers.
What they've done - it's criminal. And they've all walked
away scott free leaving the likes of us to pick up the pieces."
"I know," agreed Emma. "Pete's having to lay men off in

Caroline Jones Lewis

The Dream Robbers

the New Year. They've got families to support, too - and mortgages. He feels terrible about it but he has no choice. There's absolutely nothing the likes of us can do about it. We just have to ride it out and hope things come right eventually. Life has to go on, doesn't it?"

Michael was thoughtful for a moment, the memory of the night of Liam's birth uppermost in his mind.

No, he thought, there's nothing we can do about it that would make the slightest difference to the likes of them. One law for them and another for the rest of us.

"When I start going on about it," he replied "Helen quotes the scriptures at me. Not that she's that religious really but I think she's thinking of my blood pressure. Vengeance is mine, saith the Lord - so she tells me. Well, I hope so but somehow I doubt it. I hope they're made to pay in some way because they don't seem to have the slightest conscience. They should be made to pay back all the millions they paid themselves in bonuses. They could start a fund to help some of those they've damaged. But I can't see it happening, can you?"

Emma agreed, the effects of all that had happened to her own family all too heavy a burden.

"How is Helen? And the children?"

"Oh, they're fine. Liam's thriving and Polly just adores him. She's quite the little surrogate."

"What are you going to do for the future, Michael? To manage, I mean."

"Well, I'm going to do the framing at home to begin with. We've turned the garage into a studio of sorts. The rubbish that went to the tip and the stuff that went to the charity shop - you wouldn't believe it. I'm a terrible hoarder, I'm afraid," he chuckled.

"Not the facilities I have here, of course, but it will do for the time being. I still have a few commissions and have put the word around locally so I'm optimistic. I've put an advert in the parish mag, too. I'll have a little cash from the sale of the stock - after I've paid off the bank, of course. Helen has

Caroline Jones Lewis
The Dream Robbers

started giving tutoring at home to local children preparing for their exams. The school were really good. She went to see the Head and they put the word out amongst other schools in the area. And in the meantime I've got some evening work at a local supermarket - filling shelves. Really taxing the old grey matter," and he laughed. "A bit of a comedown from my City days, heh?"
Emma smiled in understanding.
"Still, I think we'll get by - just about. This shop was my dream, you know. I loved it. It would have worked out if"
"If it hadn't been for this recession."
"Yes. My dream The banks have reduced it to rubble. Things were going well until this credit crunch. We made a good start. We were so thrilled....."
He stopped. There was nothing more to say. He was simply repeating himself to himself.
"I'm so sorry, Michael. Perhaps some time in the future you can try again."
"Perhaps. But the dream's a bit tarnished now. I don't know quite how I feel at this minute. I don't know if I can go through all this again. Well - we'll see. Right now all I care about is being able to provide for my family. So we'll plod on together. We'll survive. That's what people do, isn't it? And survive worse than this, some poor souls. Flood, famine, war, holocaust. We've all seen the news lately. As long as there's hope for the future. Perhaps it's time for a *new* dream. We can't let them win, can we? Can't let them have it all their own way, the dream robbers. I can still do the framing and Helen thinks I should do some woodworking, too. She's very good at organising, as you've probably noticed."
Emma grinned.
"Yes, I remember. She was very good at organising us Mums at school."
"Hmm, I'm sure she was. Well, she's come up with this idea and I think it's a good one. They start a new set of courses at the local college after Christmas and some of them

Caroline Jones Lewis

The Dream Robbers

are really interesting. Woodworking. All kinds of things. I might enrol. I love working with wood, you know. It's so tactile, so comforting. Just the touch of it. I love it."

"Well, yes. It does sound a good idea. It's obviously something you have a passion for. Do you mean sculpting or furniture?"

"I don't know really. It would depend on me, I suppose. Whether I have any talent or not for one thing. I like the idea of sculpting but perhaps I'd better start with the practical stuff that will sell. Whatever earns us an income. Especially with the patter of more tiny feet in the offing."

"What, Helen?" gasped Emma.

"Oh, no," Michael chuckled. "Not Helen. I'm being facetious. It's the cat. She's pregnant. Polly is ecstatic of course. She thinks she'll be keeping all the kittens. Because that's what parents do, isn't it? They keep their babies."

Emma laughed.

"Oh, I see. You had me wondering there for a moment. Well, good luck with everything. I hope it all works out for you. I'll tell Pete about your plans. Perhaps he can put the word out at the Chamber of Commerce. You never know - it might help."

"Thanks, Emma. That's good of you. Any help would be much appreciated. Well, as Helen likes to remind me, failure is not an option."

"Yes, well, she's right really, isn't she," Emma mused. "It's what we do, isn't it, we British. We get on with it. Soldier on in the face of adversity."

Michael grimaced.

"We do. It's certainly been a rough ride this last year, though."

He sighed at the thought and said no more but in reality it had been much harder than he wished to admit. With the help of advice he and Helen had addressed their debt situation and come to terms with the measures they must take. The more they had talked the easier had come the

Caroline Jones Lewis
The Dream Robbers

solutions and the smaller the problems until they had shrank to manageable proportions. And he carried with him constantly the knowledge that he was lucky to be a free man, that no-one had discovered his guilty secret.

"Yes, I know it has," Emma was saying. It must have been a real worry - especially with a new baby. I'll bear you both in mind if I hear of anything. Teaching or framing."

He wanted to say something, to offer to offer his condolences at all he had heard of her sadness but hardly knew how to address it all. He chose his words carefully. "Nothing to what you've been through, though," he ventured. "We were so sorry to hear about your sister."

Emma pursed her lips hard, fighting back the emotion, irritated with herself for being caught unawares. Why do I do this, she wondered. Why is it always kindness that makes me crumple? I can cope with meanness. Indifference. But kindness does it every time, reduces me to a jibbering emotional wreck. Michael could see her struggle, the tears close to falling, the catching of her breath in her difficulty to keep her pain under control.

"You were close?" he asked.

"Not really," she began, her voice faltering. "We were as children. But we seemed to drift apart as we grew older. It wasn't the same. Not in recent years since she moved to London. Well, at least, I hadn't thought so."

She reconsidered. "But now - well, now I think perhaps we were still closer than I had realised."

It was true, she had acknowledged. There was so much regret, of things left unsaid, of things left undone that they might have done together, so little time spent together, so little love and laughter shared in recent years and yet still there had been an underlying closeness that had remained. Now there was a gaping hole in Emma's life left by the loss of her only sister.

"On top of your father's heart attack, too," Michael continued, turning the conversation to the living. "How's he doing?"

Caroline Jones Lewis
The Dream Robbers

Emma struggled to recover her composure, then answered, a voice thick with emotion, that he was doing alright now but of course the loss of Sophie was another blow he was finding hard to bear, as was her mother. There was nothing more that Michael could say and to cover the awkwardness of the moment, Emma glanced around the shop, studying the mish mash of items still left unsold and marked down drastically on their original price. She considered her newly acquired property at The Tythings, the dressing she needed to do in order to rent it out and earn some income.

"I like this mirror," she told him, stroking the frame of a large gilt over-mantle still displayed on the wall. "I think that would look good in the sitting room".

She bought the mirror and she bought some 'photo frames not least for a favourite photograph of Sophie that she wanted to put in the bedroom. Then feeling she had done at least something to help Michael on his way, she watched while he loaded the items into the boot of her car for her, then left him standing on the pavement with a wave of goodbye, good wishes for the future and hopes for better times in the new year ahead. For no reason she could explain the very mention of another year filled her with trepidation.

Caroline Jones Lewis

The Dream Robbers

Chapter 8 - Fated

January 2009

> *I said to the man who stood at the gate of the year*
> *Give me a light that I may tread safely into the unknown*
> *And he replied "Go into the darkness and put your hand*
> *into the hand of God.*
> *That shall be to you better than light and safer than a*
> *known way."*
>
> ***Minnie Louise Harkins***

After a subdued Christmas Emma stood on the first day of the year at her sister's graveside. The weather over the Christmas break had been bitter and her toes were nipped by cold from a thick hoar frost that crunched beneath her feet. The neatly trimmed grass of the cemetery glistened and sparkled in bleak winter light as she approached along the gravel path. Frozen fog curled around the silent headstones, wrapping the churchyard in a milky mistiness, in that eerie quietness that fog can induce. She clutched in her gloved hands a bowl of hyacinth, their leaves still curled tightly together and no sign yet in the winter coldness of the deep blue buds that would burst from inside when the first rays of warm spring sunshine coaxed them from their winter bed. Already on the grave was a pot of ruby red cyclamen left the previous day by their parents and by their side a bunch of red roses frozen and glistening inside their cellophane wrapping and brought from France on Boxing Day by a grief-stricken James.

I wish he had called, thought Emma. I wish we were able to offer him comfort. She had made it plain to him that he would be welcome.

"Please keep in touch," she had pleaded. "Please let us know how .... you know," and he had nodded his understanding. The court case, when it came.

Caroline Jones Lewis

The Dream Robbers

But he had come to the graveside alone, unable to share his grief, unable to face Sophie's family and unwanting of the intrusion. Much as he loved his parents and was grateful of their support, he had found Christmas almost unbearable, their presence at times too much to bear, the attempt at normality an affront to his grieving. He had withdrawn to his room, to what had been their bedroom - his and Sophie's - and his parents had not protested when he had announced his intention to leave for London the following day. They were at a loss to know how best to help their stricken son in a grief they, too, shared. They had loved Sophie, . They missed the glamour and sheer exuberance of her, shared his disbelief that she was gone forever. But they knew the sadness they were feeling could in no way match the despair of their son and felt impotent to help him. He needed solitude for it was only in solitude that he could indulge his grief unhindered. He had stood at the graveside, frozen to the core and feeling empty - and asked her how they had come to this, he and his Sophie? How such promise had been hijacked by destruction and despair. But deep down he knew the answer. There was no-one he could blame other than the two of them. It was Sophie who had run unheeding into the path of the taxi. It was he who had committed a cardinal sin. So she had lost her life and he was as good as dead inside. They had been the architects of their own misfortune, of the events that had followed and were still to come to an inevitable conclusion. He punished himself relentlessly. At length he had left her there, cold and silent in her grave with no answer or comfort to give him, to walk alone along his personal road to Calvary.

Emma stared blankly down at the freshly turned mound of earth, the simple cross with Sophie's name unbelievably carved into the wood and planted at its head. She could still barely believe that she was there, her sister. Alone in that frozen ground. Though the first tears of grieving had subsided now, they had left in their wake a deep abiding

Caroline Jones Lewis

The Dream Robbers

sorrow that was hard to bear, that wrapped itself around her heart, constricting her chest and interrupting the natural rhythm of her breathing.

"Oh, Sophie. How we all miss you," she whispered.

"How will we manage without you? How will I manage? My sister. My only sister."

All the things they had shared through their childhood had come back to her over recent days, their teenage angst, the pranks and scrapes that Sophie had got into. She saw the devil-may-care Sophie, head thrown back in laughter; the Robert Welling episode and the vulnerable Sophie, with eyes puffed and red from crying, the tears she had concealed from the rest of the world, her jaw set in firm determination not to let his family see her pain; the absconding to the City and a gradual fracturing in their relationship.

"If only things had worked out for you and Robert - you might still be here," attempted Emma. "But life's full of if onlies, isn't it, Soph? Truth is, it didn't. And that would be to deny James. Poor James. He loved you so much. Loves you so much. So - here we all are. Feeling lost without you."

She knelt for moments until the coldness of the air seeped into the very bones of her urging her to leave. She placed the pot of hyacinths beside the cyclamen and the frozen glistening roses.

"I hate to leave you here alone. You should be with us - at home by the warm fireside."

She paused, unable for a moment to continue. She wished that tears would come. Tears brought relief, albeit temporary. A brief release of the emotions trapped inside. But there were none.

"I hope you're happy, Soph," she whispered. "Love you always. Love you. I wish we had made up after that awful quarrel, before we lost you. But you do know, don't you. You *do* know that I still love you. That we all do. We always will."

But there was no reply. Only silence. She shivered and a

Caroline Jones Lewis

The Dream Robbers

thought struck her, reminded of a casual comment overhead in the post office.

"They do say things come in threes, don't they?"

"Please God, no," she pleaded. "I don't think I could take anything more."

******

On the morning of Izzie's return to the Academy, Pete and Emma lay in the half-light of the bedroom contemplating the day ahead. For Emma it was every bit as hard as the first time they had taken her there only this time she was to travel back by train. The events of the last year had made Emma more protective of her brood, more fearful of letting them go but Isobel had insisted.

"I'll go by train, Mum. There's really no need for you and Dad to thrash up to town in this awful weather."

"I know it's me," she was telling Pete. "I know I have to let her go. But losing Sophie has frightened me. All the uncertainty of the last year, all the uncertainty of the future even."

They faced each other in the shadow, their heads moulded into the indents in the pillows.

"Mmm, but you mustn't let her know that, love," Pete advised. "It wouldn't be fair. She has to live her life just as much now as before."

"I know. I am trying not to let it show. It's just that, well... all the certainties in life have been taken away. We would never have dreamed a year ago that the business would be close to collapse, that providing for the childrens' future would be a source of worry. Then Dad's heart attack. His health will always be a concern now. And most of all that I would have lost my sister. My only sister. It reminds you of just how tenuous life is, what a delicate thread we all hang by."

"Best not to think about it too much. That way madness lies, as someone clever once said," and Pete caressed his

Caroline Jones Lewis

The Dream Robbers

wife's face with gently stroking fingers, traced the contours of her nose and mouth to make her smile.

"I spoke to Michael Croft just before Christmas," she continued. "He's closed his gallery, you know."

"Yes, I noticed. Such a shame. It was looking a promising little business when he first opened. Another village shop that's bit the dust. What's he going to do now?"

Emma explained Michael's plans as he had explained them to her.

"Helen's very positive," she added. "Just as well under the circumstances."

"Well, they're right, aren't they. It's the only way to be. We've never given in to things, have we, Em? We've had difficult times and we've always stuck it through, come out the other side all the stronger. It's the only option."

"He's made me think, though". She paused.

"Careful now. That's not good for you, is it? Thinking. Mustn't do too much of that," Pete quipped.

"Seriously, love," she continued. "I think that Max is going to make someone redundant. And I was wondering how you'd feel if I offered it to be me."

Pete was silent. It was an unexpected turn to the conversation.

"I know what you're thinking," continued Emma. "About the money. Losing my wages just at this time. But the rent from No 8 will actually bring in more than I'm earning now. And I was thinking that I could go to college."

She waited for the reaction.

"OK. Go on. There must be a reason for all this thinking," Pete encouraged.

"It's just, well, I've always wanted to do something with my art," she continued. "and I heard this programme on the radio the other day. In the car when I was driving to the office. People who had lost their jobs through the recession ringing in to say how they had taken the opportunity to change direction. Change their career and their entire lives.

Caroline Jones Lewis

The Dream Robbers

Some of them had done really amazing things. One woman who had tried for years to get her book published used her redundancy money to set up her own publishing company. She published her book and then a big publishing house offered her a contract. Someone else had opted out of the rat race and gone into market gardening. Well, it made me think - so why not me. Perhaps now is the time for me? If Michael can find the courage with all he has to cope with surely I can."

It seemed an eternity to her before Pete made any response and she thought for a moment that he was opposed to the idea. In truth he was controlling his emotions before he spoke though he would have denied it had he been challenged.

"I'd like that," he began. "I've always felt I deprived you," he added guardedly.

"You know that isn't true," Emma protested. "I've never felt that, never thought it for a second."

"I know. I know you would never do that, Em. But I do. I've always known what you gave up when we had Izz and it's always been what I and the kids needed first and foremost with you. All these years." He paused, still emotional. "And there's another reason to do it, too," he went on.

Emma waited, aware that he was struggling, that despite his usual down to earth practicality Pete too was affected deeply by all the events of the previous months.

"I think that Sophie would be pleased," he said at length. "That she would feel she had made a final gesture towards redemption, towards making things up with you. To give you something special. Just for yourself. That her ill-gotten gains had finally, sort of, redeemed her...." He paused.

"Well, something like that," he added awkwardly.

They remained silent for a moment, each in their own thoughts.

"She hadn't done anything really bad, had she?" Emma

Caroline Jones Lewis

The Dream Robbers

mused. "She was just a pawn really in other peoples' games. It was the ones at the top that are really to blame."
"Suppose so," Pete murmured, not entirely in agreement with his wife's generosity to her late departed sister but understanding her need.
"However must they feel," Emma pondered. "These bankers. Knowing what they've caused to happen. What they've done to peoples' lives, their hopes, their dreams. Everything. The dream robbers, Michael Croft called them."
"Huh. They don't seem to care that much," Pete spluttered. "This pensions business - more millions that they've skimmed off the top."
"They must do - *surely*," argued Emma. "*Surely* no-one can be that thick-skinned."
"Oh, I think they can. They're morally bankrupt, Em. They live at a different level. Don't mix with the ordinary guy in the street. The hoi poloi, as they see us ordinary folk. Completely out of touch with the real world - the one that we and most people live in. Well, they're the losers, if you ask me. Imagine having all that money, the financial freedom to buy your way anywhere and everywhere in the world and being held in contempt by the entire population of the informed world everywhere you go. They can hardly walk down a street nowadays without being aware of that contempt, of expecting abuse to be hurled in their direction. Their photographs have been splashed across the front of every tabloid. They must have to travel incognito. Just imagine. Dark glasses, false moustache and a trilby every time you set foot outside the door."
"And that's only the women," giggled Emma, needing to lighten the mood.
"Oh, very droll," he laughed. "Well, let's see how clever you are at getting breakfast, Mrs Bailey because if we don't move soon Izz is going to miss her train."
"But it's cold out there. And it's warm and cosy in here," she protested.

Caroline Jones Lewis
The Dream Robbers

She yawned, snuggled in closer, reluctant to move from the comfort of his body.
"I know. Perhaps we can sneak just five more minutes," he conceded lazily and with little need for convincing.
"Yeah. Five more minutes," she agreed and closed her eyes smugly, sliding her arm comfortably around his waist.

They stood on the platform, the family, watching Izzie through the window of the compartment as she settled herself ready for the journey. Dumping her bag on the luggage rack above her seat, she lowered the window, grimacing at the cold wind that whistled in around her neck and caused her to shiver. The guard blew his whistle, slamming shut the last of the doors that remained open as he marched along the platform from carriage to carriage.
"Bye," called Izzie. "See you all soon."
"Bye darling," called Emma.
"Bye, Izz," chorused the rest of her family.
Izzie leaned from the carriage window as the train slid alongside the platform heading out of the station, waving her gloved hand at the four figures receding into the distance. Then she closed the window and settled into her seat for the remainder of the journey, stripping her gloves off her hands and loosening her scarf as the warmth of the carriage began to take effect. It had been a difficult Christmas, she thought - for all of them. Unreal. Sort of - disjointed. It was a relief in a way to head back to the Academy where the unreal-ness that had become home would be left behind, where people didn't know about Aunt Sophie, where people didn't keep offering their condolences. So much kindness had been hard to bear when really she wanted to scream and stamp her feet and insist that someone brought Aunt Sophie back. Back at the Academy she could absorb herself in her music, lose the emotions in the ebb and flow of crotchets and quavers and blot out the realities back home that weighed down on her shoulders. Everyone should have that, she

Caroline Jones Lewis

The Dream Robbers

thought. Something, some way of blotting out pain that was too much to bear. She wondered at her parents and her grandparents. What did they do, she wondered? What was their escape? Hannah would shut herself in a book and Joe got out his foottie. But what about her parents - and her grandparents? How did they cope in the face of overwhelming grief?

On the platform, the four of them watched the face at the window disappear into the distance, watched it becoming smaller and smaller until its features were beyond distinction.
"Come on, let's get home in the warm," encouraged Pete. "This weather is just unbelievable."
"Will she be alright without us," Hannah questioned, a Hannah softened of late by an avalanche of pain and uncertainty. "She's still really upset about Aunt Sophie."
"Yes, she'll be alright," her father assured her. "We're all still upset about your Aunt Sophie, Hann - but we just have to get on with life, don't we? There's nothing else we can do. And anyway, it's what your Aunt Sophie would want, isn't it? She would want you to get on with life and have fun. Remember her, yes. But not with tears and sadness. We have to remember the good times we had with her, the happy times we shared," and he took his daughter's hand and squeezed it in his own.
They walked steadily back to the car park, a family together.
"Life goes on, Hann," said Emma with a sigh, clutching her daughter's other hand closely and placing her other arm protectively around Joe's shoulder. "It will get easier. You'll see."
"Will everything be alright," Hannah fretted. "With all this money stuff that everyone's talking about. It's on the news all the time. Some of my school friends, their Dads have lost their jobs. What will they do? It's all bad news, all the time."
"Well, they'll manage somehow," Emma insisted. "That's

Caroline Jones Lewis
The Dream Robbers

what grownups do - manage when times get tough. They'll look for more work."

"But will they find any?"

"We hope so," Pete assured her. "There's always hope, love. As long as there's breath in the body there's hope. When all this is over, things will have changed for the better. Some of the bad things will have been blown away. That's what we hope. You'll see."

Emma glanced him a 'let's hope so' look.

"Do you really think so?" Hannah insisted.

"Yes I do. Now I don't think it's something you should be fretting about," Pete continued. "You have a busy year ahead of you, young lady, with all your exams to think about. Let's concentrate on those, shall we?"

"I'm sorry," Hannah blurted.

"What for?" Emma asked, surprised at the apology.

"I've been beastly," Hannah ventured. "Just thinking of myself all the time. I won't any more - I promise."

Emma squeezed Hannah's hand and shot a questioning glance at Pete, concern written on her face but a wry grin on his.

"'Till the next time," his expression was saying. "Till the next time!"

Back at the house, Emma closed the door on the outside world. She wanted time away from the wider world, time in the safety of her own world to recover. She lived each day now with a tremble inside her threatening to emerge at the slightest hint of trouble, so unlike the way her life had previously been, and though she tried to hide it beneath the routine of normality she knew the self-assured person she had been had taken a severe knock. There was an insecurity where once there had been assurance. With Isobel on her way back to the Academy and her career aspirations, with Hannah on the brink of the exams that would determine hers, Emma wanted time to savour all of her family, to wrap them in her arms and hold them there so tightly no more harm

Caroline Jones Lewis

The Dream Robbers

could ever reach them. So much had happened since that day the letter from the Academy had fluttered onto the doormat. It had all seemed to start that day, all the anxieties, the differences that would create a rift that would eventually lead to the loss of one of them.   It was hard to believe the devastation that had taken place in such a short period of time. There were still challenges ahead - for others more so than anything she had to face. Pete was right. There was hope. Hope that the world would be a better place, that people would be better people and rebuild a better society. That all this terrible greed would stop. It had to be. Otherwise, all this pain would be for nothing.

She hung her coat in the cloakroom in the hallway, put the kettle on in the kitchen and gathering together all the courage she could muster, joined the remainder of her family who had congregated in front of the TV.
"OK guys," she began. "What do you fancy for lunch, all of you?"
How could she know there was a further desperate chapter to come.

******

Outside the air was tranquil. There was little breeze and what there was lapped lazily across the valley to the farm beyond. With the severe drop in temperature, a quiet stillness had settled over the landscape like the calm before the storm. There would be more to come, more change, more businesses failing, more job losses, more houses repossessed, more wars and more bloodshed. The purge would continue. For some the worst was not yet over. The winds were only resting. They were not gone. But there was awareness now. That changes must be for the better, cathartic and cleansing, and the actions of the few must not be allowed to cause the destruction of the many. It was a tall order but must be achieved if lessons were truly

Caroline Jones Lewis

The Dream Robbers

to be learned. So far, the perpetrators remained unpunished, the financial institutions still failing to respond to the call to reform and assist. There were those that must be brought to brook. There must be some justice. Yes, indeed there was more to come. Out in the Atlantic, chill winds regrouped and gathered momentum, gathering energy for a new season.

In Washington DC, on the cold morning of 20th January 2009, Barack Hussein Obama took the oath of allegiance to become the 45th President of the United States of America.

The Mall leading to the Capital Building was crammed with millions of celebrating citizens of all creeds and colour. His inaugural address left them in no doubt as to the difficult days ahead, the problems to be faced and the sacrifices that would have to be made.
"My fellow citizens: I stand here today humbled by the task before us, grateful for the trust you have bestowed, mindful of the sacrifices born by our ancestors." But he inspired them with hope, for a better tomorrow, a better world, a better America.
"Let it be said that when we were tested we refused to let this journey end, that we did not turn back nor did we falter; and
with eyes fixed on the horizon and God's grace upon us, we carried forth that great gift of freedom and delivered it safe to future generations. Thank you. God bless you. And God bless the United States of America."

He walked along Pennsylvania Avenue, his wife Michelle beside him, their daughters Melia and Sasha waiting inside as they entered the White House to begin the tasks ahead, the changes that the he and the rest of the world must make. Change had come to America and the world, and

Caroline Jones Lewis

The Dream Robbers

change remained the order of the day.

Across the Atlantic in the streets of Paris, on a blustery January evening, the anger and frustration that had been brewing over the weeks spilled out into the streets in a riot. Ordinary people demanding justice, demanding help for the victims and retribution against the bankers, vent their fury as financial instability threatened to de-stabilise the Eurozone. People power was on the march and change must come to bring hope, to restore the dreams of a generation.

******

Blown in on a westerly from the frozen plains of Siberia, the greatest snowfall for many years came in an overnight blast, settling across the country in a silent blanket. The entire United Kingdom slid and slithered into the usual chaos occasioned by a sudden change of weather. Roads were impassable, traffic disrupted, schools closed and workers unable to get to their place of work. At night the frosts and winds were bitter, adding ice hazards to the already treacherous conditions. By day, children played with their sledges, building snowmen and laughing as they pounded each other with snowballs and their parents muttered and mumbled as they stumbled their way through the daily routine. Snowfall followed snowfall. In the City of London, the 'buses and the underground ground to a halt and traffic slithered and slewed through the narrow streets.

As the snow turned to slush and melted, the four disgraced bankers who had broken the banks appeared before a bipartisan House of Commons Select Committee to attempt an explanation of their conduct. They offered a weak and unimpressive apology for their failure and all the consequences they had brought about. It left the general public unimpressed and demanding that they should be

Caroline Jones Lewis

The Dream Robbers

stripped of their titles, stripped of their ill-gotten gains and thrown behind bars. They left after one full day's grilling unaquitted and in no doubt that they would be called upon again.

A trail of complicity led to a would-be independent regulator appointed by the Government who in reality was one of their own, a comfortable little gentleman's club feathering their own nests and shielding each other's ineptitude. They had been warned of the risk their banks were taking and chose to ignore the warning. Not only that but the counsellor who had issued the direst of warnings to one of the stricken banks had been rewarded for his diligence and clear thinking with dismissal, fired from his job for his audacity of questioning the actions of his peers. The public mood was black and became blacker with the knowledge that the footprints led to the very door of the Treasury. The blood-letting would go on.

The snow thawed into rivers that swelled the gutters and life took on a steady pace of downturn. Redundancies here, reduced hours or pay cuts there, businesses struggling to survive. In contradiction the continuing revelations of massive pension pay-outs to disgraced bankers fuelled public discontent. Demands were made for the monies to be returned - or withheld in the first place - but the bankers refused to concede and the lawyers scanned contracts in vain for a means of enforcing the request.

March blew in like a lion, the winds refusing to ease and the rumblings of discontent forming into organised protest as London prepared for the G20 summit. So that world leaders flew in to a sea of protestors flooding the streets of the City of London.

******

Peter Bailey studied his face in the bathroom mirror as he

Caroline Jones Lewis

The Dream Robbers

brushed his teeth vigorously. In recent months fine creases had appeared across his forehead and dark circles were evident around his eyes made all the more noticeable by an unhealthier than usual pallor. He had not historically been of an obsessive nature but on the issue of the banks and on each and every occasion the economic crisis was broached irritation churned. He fumed over every indiscretion that big business had been found to have committed, a subject on which Emma had commented to her mother with concern.
"He's so wound up about everything these days. I've never known him like it. He gets angrier every time another financial scandal comes to light. I'm sure his blood pressure's up and that's why he's getting these headaches."
"Has he seen the doctor, dear?"
"I have asked him to, Mum, but he keeps putting it off. I think I'll just make an appointment and hope he doesn't have a meeting, or something."
He had agreed to go.
"We need a break," he thought. "All of us. Somewhere warm and relaxed."
Emma too was pale and strained after the traumas of the previous year. The auction of the properties at The Tythings had relieved their finances somewhat and though they still needed to conserve as much as possible, maybe they would all benefit from a short break in the sun.
"I'll talk to Em about it this evening," he promised himself. But first he had to get through the day. He was not looking forward to today.

.

The previous evening had brought an urgent appeal from Izzie.
"Mum, I left the sheet music with all my notes on it at home and I really need it for this weekend's concert. Can you courier it up to me or something - please, Mum?"
"Yes, of course, darling. I'll find a way of getting it to you safely. I'll let you know."
Pete suggested what he thought was an easy solution.

Caroline Jones Lewis
The Dream Robbers

"I have to go to town in the morning, Em. Meeting with the architects."

"What, on a Saturday?" Emma grumbled.

"Afraid so. They're really busy at the moment; tied up on problems with some big project or the other. They're not happy about working on a Saturday, either. But there it is. I'll take it to Izz. I can give it in at reception if she's busy." And so it was settled. It was only later that he realised the G20 summit was taking place the same morning, accompanied by a mass demonstration that meant his route across town from one appointment to the other would cut right through the middle. He was not looking forward to his day.

The meeting with the architects was much as he had anticipated. To change the plans for the site at Burwash meant considerable outlay for revised plans and an even more considerable delay for planning approval. Though time was not an issue due to the state of the market, the additional outlay and potential reduction in profit of a less lucrative development required careful consideration. He left their offices undecided as to the course of action to take and walked steadily and in deep thought along the Embankment. His briefcase was heavy, pulling on his arm and shoulder and he remonstrated with himself for not having taken time to discard unwanted items before leaving home, a brick sample for conservatory construction that Emma was contemplating for the new house at The Tythings and some tile samples for the downstairs cloakroom at home. "Stupid of me," he had told himself. "I'll dump them when I find a suitable bin."

At the Academy he had left the parcel for Izzie at reception as he knew she would now be engrossed in rehearsal and he texted her mobile to let her know it was there. Now he had time to kill before his train home was due and he measured his options of taking a walk in the park or slipping into a coffee house for a good strong coffee. Protestors were

Caroline Jones Lewis
The Dream Robbers

flooding the streets around him now as the demonstration fractured into disarray. Ahead of him he could hear the buzz of angry chanting voices and the sound of splintering glass. His curiosity was aroused but caution deterred him from joining the melee.
"However much you sympathise with their cause," he told himself, "remember the blood pressure. Remember the family."
But temptation taunted him and a thin voice of conscience called him a coward.

******

On a coach trundling its way into Victoria, Peggy was reading a newspaper that outlined the itinerary of the day. Why she had bought the newspaper she could not say. They were an unnecessary extravagance in her normal daily budget but today was different and despite the reason for her journey, the very event in itself seemed to give the day an air of adventure, of venturing forth from her little world into the wider. She had given in to a feeling that today anything was possible, a lifting of the spirit and she felt an air of optimism she was unable to justify.
The newspaper was full of comment on the protests and protesters but she gave them little heed, her mind focused on the event in her own life that was bringing her into town.

The call from her cousin had been quite unexpected and intuition had warned her in an instant that its reason must be bad news. Why else would her cousin bother to ring? And so indeed it was confirmed. Her aunt's demise had been quite sudden, a stroke two nights previously which had lapsed her into an unconscious state from which she had not recovered.

Peggy had offered her condolences. At first she had thought it unnecessary to attend the funeral, her relationship

Caroline Jones Lewis
The Dream Robbers

with the remainder of the family being a virtual estrangement but on second thought she had reconsidered, acknowledging that her aunt, at least, had shown some care of her existence, albeit small. This was her mother's last sibling and although they had never been really close, even so her absence might well be regarded dimly. On behalf of her mother, she considered, why not go? Surprisingly the funeral was to be on a Saturday, an unusual situation necessitated by a backlog caused by the severe winter weather. Nothing she had tried had resulted in even the faintest glimmer of employment, and in any case no prospective employer would be calling her on a Saturday. Since she had little else to do, and even her close friend Ruby was at present away, luxuriating in the warmth of Tenerife sunshine on her annual escape from the British winter, the decision was made. Peggy had managed to keep by some of the money given to her by the banker's wife on that fateful evening of the fire and decided she would indulge herself by turning the journey into an outing once her duty had been fulfilled. Perhaps one of those tour 'buses that would take her past the Palace. Who knows, she might even catch a glimpse of one of the royals on their way to and fro? She had listened intently to her cousin's impassive and explicit instructions when confirming her attendance and written them down in the back of her diary. So here she was, city bound on the coach to Victoria and watching the landscape of outer London slide by in a virtual state of trance. It was unreal, she thought. The end of an era, of her mother's generation and with it came the recognition that, given the lack of attachment between her cousins and herself, from now on she would be - too all intents and purposes - entirely alone in the world. She alighted from the coach and made her way towards the tube station for the next stage of her journey.

******

Caroline Jones Lewis
The Dream Robbers

In another part of London the G20 protestors were running into trouble. It was well into the protest that the trouble began. From his place amongst the ranks of peaceful demonstrators, Michael Croft could see what was happening ahead. Frustration overflowed into violence at the Royal Bank of Scotland where a minority of vandals intent on making trouble attacked the building with any weapon they could lay their hands on, smashing the glass façade to leave the pavement littered with its fragments. Wolves in sheep's clothing, thought Michael. He gave the violence a wide berth with Helen's words uppermost in his mind.
She had been pleased at his determination to go, announced at the breakfast table a few mornings previous. A new Michael, she had thought, a more confident, positive Michael ready to take a stand.
"Michael the militant," she had teased grinning.
"Why not," he had responded. "After all we've been through because of these people, because of this society they have developed. Things really do need to change, Helen. These politicians need to understand that. For our sake. For their sake," and he had pointed to Polly, stirring Rice Krispies in a cereal bowl and lolling her head to listen for the snap, crackle and pop. Baby Liam sat contentedly in his baby chair sucking his thumb and on the verge of sleep. "We want a better world for them."
She had approved wholeheartedly. Only then she had become just a little anxious of events that could escalate outside of their control.
"I know you really want to go, darling," she had encouraged. "But you'll stay well away from anything that looks like trouble, won't you? You know what it's like. There are always just those few who go especially to hijack the whole thing to make trouble. It's always the innocent bystanders that get hurt, caught up in the crossfire. They're not there to support the cause at all, those types. Please don't get hurt or anything. We need you," and she had smiled that smile that had always pierced his heart. The smile that said I love and

Caroline Jones Lewis

The Dream Robbers

need you."

"Of course I won't," he had assured her. "I promise I'll keep well away from anything that looks like it's heading towards violence. The organisers are intent on a peaceful protest so I'm sure we'll be steered well clear of anything else."

He had kissed her forehead as he left her there in bed this morning, Polly asleep on the duvet beside her and baby Liam at her breast.

"See you later, darling."

She nodded.

"See you later. Take care."

Now that trouble was brewing ahead of him her words echoed in his mind and he made a deliberate attempt to move away from the obvious centre of dissent. The crowd was jostling now, herded in the opposite direction by police in heavy riot gear and as he tried to make his way across the street towards the river, the banner he had been given to carry was knocked from his hand. As he bent to retrieve it, the placard was trampled on so that he found himself with just the wooden stave left in his hand. The placard itself disappeared beneath an army of feet as he was shoved forward by the host of bodies surrounding him, stumbling and struggling to regain his balance. He left the placard where it lay and pushed himself forward away from the Bank of England. It was approaching noon now and the genuine protest was almost over. People were already beginning to drift away, back towards the Embankment and The Treasury where it had all begun. Soon he found himself detached from the main group of protestors that he had marched with. He realised that he was hungry now, and thirsty, in need of a break from the crowds and the noise that had accompanied him all morning, unused as he was these days to the hustle and bustle of town. In his backpack were the sandwiches and the bottle of juice that Helen had insisted he bring and for which at the time he had protested but now was entirely

Caroline Jones Lewis
The Dream Robbers

grateful. On a sudden whim, he took a taxi to Hyde Park and made his way towards the Serpentine to find a quiet spot to eat and drink and contemplate the usefulness of the day. He had played his part and to Michael that was a matter of pride and satisfaction. He found a seat beside the lake and settled comfortably and with contentment.

It was a while later that, replete from his snack, he wandered aimlessly along the banks of the lake, his backpack returned to his back and the wooden stave that had once supported the placard still in his hand. He wondered what he should do with it, reluctant to be burdened with it all the way home. Dump it perhaps, but in a litter bin, not just littering the park or a pavement. His attention was caught by a clutch of baby ducks with their mother and he meandered towards them. He thought of Polly and the delight the sight of them would bring were she here. It was then that he saw him. The Banker. Sitting on a bench under a willow tree, a briefcase by his side. It was unmistakeably him. Michael would know him anywhere for he had contemplated that face many times in recent weeks, a face emblazoned across the pages of the tabloids, a face he recognised from his own village, a face that had haunted him on the night of the fire. The face of a man that embodied a culture that had robbed him of his dream. The dream robber, the bringer of pain to him and his beloved family. He was there right before his very eyes. The anger that had gripped him on the night of the fire began to bubble under the surface of his composure and for a moment he faltered in his steps, torn between walking on and walking away or confronting the man with a red hot torrent of anger. Remember Helen, he told himself. Remember Polly and Liam. Walk away. Walk away. But his anger was pulling him like a magnet towards the dream robber, tugging at his sleeve like a demon whose whispered voice was urging him on.

******

Caroline Jones Lewis
The Dream Robbers

The banker had arrived in Hyde Park by an unintended excursion on the underground in a bid for anonymity. In recent days he had become increasingly convinced that he was being tailed and had more than a suspicion that his 'phone was being tapped. There was that echo on the line, a slight delay when he dialled out that he was sure had not been there before. At first he had told himself it was imagination, paranoia, but the feeling of being watched just would not go away. Since the death threats and the fire at the cottage he was constantly looking over his shoulder. He had become accustomed to the gutter press, as he called them, dogging his every move but this was different and he regarded it as sinister. His family, to whom he had confided his thoughts over the telephone, were unconvinced, regarding it as paranoia fuelled by his guilt or a bid to coax his wife back from their daughter's. They put it down to the use of any tactic to get his way. His wife had not been swayed.

Today he had met with his lawyer to discuss his pension payout and the constant pressure he was being put under to relinquish his rights. But his contract was quite clear and in his favour and he refused to concede. After their meeting he left his lawyer's office and convinced again that he was not alone, he hailed a taxi swiftly and leapt into the rear with a furtive glance behind. Approaching Knightsbridge Tube Station, he told the driver to pull over to the curb and swiftly thrust a £10. note into his hand. Telling the driver to keep the change, he clutched his briefcase against his chest and hurried down the steps into the depths of the station, dodging in and out of other travellers to shake off the would be follower in what to him was unfamiliar territory. His nostrils flared with distaste at the smell that wafted from below to greet him and he steeled himself to go on. Reaching the bottom of the escalator he sidled into a tunnel to the right of him until he found himself on a platform. He hugged back against the wall in an attempt to be

The Dream Robbers

Caroline Jones Lewis

inconspicuous, hunching down behind a group of young backpackers engaged in animated conversation. When a train trundled alongside the platform he boarded under the cover they afforded him and dropped into the only empty seat in the crowded carriage. Feeling sure that he had jettisoned anyone tailing him, when the train slid to a halt at Hyde Park Corner, he alighted onto the platform at the very last moment for good measure, just as the doors were about to close.

Standing on the pavement in the clean fresh air above, he felt the need for some quiet moments to recover his composure. His heart was thumping madly and he was beginning to question his own sanity. Without the calming influence of his wife and children around him, his dominance as the head of the family and the status of his former position in business, his self-esteem had become a little shaky despite all outward signs that he clung to his convictions. Behind him in the distance was the noise of what he guessed to be the protesters at the G20 summit, a rabble he had no desire or intention of confronting. On an impulse he headed for the gates of the park to find a quiet seat for a few moments contemplation.

He had walked some way before he spotted a bench half hidden beneath a willow tree. He headed gratefully for its cover. The soft green tips of new leaves peeped from the branches brushing his cheek as he sank gratefully onto the seat.

******

After the funeral Peggy returned to her aunt's house with her cousins and a few remnants of friends and neighbours. Surprisingly she learned that her aunt had left her a legacy. Small though it was to her cousins, to Peggy £500. was a fortune that had been beyond her wildest expectation.

Caroline Jones Lewis

The Dream Robbers

Indeed, she had expected nothing at all and wondered what had prompted her aunt's generosity. She received the news with quiet dignity and gratitude, ignoring the patronising tone of her cousins as they gave her the news from their loftier and wealthier positions in society. They drank tea and ate sandwiches in polite conversation but there was little warmth between the members of the gathering. They were not a warm and loving family. She made her excuses ready to leave.

"Oh, just one more thing, Peggy," her cousin was saying. "We've started clearing the house. There's no point in waiting, is there? It has to be sold."

Yes, I 'ave noticed, thought Peggy, the collection of fine porcelain figures that had graced her aunt's display cabinet conspicuous by their absence and here and there the indents in the carpet that betrayed the absence of the better pieces of her aunt's antique furniture now removed.

"Mother always wanted you to have something. You know - a little memento."

"Oh," was all that Peggy managed to say.

"So we thought you'd like to have this," and her cousin produced from behind the sofa a cheap plastic carrier bag that she thrust into Peggy's unprepared hands, her husband standing alongside her, the two smiling self-congratulatory smiles as though they had invested upon her a great and valued honour. Through a gap in the top of the bag and the weight that caused her arms to fall, Peggy recognised a heavy, ungainly statuette of unidentified metal that her aunt had disliked immensely and, if Peggy's memory served her right, was always kept at the back of the cabinet as far out of sight as was possible but ready for display should the donor decide to call. She thanked her cousin as genuinely as she could muster in face of the unwanted and condescending gesture and left, heaving a grateful sigh and with the fervent hope that she would never have to see them again. Outside the air smelled fresh and clean following a light shower that had washed the landscape. Peggy breathed in the sweet air

Caroline Jones Lewis

The Dream Robbers

with a gentle smile.

There was an hour or two yet before her coach back to Tunbridge Wells and she reinforced her decision to make the most of her time in the City, to turn her usual aversion to the hubbub of town into the rare gift of an outing now that the sombre proceedings of the day were concluded. She drank in the euphoria of the moment, at the surprise financial bequest, the feeling of unexpected wealth turning the usual dull and anxious greyness of her life into a sunny day. It was the second act of unexpected generosity she had received in not many more months and it raised her spirits and her opinion of her fellow men. Clutching her handbag in one hand and the hideous statuette in the other, she walked from the house towards the Embankment and along the river until she reached the gates of Hyde Park. On a whim, she turned into the park and followed a lone mother walking with her children towards the lake. They paused to feed the ducks with dry crusts of bread produced from a plastic bag, and a courting couple walking their dog strolled by arm in arm and engrossed in conversation, the collars of their coats turned up against the chill of a winter wind that was refusing to relinquish its grip and give way to an overdue spring.

The banks of the Serpentine were a scene of tranquillity save for the brisk wind rustling the trees and gently ruffling the surface waters of the lake. Peggy walked on content in her own thoughts. As she circumnavigated the lake, the company of even the few other walkers fell away and she soon found herself a solitary figure in the expanse of parkland. It was then that she saw him, espying the Banker sitting on a bench beneath a willow tree with his briefcase clutched in his hands. It came as a shock that snapped her out of her reverie. That man. That wretched man that she so despised. She railed against him in her mind; greedy, deceitful, corrupt, disgraced. He had treated her with such condescension in her decent, honest, hardworking ways. A

Caroline Jones Lewis

The Dream Robbers

man now stripped of any semblance of the decency and integrity she and everyone she knew had always been expected to live by. The sight of him transported her in an instant from the serenity of the former moment to a new and unfamiliar place of torrid emotion. A place populated by deceit. By betrayal. A place devoid of morality. His place. And the sight of him brought her to a standstill. In a split second she was faced with a choice - of passing by, of turning the other cheek and walking away or of giving vent to a cocktail of emotions that were building to a crescendo inside her. A voice was warning her. Remember the politician. Remember the paint can and the car. Remember what anger can do to you. Walk away. Walk away. But her anger was taunting her like the tongue of a serpentine devil.

******

The banker had not registered the footsteps approaching along the path until they had come to a halt. Someone was there - near to him. He could feel their presence. Feel their mood. It carried itself to him on the wind that brushed his face and ruffled his greying hair, a hostile mood that sent a tremor juddering through the air. He turned to see the owner of the footsteps, saw a face that he recognised from a splintered past that was rapidly disappearing into the distance; a vaguely familiar face from the life that he once had enjoyed but lost to the unfamiliar territory that he now inhabited, that his life had ventured into. The angry torrent of words that was thrust in his direction rendered him temporarily speechless. It was becoming a regular event these days. Anger and resentment from people who thought they knew him, the man he was, but that in reality, he defended to himself, did not know him at all.
"I don't have to put up with this," he mouthed into the wind. He turned away muttering to himself.
He stooped to pick up his briefcase and as he did so, a blow

Caroline Jones Lewis

The Dream Robbers

to the back of his head took him by surprise, then before he had time to recover came another that sent him reeling forward, arms flailing, falling, falling. Then the darkness came, then the water. The briefcase, released from his grasp, slid down the bank to the water's edge. All became blackness. All became cold.

A little while later the courting couple on their return journey were shaken from their intimacy by the barking of their curious and exuberant tail-wagging dog. The sight of the banker's body floating against the reeds caused them to shrink back in fear.

On his arrival, the detective chief inspector considered the scene with his sergeant.
"Well, there's no CCTV to go on. Grass is dry and long so there's no footprints to speak of. No murder weapon in the vicinity. And with all these G20 protestors at the entrance to the park God knows how we're going to identify any suspects. It clearly wasn't robbery. There's money in his wallet and all sorts of stuff in the briefcase a burglar might have been interested in."
"Definitely murder, then, sir?"
"Definitely," came the reply. "I doubt even someone of his ability could inflict wounds like that to the back of his head. Pathologist's initial opinion is drowning following blows to the back of the head. He would have been unconscious when he hit the water. We'll have to wait for his full report after the autopsy, of course, but doesn't seem any doubt that it's murder. Can't have happened long either. The body's barely cold."
"Do you think it's anything to do with these protesters, sir?"
"Who knows? He wasn't the most popular of people these days, was he? All the publicity this pension business has had in recent days on top of everything else his bank got up to. Much good all that pension's going to do him now, heh. It would be a sort of poetic justice if his death had been

Caroline Jones Lewis

The Dream Robbers

natural. Murder, though. That's different. We know there were trouble makers amongst the demonstrators. We did arrest some after the break in at RBS but probably not all of them. It's going to be like finding a needle in a haystack."

He sighed and shook his head.

"Well, best go and find the wife and family to break the news. We'd better get that over with for a start. Then get the incident room set up smartish. The press are going to be all over this one like a rash. Come on. Let's get back to the car and leave SOCO to it. There's nothing more we can do here. I'll be glad to get out of this bloody cold wind. My ears are aching."

******

Back in the village, Michael Croft related the events of the day to his wife over a mug of hot chocolate. Propped up in bed on a bank of pillows they discussed the achievement or otherwise of the demonstration, abhorred the vandalism of the few which they hoped had not detracted from the good intentions of the many and felt a general satisfaction at the outcome. Polly slept firmly in her room and baby Liam slumbered contentedly in his cot against the wall in the lull before the next round of gusty yells that signalled time for another feed. Michael omitted all mention of his encounter with the banker, a meeting that he had already buried in the recesses of his mind and memory as firmly as the events of the night of the fire. The banker in the park with his briefcase was no longer a matter of his concern. The wooden stave he had discarded determinedly just before he left the park to head home. He had thrust it downwards into the water to lodge in the mud on the bed of the lake. Over the coming days, he closed his ears resolutely to the gossip that percolated around a village enthralled at the discovery of the banker's body and avoided any contribution to the inevitable speculation as to who, how, why the man had met

Caroline Jones Lewis

The Dream Robbers

his death. To Michael there had been a modicum of natural retribution that the man so intent on thieving millions from the taxpayer in a pension payout had not lived to enjoy the proceeds. The violence of the untimely loss of a still youthful man barely bothered him as he focused his attention firmly on his own life and family.

******

Peggy had left the park and with all thoughts of exploration now abandoned, she made her way swiftly to Victoria. A light drizzle had begun to fall silently and gently in the descending gloom of dusk and out of habit she delved into her handbag for her umbrella. The umbrella stuck and she yanked it several times before it opened properly.
"I'll buy myself a new one," she muttered to herself. "A celebration of my inheritance. Something more cheerful than the old one. But not today."

At home a little later, tired and a somewhat overwrought by the emotions of the day, the emotional roller-coaster it had proved itself to be, she made herself a light supper and a mug of Horlicks before going to bed. She switched out the bedside light and fell into an exhausted sleep until the light of morning sneaked around the folds of the bedroom curtains. When at last she emerged from her slumbers, the events of the previous day were a distant memory that she locked firmly away in her subconscious. She had things to do today. Things for herself and her own life, a future that she had suddenly begun to view with optimism.

Over the coming days the village buzzed with gossip. The news of the banker's death had burst onto an unsympathetic world and in the post office, Ruby, who had now returned from Tenerife and was most annoyed to have missed by hours the main event, gushed animatedly to Peggy with all the gory details that she had gleaned from the morning's

Caroline Jones Lewis

The Dream Robbers

tabloids.

"Fancy," she exclaimed to her friend. "Just fancy, Peggy - you could still have been working for the man if it hadn't been for that fire. The police would have been here asking questions again - here in the village, like they did after the fire. Only the Met this time. They may still come, don't you think?" and she bristled with anticipation.

Peggy said nothing, keeping her own counsel. Since no-one knew of her visit to the City, of her aunt's death and the funeral, much less of her sighting of the wretched man in the Park, sitting there on that bench large as life and without a shred of conscience, there was no need to say a word.

"I need a stamp," she said blankly, "first class" and passed the money through the screen without any reference to the matter that was so intriguing her friend. She was more concerned with the letter that she wished to catch the morning post.

She had decided to apply for the extra money from social services that people had told her she could claim. She had decided that it was time for a state that had so let her down to look after her. She had decided, too, that it was time to celebrate living, to leave behind the angst and the hardships of the past and enjoy a new way of living before it was too late. Like a snake shedding its skin, she was casting off her old pride and prejudices to encompass the new. After all, had she not worked a lifetime to contribute to the public purse? Had she not led an honest life without taking so much as a penny she was not entitled to? Save for a brief lapse with a can of paint and a limo, she had led a decent and honest life. Not like these greedy, deceitful people in public life who lacked even a crumb of integrity and conscience. To Ruby's amusement, Peggy licked the stamp and stuck it firmly onto the envelope with a thump and passed the envelope to Ruby to drop into the mail bag. There, she thought. It's done. She had justified her intention to her own satisfaction and done the deed.

Caroline Jones Lewis

The Dream Robbers

"Important letter, then?" queried Ruby.
"Yes," replied Peggy, " important letter" but elaborating no further.

It had been Peggy's intention to invite Ruby for their usual tea, but in Ruby's present highly excited state about the murder, her company, she decided, would be too much to bear. All that prattling on about things she herself did not want to hear. The banker and his sticky end were of no interest to her now, her last sighting of the despicable individual buried in the deep recesses of her memory, along with a long lost memory of paint splashed across a car. So she excused herself from Ruby's company on the grounds of feeling a little unwell in the chill weather, that maybe she had a cold coming or perhaps was just overtired. Ruby accepted without hesitation and Peggy made to leave the post office in haste and with a promise to see Ruby in a day or two when she was sure she would be feeling better - and when hopefully, she observed to herself, the gossip may have died down a deal.
Ruby was a little flummoxed.
"Are you sure you're alright?" she had probed. "You have got your heating on, Peggy, haven't you?"
"Yes. I 'ave," Peggy insisted. "I just 'ave a bit of a snuffle, that's all. But if I 'ave gotta cold coming I'm sure you don't wanna catch it. Don't wanna spoil your 'oliday by getting a cold the minute you get back, eh Rube? A bit of TLC will put me to rights. I'll see you soon."
"I'll call round in the morning, just to see you're alright," Ruby insisted and watched her friend leave with a little concern.

"She looks peaky," she thought. "As though something's bothering her."
As she was leaving, Peggy noticed an advert on the notice board. *Wanted*, it said. *Good homes for five pretty kittens*, and there was a photograph, five bundles of fluff snuggled

Caroline Jones Lewis
The Dream Robbers

around their mother and the address of the Croft's cottage just a little way down the lane. "It'd be quite nice to 'ave a cat again," she thought. "Good company."
And now she wasn't working, she could look after it properly. She had had a cat once before, when she lived in her little house and had a garden. But it had been killed on the road outside and her distress had been palpable. She had hoped he had not suffered, that his death would have been quick and without an agonized lingering. She had vowed never to go through that again. Never, never. It had been just too painful. She had loved her cat. A beautiful ginger tom who came and settled on her lap in the evenings, wrapping its tail around her chin in a caress as he curled himself into a comfortable ball, purring loudly like a traction engine at full throttle. Yes, it would be quite nice to have a cat again. The pretty grey tabby one, she thought, peering closely at the photograph. She went straight away to the cottage and knocked on the door.

Leaving the Crofts cottage a little while later with the furry grey bundle curled sleepy inside her overcoat she almost collided with Emma Bailey and on the spur of the moment, amidst the giggled apologies each made to the other, she blurted another.
"I was rude," she ventured. "That day you called. You were only being kind an' I was rude."
"That's alright, Peggy," Emma replied. "I understand. But people care about you, you know. Would you let me call on you from time to time, just for a chat, just so that people know you're alright? And if you're not well, well you might need something, mightn't you? Some shopping or something. A letter posting. Anything."

Peggy paused momentarily, then "that would be nice," she agreed. "Praps you could stay for a cuppa tea."
"Lovely," smiled Emma. "See you soon then," and Peggy walked on, feeling good about herself and glad she had had

Caroline Jones Lewis
The Dream Robbers

the opportunity to put things right.

The police came to the village but at first it was only a brief sojourn in their enquiry. There seemed no-one really connected with the man who was of interest, only an ageing ex-housekeeper now redundant since his property had been torched and who they were assured rarely left the village and certainly ventured no further than the town a few miles away. The fire remained a mystery that they now suspected to be a foiled previous attempt at his murder. Conspiracy theories began to circulate, the gentlemen of the press speculating wildly, all manner of imaginings as to who, what, why. Lurid stories followed dramatic headlines, all of them apocryphal but that mattered not a jot. It was certainly not the family. That was identified beyond a doubt and their shock and grief was evident. The wife and children were well accounted for and it was they who had recounted the banker's conviction that he was being followed, that his 'phone was being tapped, that someone, somewhere was out to get him. Investigation gave credence to his suspicion. His 'phone was indeed bugged though no party would admit responsibility. Westminster was alive with rumour and questions were raised in the House. There were, of course, many likely candidates given the events of the previous year but all enquiries were met with stringent denials.

"If it is any of them it's unlikely we'll ever find out for sure," the DCI observed glumly. "These agencies are expert at covering their tracks."

The investigation was floundering in a mire of rumour and hypothesis - until a sharp eyed member of the team spotted a vaguely familiar face.

"It's here, guv," they told the detective chief inspector. "I picked this up on the CCTV," and he pointed to a frame frozen on the screen.

"From the banker's diary we know he had an appointment with his lawyer that morning. The lawyer has confirmed it

Caroline Jones Lewis

The Dream Robbers

and the timings, etc. We picked the man up making his way along the embankment after the meeting. See this guy here, just behind him. I was sure I knew him but I couldn't think where from."

"You think he could have been following him, this man?"
"Could be, sir. It bugged me. I couldn't get it out of my mind. Then I remembered. He lives in that village - you know, where the victim's property was torched. Or just outside it, anyway. I interviewed him at the time. So I looked back through my notes and I'm sure it's him. He's in property development and his business was struggling at the time because of the recession. Bailey, his name is. Peter Bailey."

******

As the year rolled on the winds continued on their course, continued to blow away the cobwebs from a world still riddled with corruption and deceit. They swept through the corridors of Westminster, swirling into every nook and cranny and exposing, in yet another scandal, malpractice by its Members in the MPs expenses affair. Dishonest claims amounting to thousands were laid bare. A disillusioned British electorate who themselves were suffering potential financial disaster because of the actions of the banks were incensed to find that the very people they had voted into office to represent their interests had themselves had their noses in the trough. Revelation after revelation left the British public reeling and the reputation of Parliament lay in tatters. Ministers were removed from power either by their own hand or that of others, Members of all parties fell from grace for disuse of the system, a claim here for building a house for the ducks on a duck pond, a claim there for cleaning out a moat, while members of the British pubic were rendered jobless and redundant with the threat of homelessness by repossession. Claims for items as

Caroline Jones Lewis
The Dream Robbers

trivial as new toilet seats and light bulbs - that any member of the voting public would have replaced from their own funds without a second thought; misuse of the second home allowance that enraged working people faced with losing the only home they had, all too much to bear. The press had a field day and the public tut-tutted with disgust. The scandal cost the Government dearly in a bi-election and with a general election pending in the not-too-distant future, the winds of change that were already poised to revolutionise the banking industry had the power yet to bring down the Government of the day.

At long, long last those responsible for the deception over Northern Rock's tenuous financial position were brought to brook in court, heavily fined and banned from working ever again in the finance industry. They accepted their fate unequivocally and responded with an all but pointless apology.

******

The knock on the door was answered by Emma Bailey who was not so much surprised at the visit of two policemen, given recent events, as by the fact that they were asking specifically for her husband.
"He isn't in at the moment," she informed them. "Can I help you?"
"Perhaps if we could come in?" enquired the DCI.
Seated in the sitting room, a feeling of unease, prompted by the gravity of their composure, began to unsettle her.
"Can you tell us where your husband was on 28th March?" they asked.
She fetched her diary from the study.
"That was the day of the G20 summit, wasn't it?" she asked. "The day that banker was murdered."
"Yes, Mrs Bailey. It was," replied the DCI.
"Yes, my husband went to London that day. He had a

Caroline Jones Lewis
The Dream Robbers

meeting with his architect. I remember because they'd made a special concession to meet him on a Saturday," she volunteered. "And he had to drop something off for our daughter. She's studying at a London academy."

"What time was his meeting? With his architect," the DCI continued.

Emma pondered.

"I can't remember exactly. I know it was in the morning. I'm sure it will be in his diary but he carries that with him. Why do you want to know?"

"Just following up enquiries," answered the Sergeant offhandedly.

"How was he when he arrived home that day?"

Emma was startled.

"Fine. Well, as fine as he ever is when he's been up to London. He doesn't really like going up to town. Especially giving up part of his weekend to do it. And the meeting with his architects wasn't easy. He had things on his mind. About the business, that is."

She stifled the desire to let her tongue run on, unnerved by the official tone of their manner.

"Where is your husband now, Mrs Bailey?"

It was the DCI again.

"Well, out on business," Emma answered. "I'm not sure exactly where he will be right now. Maybe at the yard - or on site. I'm not sure."

"And what time do you expect him home?"

"He's usually home about 5, but it depends on how his day goes. If he's going to be late he sends me a text. Why? What is this about?"

"We'll call back later then. Just a few questions. He may have seen something that's relevant to our enquiries."

The DCI smiled and stood to leave. Emma closed the door behind the two men, frowning. She retrieved her mobile 'phone from her handbag in the kitchen and rang her husband.

Caroline Jones Lewis
The Dream Robbers

Peter Bailey was as surprised as Emma to be interviewed by the police in respect of a man he disclosed having met on only one occasion and as a follow up to their previous enquiries regarding the fire. It was late in the evening when they returned, by which time he had assured himself that they had abandoned their earlier intention and had relaxed on the sofa to watch the evening news on TV. It was unnerving to be disturbed so late in the evening.

He advised them that he had not even noticed the banker ahead of him along the Embankment on his visit to London and became irritated when they intimated their disbelief.
"Why should I recognise *him*?" he grumbled. "I can only remember meeting him once and that was some time ago. I had virtually nothing to do with the man."
"You say that as though you disapproved of him," the DCI said, looking at him directly.
"I disapprove of the things he did," Pete retorted. "I didn't know 'the man'."
The DCI raised his eyebrows pointedly.

When the questioning turned to the night of the fire, Pete became even more irritated.
"I was at home. In bed. With my wife. Where else would I be?"
"Where indeed?" the DCI questioned.
"He was," chimed in Emma, trying to calm Pete's growing annoyance, at which point it was suggested by the DCI that the interview should continue down at the station. As her husband was led away in the gloom of evening, Emma was incredulous. She rang her mother in a state of distress.
"But they've taken him to the station for further questioning," she stressed.
"We'll come over," her mother insisted. "Just stay calm, Emma. It's probably just routine, or a mistake of some kind. We'll come right away. Where are the children?"

Caroline Jones Lewis
The Dream Robbers

Emma replaced the receiver and sank into a chair.
"Where's Dad going?" Hannah asked.   She was standing in the doorway in her dressing gown, disturbed by the commotion, her hair tousled from her bed.
"Who were those men?"
Words overheard in the post office sprang into Emma's mind.
"Some people seem to get it all, don't they, dear? And they do say things come in threes."
First her father, she thought.   Then her sister.   Now her husband.   It was ridiculous.   Preposterous.   How could the police even consider such a thing?   It was unbelievable. But they had taken him all the same.   She had visions of an announcement on the early morning news, that a man was helping the police with their enquiries.   And it would be him, her husband and the father of her children.   Her Peter. She had to be there, down at the station waiting for his release.   She turned and spoke to Hannah.
"It's alright, love.   He's just had to go out for a while. About the business, that's all.   And I need to go with him as soon as Gran and Granddad get here.   Go on back to bed, sweetheart.   It's nothing to worry about."

In the early hours of morning Pete was released from custody, then called back later, then released and called back several times over the coming days while the police fumbled their way through the only possible lead they had.   The tabloids descended on the village rummaging for information, embellishing the story to Pete's disadvantage, while Pete and Emma tried to protect Hannah and Joe and insisted that Izzie stay in London and out of harm's way. But life was turning nasty - very nasty indeed.

While Emma fretted about the effect of his situation on Pete's blood pressure, Kate worried of the effect on Andy and his already fragile heart.
"How is Dad?" Emma asked her during their daily 'phone

Caroline Jones Lewis
The Dream Robbers

call.

"Well, he says he's fine but it doesn't stop me worrying," Kate told her. "It's bound to be affecting him. I'm just worried all this stress will prompt another heart attack. How are you coping, dear? All of you."
"Bearing up, Mum. Trying to keep positive. And trying to keep the kids on track. There were so many press here yesterday I had to keep them off school. I just couldn't face running the gauntlet. But it's really bad for Hannah. She can't afford to miss any school now with her exams due in May."
"What about Pete?"
"I think he's punch drunk, Mum. Reeling with the shock of it all. And disbelief, like the rest of us. What on earth are the police thinking of? They really can't believe he was anything to do with the man's death, surely."

******

The diagnosis did not impress itself on Peggy. The first symptoms began only days after her return from London and were so violent as to need an urgent visit to her GP. The speed at which the tests at the hospital were arranged rang warning bells for Ruby but Peggy herself seemed unconcerned. She was unruffled by delays between tests and results and a further wait for an appointment to see a consultant at the hospital requested by her GP as the wheels of the NHS turned at a steady but unhurried pace.

In the intervening weeks following her aunt's funeral and the surprise inheritance, she had determined to release herself from the strict disciplines that had hitherto ruled her life and was looking forward to enjoying every moment of her remaining time. Having resolved to live her final years in a relative comfort provided by the tax payer, with Tigger the kitten her already much-loved companion, she had become

Caroline Jones Lewis

The Dream Robbers

cheerful about her prospects once the initial bout of illness had subsided. Her grey hair grew longer and untidier and she took to wearing bizarre combinations of dress, most of which were purchased in the local charity shop. Her hitherto serious expression gave way to a smiling, almost girlish expression and all in the village welcomed her with affection as she went about her usual shopping routine. There were those who regarded her as uplifted by eccentricity and those who insisted it was a decent into senility. Whatever the view, all in the village treated her with respect.

"I don't know what 'e's making all this fuss about," she insisted to Ruby while awaiting another visit from the GP following yet another bout of ill health.

"Probably nothing but a touch of dicky tummy. I don't know why I couldn't'ave just gone to the surgery for some pills."

Ruby sat quietly at her bedside.

"Do you have any family, Peggy?" the doctor had asked her. "Someone who can be with you when I call."

"No," Peggy had replied bluntly.

"Or a friend maybe?" he had insisted.

"Well, I could ask Ruby, I 'spose," she had considered. "Why? What do I need 'er 'ere for?"

"Well, you may forget things that I tell you. About medication. That sort of thing," he had answered. "If you had a friend with you she may remember more. You know, Peggy. Two heads better than one, heh?"

"If you say so, doctor," Peggy had agreed reluctantly and Ruby, already anticipating bad news, had of course agreed to come.

"You seem to be getting these upsets quite often these days, Peg," Ruby said. "Best not take chances. I'm sure the doctor knows what he's doing."

At first Peggy was inclined to doubt what he was telling her. "Pancreatic cancer?" she queried. "But it's only a touch of diarrhea," she insisted. "I'll be up and about again in no

Caroline Jones Lewis

The Dream Robbers

time."

"What's the real situation, doctor?" Ruby asked in Peggy's little kitchen.

"It's very advanced, I'm afraid," he told her. "Nothing that can be done. We're talking weeks rather than months."

"Oh."

Ruby sighed, gripping the back of the kitchen chair she was leaning on so hard that her knuckles gleamed white. The colour drained from her face and she had a sudden feeling of light-headedness as the room seemed to sway around her. She steadied herself to speak.

"But she doesn't seem to have taken it in at all,.."

"Well, nature sometimes has a way of protecting people," the GP answered. "Best let her go on that way if it makes it easier for her. I'm arranging nursing support and any other help she's going to need but we'll get her into the hospice as soon as we think it necessary. In the meantime, will you be able to help her?"

"Of course," Ruby answered. "Anything she needs. I'll be here every day. I can call before I go into the post office in the mornings, and then come after."

******

For Michael Croft, the dilemma grew daily. As the pressure on the Baileys intensified, and according to village rumour and the wild imaginings of the media, Peter Bailey was suspected not only of murdering the banker but of torching his country home in a previous unsuccessful attempt. Michael knew the day of his reckoning could be nigh. He knew he could not stand by and see an innocent man, whether of his acquaintance or not, go to prison for something he himself had done. If it were proven to the police that Peter had not been responsible for the arson, so too they may understand that he was not guilty of the murder, for no-one that knew the Baileys could doubt his innocence. But Michael realised too that once admitting

Caroline Jones Lewis
The Dream Robbers

the arson and then the fact that he had been in London on the day of the murder, there was no doubt that he himself would also become the prime suspect for the murder.

"How on earth can the police even consider Peter to be capable of such a thing," Helen exclaimed. "And the tabloids. Have you seen some of the headlines, Michael? I read them in the supermarket this morning. They're outrageous. They have him tried and convicted already."

Michael agreed but said no more. His growing dilemma was with him every waking moment of every day. He had determined to wait and see if Peter were charged, at which point he would have no alternative but to go to the police and disclose all. It was a moment he was praying would not come but in the meantime, he relished every precious day of freedom with Helen and the children. Several times he had been on the point of blurting all to Helen but somehow had restrained himself. It was to him a heavy burden to bear.

******

Some days later on a visit to the hospice where Peggy was now comfortably installed, Ruby was somewhat vexed by a conversation with her friend.

"Do you think I'm a good person, Ruby?" asked Peggy.

"Of course you are, Peg," she answered. "Whatever makes you ask such a thing, I don't know, I'm sure."

Peggy clasped Ruby's hand and looked earnestly into her eyes. Ruby leaned forward, sensing her friend to be in distress. Peggy's face was pallid, prink-rimmed eyes that were watery. She was thin now and the hand that clasped Ruby's wrist so fiercely was bony and skeletal.

"I 'ave to tell you, Rube," Peggy gasped. "I 'ave to tell you."

"Peggy, what is it? You're fretting about something."

Peggy steadied herself, tried to calm her breathing. And then began.

"When you were in Tenerife on 'oliday my auntie in London

Caroline Jones Lewis

The Dream Robbers

died an' I went up there for 'er funeral. She left me some money, which was a lovely surprise. I don't know why she did. I'd never expected that. But she left me something else as well. At least my cousins gave me something of 'ers.

"Hideous it was," she gasped, emphasising the 'h' that she struggled always to remember to pronounce. "A statue thing that my auntie'd never liked . Nor me. She'd wanted me to 'ave something of 'ers, they said and they'd taken all the good stuff of course. Typical of that greedy lot. Well anyway Rube after the funeral I went to 'yde Park for a walk 'cos my 'bus wasn't due for ages. And there 'e was. That man. That banker chap. Well …."
And so she went on.
She had not intended to kill him, she said. But when she had seen him sitting on the seat in the park seemingly untouched by all the devastation he had caused, financially secure himself and showing no sign of remorse, the anger their encounter fuelled had just been too much to contain. Every condescending word he had ever uttered to her had returned to her memory to prick her like the barbs on the rose trees in the garden of the little house that she had lost. She had called his name
"I didn't sound angry, Rube," she said. "I didn't shout. I must've sounded quite calm at first. But once I started I just couldn't stop meself."
He had turned to see her standing there looking at him with his '*down 'is nose'* expression, she explained.
"Oh, it's you. What on earth are you doing here?" he'd said.
The disdain implied had not escaped her and the latent anger she had been keeping under control had flared into life. She had railed at him, her voice thick with emotion, accusing, insulting, every name she could think of to express her contempt of everything he had done and stood for.

Caroline Jones Lewis

The Dream Robbers

"I don't have to listen to this," he had spat. "The ranting of a bitter old woman," and he had turned from her, bending to retrieve his briefcase in a bid to walk away.
''e turned 'is back on me,' she whispered tremulously.
'Just dismissed me as a bitter old woman.'
She had stepped forward in an instant of reaction, raising the hand in which she held the hideous statuette wrapped inside the cheap plastic carrier bag. She had hit him full force on the back of his head, then a second blow as his body froze momentarily at the shock. The second blow had sent him reeling forwards, the briefcase released from his grip and sliding on the bank of the lake. Without waiting to see the results of her attack, she had turned and walked quickly away, venting her fury by thrashing the reeds along the bank as she went, the splash as his body hit the water the only clue she had of his fall. The plastic bag around the statuette was bloodstained and the sight of the blood snapped her back to her senses. She had looked around her, realising suddenly what she had done and that someone might have seen her attack, that even now they might be rushing to arrest her - a citizen's arrest . But there was no-one around. Not a single soul at that moment to bear witness to her crime. She had flung the statuette with all the strength she could muster into the murky waters. The plastic bag wrapped around it had stuck fast, welded to its contents by the clotting blood that had seeped through a hole to form a sticky matt.
The entire package had sank in an instant towards the mud on the floor of the lake.

It still had not occurred to Peggy that he might die and it was only as she had walked swiftly from the park that the potential consequences of her actions had begun to dawn. She was numb. The blood from the statuette had brushed onto the front of her coat and she had felt a rising panic, gripping her handbag close to her to cover the stain. Just outside the gate she had stepped off the kerb without looking in either direction for oncoming traffic and an approaching

Caroline Jones Lewis

The Dream Robbers

taxi to the right of her had blasted its horn as she had
narrowly missed stepping into its path. It had jolted her
back to the moment and she had hesitated, calming herself
before crossing to the opposite pavement. As she had
walked, she had calmed herself further and contemplated
future events.

He would identify her, of course, she had reasoned and she
would be arrested and go to prison. Assault. It was a
serious matter. He would spare her no mercy, that man.
He would want her punished without a doubt. Well, she
would take her punishment. And she would tell everyone
why she had done what she did, what he had done to her,
what he was like and the way he had treated her. She would
tell the court and everyone would be listening. It would be
in the newspapers. On the tele. Everyone would know.

She had walked on towards the bus for home, slipping into a
feeling of light-headedness. How strange, she had thought.
She had no fear. No fear at all. A slight drizzle had begun
to fall in the gathering gloom of dusk and she had reached
instinctively for her umbrella in her handbag. It was
damaged and had stuck when she tried to open it so she had
to fiddle with it to get it to work.
"I'll buy myself a new one," she had promised herself. "A
celebration of my inheritance. Something more cheerful
than the old one. But not today. After all, if I'm going to
prison I won't need it just yet."

At Victoria she had still had time to wait for her coach and on
an impulse she had gone into a small café for a cup of tea.
There was a television in the corner and the voice of a
newsreader droned quietly in the background above the
hushed conversations of the diners at their tables. The only
table free had been quite close to the screen and she had been
able to hear the newsreader quite clearly, to see the screen
unhindered. Stirring a lump of sugar around in the tea cup,

Caroline Jones Lewis
The Dream Robbers

she had watched absentmindedly until the realisation of what the newsreader was saying had penetrated a mind switched to automatic pilot. A picture of the banker appeared on the screen with the words 'breaking news' in red lettering flashing across the bottom. She had listened more intently as the newsreader announced almost breathlessly the discovery of a body in Hyde Park rumoured by the media to be that of the banker. At first she had not believed it. It was only on the 'bus journey home that it had impressed itself upon her that she had killed him. She was a murderer. A murderer. When they sent her to prison they would throw away the key. But then another thought had thrust itself upon her almost as quickly. The only witness to her assault, to the identity of his attacker, was now dead. Unbelievably, for a second time in her life, fate it seemed had offorded her protection. And as time went by without any hint of suspicion falling upon her, more and more the matter had slipped to the darkest recesses of her mind. Until Peter Bailey became the prime suspect
and she had known that she could not let him take the blame. She knew that she must confess. And as it had now turned out, there would be no prison to face.

"I must make sure, Rube," she insisted "that Emma's 'usband isn't charged and punished for what I've done, nor anybody else neither. I've got to tell the police. I need you to ring them for me. Please, Rube."

Ruby was not sure she believed Peggy's tale and half-suspected it was Peggy's way of helping Emma and her family by taking the blame. But she knew she had to respect her friend's request.

"Please, Rube," Peggy repeated in distress. "I've got to tell'em."

"Alright, Peggy. Don't fret now. I'll ring them."

The DCI listened carefully to Peggy's story and his sergeant helped Peggy to make a formal statement. Neither of them were convinced. They viewed the confession with

Caroline Jones Lewis
The Dream Robbers

suspicion, the ramblings of an old and dying woman wanting to protect a family she cared for.

"What do we do now, then, sir?" the sergeant enquired.

"Well, we'll have to follow it up," came the reply. "We have no choice. We'll have to look for evidence to support the story."

"Not drag the lake, sir? That's a big area."

"Yes, well …. We'll check out the details first. The funeral, etc. And we do know which part of the lake to concentrate on to find this statuette thing, if we have to. They can start at the murder site and work their way outwards. If everything else fits we'll have no option. Check out the details first and get back to me. We'll take it from there."

He paused considering.

"It's all the details, you see."

He spoke quietly, as though to himself rather than his sergeant.

"They seem to fit, don't they? The two blows to the back of the head. The weapon she described. The timing even. It all fits."

"Do you think she got that from the papers, sir? She doesn't seem … well, strong enough," his sergeant emphasised. "I know she's ill but even so. We're only talking a short time ago. Would she have been strong enough even then? She's a friend of the Bailey woman. She could be covering for the husband. After all, she's got nothing to lose, has she?"

"I don't recall the details of the death being given out in the press. But the friend's husband could have provided those; persuaded her to cover for him. Since she's dying she has nothing to lose but her good name. People do cover for others they care about in those circumstances. Check it out anyway. The tabloids in particular. But we have to remember, sergeant; cancer does that to people. People can go downhill in no time at all. Like I said, check out the facts about the funeral and her trip to London and then get back to me. We'll take it from there."

Caroline Jones Lewis

The Dream Robbers

******

Though the police still officially seemed interested in Peter Bailey, the conspiracy theorists were once more favoured by tabloids that preferred the sensationalist implications to the likelihood of his guilt. Was there really a need for Peggy to reveal this now, Ruby wondered? Did the police seriously consider either her or Peter Bailey to be guilty? Ruby's friend had suffered much misfortune during her lifetime because of the actions of others. To bring her name into disrepute in death was more than Ruby could bear, to have her gossiped about in the village like a common criminal. It wasn't fair.

But "just remember. If it's true then she's killed a man," she chided herself. "She didn't mean to, she says, but she still killed a man and that's not right."

She sat in Peggy's little kitchen later in the day after calling in to check the mail.

"Well, Frank," she confided to her long-departed. "What do you think about this then? Do you think it's true? 'Cos I don't know what to think. Do you think she's made it up to protect Emma's husband? She likes Emma, you know. She could have done. And she's really odd at times now, with the drugs and the illness and all. But all the details. I really don't know. I just don't want people to think badly of her. To disrespect her memory when she's gone."

She fussed around the kitchen, making herself a cup of tea, a habit in times of crisis and sat once more to think while she sipped the steaming liquid. Ruby was renowned in the village as a gossip, but there was a side to her that people did not know. To Ruby there was gossip - but then there was gossip.

There was the time she had left the village pub after a quiz in aid of the local hospice, click clacking her high heels along the pavement, jangling her bangles as she clutched the collar

Caroline Jones Lewis

The Dream Robbers

of her fake fur jacket around her. She had come across the vicar's son slumped unconscious in the 'bus shelter. By his side was a syringe and she knew instinctively what he had done. Oh, how sad, she had thought. Such a nice young life blighted by this rubbish. She had wrapped the syringe carefully in a handkerchief retrieved from her handbag and gone with all haste to the vicarage to fetch the vicar. The vicar had expected the details of this encounter to be related to all and sundry, he had expected to be harangued with unwelcome comment from anyone he met next time he ventured outside of his own front door. He had been a critic of Ruby's hobby of gossip since his arrival in the village some years before, a frequent tut-tutting at some piece of tittle-tattle she had transmitted or another.

"That woman," he had been heard to utter in exasperation. "She needs telling a home truth or two."

But to his surprise not a word had been spoken. The next time he saw Ruby he had thanked her for her discretion.

"Well, vicar," she had told him, "there's gossip - and then there's gossip, isn't there? I would think you've got enough on your hands to cope with - with your young lad and his problem. I'm sure you don't need every tom, dick and harry in the village sticking their nose in."

"How right you are, Ruby," he had told her. "How right you are. And thank you again."

On reflection he had realised that indeed she was right. The gossip she transmitted had always been innocuous, nothing of great value or distress to anyone as far as he could remember. He had paused and looked at her quizzically.

"You keep your compassion a closely guarded secret, Ruby."

Ruby had grinned.

"Well, vicar - I have a reputation to maintain," and they had parted conspirators with their closely guarded secret eternally binding.

There had been the night, too, when - an incurable

Caroline Jones Lewis
The Dream Robbers

insomniac since Frank had died - she had sat at her bedroom window in the early morning hours watching the wind and rain raging, searching in vain above her for the stars she so loved to see and talking to Frank whose photograph took pride of place at her bedside. And she had seen something that night that had impressed itself upon her - but it was not the stars. She had seen Michael Croft that night, the night that little Liam had been born. He had driven past her cottage three times that night, not just once, first in one direction and then the other, then back again. The night of the fire, she had recalled. She had made a guess at what he had been up to. Poor Michael, distressed at the loss of his business and with a family's needs to meet. What good would it have done to say? What good to anyone? She had mentioned not a word to a soul, least of all the police. There had been no damage done apart from to property, no lives lost - that would have been different - and no real distress. The family of the banker were like the Queen and her annus horribilis. They had other homes to go to, other places to lay their head. After much soul-searching, she had kept her own counsel.

******

To great surprise, the discovery of the statuette embedded in the lake gave credibility to Peggy's story. When specks of blood were scraped from indents in the sculpture and confirmed by analysis to be that of the banker's, all speculation ceased. The DCI and his sergeant would have no option but to accept Peggy's confession and charge her with the murder. They arrived at the hospice for the unpalatable task with a female PC to remain at her bedside only to be told that Peggy had passed away not five minutes before. They left a sorrowful Ruby to cope with the formalities.

With compassion and discretion by police officers

Caroline Jones Lewis
The Dream Robbers

themselves suffering economic difficulties prompted by the banking crisis, a press release simply disclosed that the banker's killer had been identified as an assailant who was now deceased. It was only to the family that the identity was disclosed. And the banker's wife, now grieving for her husband, could not resist a degree of compassion and grieving for Peggy too. The press in their comparative ignorance remained sceptic. The conspiracy theories remained rife.

"The press don't believe it, do they, sir?" observed the sergeant. "They're still running ragged looking for an alternative."

"Shouldn't let that worry you," the DCI responded grinning wryly. "It gives me a degree of satisfaction to get one over on that lot. Leave them chasing their tails for nothing. Anyway, they'll be happy. It will sell far more newspaper than the reality."

The Bailey family were told that Peter was no longer a suspect. Emma was in a virtual state of collapse with relief. As the news became known, Michael Croft could not believe his good fortune and swore to a God he was sure he now believed in that his life from now on would be led in an exemplary and law-abiding manner.

******

April 2010

With election time approaching in Great Britain, the two main parties began a tit for tat rhetoric to discredit each other's proposed solutions to the country's ills. The opposition party launched their campaign with a slogan of change alongside a picture of their leader.
"He thinks he's Barack Obama," exclaimed Andy Gray in jest.
"He's the best alternative we've got to the current PM,"

Caroline Jones Lewis
The Dream Robbers

insisted Peter Bailey.
In relaxed and friendly banter, they voiced their opposing views already known to and tolerated by each other but in reality, apathy was the overwhelming emotion dominating an electorate split down the middle and who wished a plague on all their houses. A hung parliament was predicted by the pollsters.

The weather continued to vent disaster upon disaster on a world population that suffered in its impotence to call a halt. Record breaking snowfalls crippled communities, floods swept away holiday tranquillity and the planet itself shuddered and inflicted mass devastation as an earthquake hit an already poverty stricken Haiti. Buildings that had been badly constructed by greedy developers, skimming off large profits attained by using inferior materials, collapsed killing thousands who should never have died. Thousands fled from the coast of Cuba in fear of the threat of a tsunami around the Pacific rim and a minor tsunami hit Southern Japan. The scientists themselves could not agree on the projected temperatures of global warming and their anticipated effect causing sceptics amongst the general population to question the entire theory.

In Greece riots broke out on the streets of Athens as the Greek people protested against austerity measures proposed by its Government. These measures were vital, the Government argued, to save the country from insolvency as financial instability caused by the banking crisis spread across the Eurozone. Tear gas and water canon were used to break up violent demonstrations and restore calm, but the mood of the people remained ugly.

******

As the winds rested the world enjoyed a temporary respite

Caroline Jones Lewis
The Dream Robbers

and lives moved on. On a Sunday morning Emma Bailey stood at her sister's graveside clutching a bouquet of spring flowers, expressing her approval of the newly completed headstone. Her husband stood beside her, his arm protectively around her shoulders.
"You ok, Em?" he asked.
She nodded.
"I still can't believe it sometimes. That she's not here. Something happens or someone says something and I think, I must remember to tell Sophie that. And then I remember and the sadness comes. But I'm afraid that if I stop feeling that I'll forget things about her. What she was like. What she looked like. Sometimes I find it hard to see her face. But other times it's as clear as day."
"Of course you won't forget," Peter reassured. "The pain will fade but not the memories."
"I know. I know you're right. But sometimes it frightens me."
He kissed her head and squeezed her shoulder.
"Come on," he said. "Let's go home. This is your last working week. Then you'll be at college. You've something positive to look forward to. That's thanks to Sophie. You can remember her that way."

******

On her last working day at the agency, Emma arrived at the office early, hoping for some quiet time before the rest of the staff arrived. She knew there would be the usual leaving celebrations, the cards and the presentation, for which she was grateful but also aware that it would be an emotional day. She sat at her desk and looked around the office fondly in the quiet of the moment. She had seen happy times here, love and laughter with colleagues who were friends. Those same colleagues had been there for her through the recent bad times. She would miss them all, not least of all Max who had supported her and kept her job open at times when

Caroline Jones Lewis

The Dream Robbers

he could have used enforced absence as an excuse to not. But today was not only the end of one era; it was also the start of an exciting and new.

On the dot of nine o'clock she turned the closed sign to open and unlocked the front door. To her surprise a familiar figure entered without delay.

"Good morning," she said smiling. "Mrs. Carpenter. We haven't seen you for ages. How are you?"

"I'm fine, thank you," replied Mrs Carpenter. "It's Emma, isn't it?"

Emma nodded.

"Emma, I've come early as I wanted a chat with someone. Confidentially, I mean. Can we ..?"

Emma nodded.

"Of course. There's no-one else in yet. We won't be disturbed for a little while. Take a seat," and she indicated the chair beside her. "What can I do for you?"

There was a difference in her, Emma noticed. A more confident manner and in the way she looked. Nothing major, but the once unruly hair had been tamed into a topknot, the blouse and voluminous skirt of the past replaced by a neater version and most noticeably the pumps had given way to a pair of court shoes. Emma recalled the striped fabric bag, the handle of which had once been twiddled nervously in Mrs Carpenter's fingers. A small leather bag now rested calmly from its shoulder strap at her side.

"I wish to put the house back on the market," she began.

"And I need to find a property for myself and the children."

"Are you looking for the same type of property as before?" Emma began.

"No," came the reply. "My husband and I are divorcing so I'm looking for something smaller. Something modern and easy to maintain,"

"Oh, I'm sorry," Emma offered.

"Don't be," Mrs Carpenter insisted. "There was a time when I would have been distraught. But not now. It's

Caroline Jones Lewis
The Dream Robbers

funny how things turn out, isn't it? I think he's probably done me a favour. I'm finding my own life and really enjoying it. I've got a job which fits in with school hours and I'm loving being back in the workplace. He never wanted me to work, you see. I suppose I lost some of my identity, if you know what I mean, And confidence in myself. I think I'd lost all of that. I'm ready to move on now."

"That's good," Emma encouraged. "It's sad when marriages break up but ... well sometimes it turns out to be right for people, doesn't it?

Mrs Carpenter nodded.

"The only thing is, he and his new 'lady' live just down the road. She's a neighbour and he's just moved in with her. I have to admit it hurts to see them together and it really isn't good for the kids to be so close. So ..... Well, we need to move as soon as possible. I need a valuation on ours, details of new properties, and an appointment with Gavin to talk about mortgages. Most of the equity in our current property will come to me so I'll have a good deposit. I just hope Gavin can help me. I know mortgages are difficult right now."

"Yes, but if you have a big deposit he should be able to do something for you," Emma reassured. "Let's take all the details and we'll get the ball rolling."

Mrs Carpenter left with a sheaf of property details and a spring in her step that had not existed at their last meeting. Emma watched her leave.

"Amazing," she thought. "Amazing how resilient people can be."

She doodled on her blotter as she pondered the past and contemplated the future, great trails of blossoms spreading across the whiteness of the pad.

"Amazing how we are. My family. After all we have been through."

With Isobel now placed with an orchestra and about to embark on her first tour of the country and Hannah's first

Caroline Jones Lewis

The Dream Robbers

GCSE exam only weeks away, it was, she pondered, remarkable how they had each clung to their individual dreams and yet achieved them as a family, giving and drawing strength from each other to get through the darkest hours.
"They had not won, the dream robbers as Michael would call them," she mused. "They had not won at all."
She drove home later in the day emotional from the departure, excited at the prospect of the new life ahead.

******

With no overall majority won by any party, coalition was the only option open to politicians struggling to maintain credibility to a disillusioned British public. A new experience for the country was the hope of the electorate. Only time would tell if it was the answer. As the winds began once more to pick up speed, more changes loomed ahead, more exposures, more illegality and more immorality, uncovered for public condemnation not only in Britain but across the world. The journey continued unending and with hope its companion, change for the better remained the order of the day.

Made in the USA
Charleston, SC
14 December 2016